By Rosemarie Heinrich

Hello Fräulein

Across The Ocean

Generation Gap

See You Tomorrow

Hello

Fräulein

Book One.

Contact Info: rosemarie.heinrich@gmail.com
Front Cover Design by: Brittany Angell, Melissa Angell
Model Photography by: Elizabeth Macy, Matthew Angell
Author Photo: Elizabeth Macy

ISBN: 979-8-9901849-0-9 (paperback)
ISBN: 979-8-9901849-1-6 (hard cover)

First Edition: February 2024
Second Edition: April 2024

For Rudi and Maria Heinrich, my beloved parents.

Prologue

RUDI HEARD THE WHISTLING SOUND OF incoming artillery shells one after another. He quickly turned to his friend, tugging on his coat. "Run! Dive for the Schützenloch!" Gunther was stunned. He couldn't hear Rudi's words or the high-pitched sound of the multiple shells in the air passing overhead. The gunfire on the ground was too loud. Moving slowly, he tried to follow Rudi's lead, but the incoming barrage of shells had already started landing around him. The unmistakable thud, like heavy rain pellets on the ground sent terror through Rudi's very soul. Then silence.

Deafening silence. Rudi waited for the explosion of bullets. He knew that he could only escape within inches of his life by diving headfirst into the safety of the hole. Amazed that he was still alive but feeling the burn of blazing shrapnel searing through his leg, he raised his eyes above the foxhole that he and Gunther had dug. Forgetting himself in the moment of panic, he tried to find his friend, only to witness Gunther's body being all but ripped apart by the enemy's surprise attack.

"No!" Rudi shouted with every strain of vocal cord that he possessed. As soon as the explosions stopped, he scrambled out of the foxhole, against orders, and picked up his friend holding him in his lap. He was still alive; barely. Blood was pouring out of his gut and his legs were all but gone. The stench of fresh blood suddenly overwhelmed his senses. He leaned over to his side, unable to control his need to vomit. They were fighting against the Red army on the Oder River and the Balkans; the collapse of the southern part on the Eastern front of Poland meant that the Soviet Army had sent its best forces. The inability of the German Army to defeat the Soviets was starting to turn the tide for the outcome of the war. Rudi knew their time was short, one way or another. Hitler had decided that his fresh drafts – of which Rudi was included thanks to his refusal to become an SS soldier – were being sent to the front line to reinforce the Oder and hold off the imminent invasion and Soviet overturn of

Berlin. He was eighteen, a reluctant draft from the previous year. Gunther had been 'gifted' with the same post, but they were thankful to at least have one another; best friends and bandmates from their youth. Rudi played the accordion, and his friend, a percussionist. Neither one of them conscripted to the ideals of the Third Reich, each refusing to take part in the political Nazi military; wanting merely to defend their home country. They couldn't go along with the 'Aryan race' propaganda, having witnessed the bloodbath in the wake of SS savagery on people who weren't willing to say they were full-throated Nazi's.

As Rudi sat holding his best friend in his arms, he felt as if he were transported in time. Memories of their childhood and youth flooded in. He wasn't able to process the reality of the moment. It seemed surreal. Grappling for encouraging words, Rudi thought of their plans.

"Hey Gunther – Remember you said you were going to propose to Anna when we get home." Gunther was unable to respond. He simply closed his eyelids a moment, avoiding the pain of his inevitability. He forced them open again, clinging onto every second of life. "You were a hero, Buddy." Rudi heartened, ignoring his own pain. He felt his own body shaking, also afraid of the imminent fate of his friend. Tears flooding his eyes and streaming helplessly down his face, he tried in vain to pull himself together. "We were strong out

4

there together." He looked up toward heaven, silently begging God not to take his best friend. He fumbled for words wishing that he could extend time for his friend and at the same time desperately wanting this moment to be over. Struggling to keep his own position, Rudi bit into his bottom lip. Gunther's head lay on his wound, but he didn't dare fix his hold. "You know you'll always be with me, everywhere I go. I'm proud of you Buddy." Even though the gunfire would've killed anyone left on the field, Rudi wanted to make his friend's last breaths, ones of feeling accomplished and worthy.

"You're my best friend, Gunther. I don't know what I'm going to do without you." He spoke out loud, voicing his own fear. At that moment Rudi saw the terror coming into Gunther's eyes; the reality that he was about to leave this earth. It caused Rudi to change his focus away from himself, still hoping against hope for a miracle. He sat helplessly cradling his best friend's head in his own lap, not allowing himself to look at the rest of Gunther's body. "You got this Gunther! Hold on. You've got to hold on. We'll get you back home and you're gonna make it." Again, he glimpsed the fear in his friend's eyes, mirroring what was in his own heart. "Don't be scared, Buddy. You won't feel any more pain. Just hang on." Rudi didn't know how to talk to someone who was dying. He never had someone close to him die, until now. It made him think of how he froze in horror the first time he saw a dead body. His commander yelled at him, calling him stupid and told him to get used to seeing a lot more. He never thought that he'd be staring down at his best friend to witness a moment like this. Gunther looked terrified. Rudi held him close, feeling his life slipping away.

"I'm here Gunther. I've got you." He simply said. In less than a minute, what was left of Gunther's body went limp in his arms. Rudi remained on the ground holding him in disbelief, feeling helpless. Ten minutes ago, they were standing side by side. Rudi was in shock.

It was only a few minutes, which seemed like an hour to Rudi, when someone pushed him forward causing him to fall over his friend and mistakenly drop his body on the ground. It caused a soul-deep anger to well up in him; partly a symptom of grief and partly because it was an asinine thing to do.

"Stand up Nazi!" the foreign soldier commanded. Suddenly, he realized it was the wrong end of a gun on his back. Rudi struggled to his feet, taking one last look at his dead friend. It was Rudi's turn to be terrified. He may've escaped death, but now he was in enemy hands; he didn't know which was worse. The gunman prodded him forwards forcing him to tread over dead German soldiers on the battlefield, evidently enjoying treating Rudi with disdain, taunting and prodding him along. He was muttering 6something in Russian and periodically burst out with an uncontrollable wicked laugh. Rudi was mute with silence, consumed by the anger burning inside his heart. He didn't understand the Soviet soldier's words, but he imagined that his insults were foul, exalting himself against his sworn enemy; all German people. One fleeting thought crossed Rudi's mind: War is useless.

He joined his comrades at the edge of the battlefield on a dirt road where they were lined up to walk in step behind the Soviet tanks. Rudi took his place at the end of the line, but not for long. He was unable to walk any further, having taken a hit in his right leg.

***

NOT KNOWING WHERE HE WAS OR HOW HE GOT there, Rudi awoke in a very clean, sterile, white room. The sound of steel medical instruments being picked up and seemingly sharpened rang in his ears like a knife scratching a plate and alerted him that he was in a hospital. Suddenly, memories of Gunther's face staring up at him as he lay dying in his arms came flooding to his mind. For a moment, he wondered if he was also in the afterlife. Suddenly, the urge to pee forced him back to the present moment. Looking to his left, he saw silhouettes of doctors and nurses on the opposite side of a curtain separating his room from other sick or injured soldiers. Sitting up in his bed, he struggled to get up, needing to find a bathroom.

Suddenly he was reminded why he was in a hospital.

"Of course it hurts, I was shot!" he whispered to himself, still determined to go use the toilet. The nurse heard him and quickly ran over, pushing him back into bed. Resisting, he tried to explain that he needed to pee. She handed him a plastic tube and made him lay back down. Apparently, this was how it was done. When he took care of business, a German speaking doctor explained to him that his unit of the Panzer army that Rudi was assigned to, surrendered to the Americans, and once he was medically cleared by the doctor's own determination, he would be used productively and legally in a forced labor camp.

"You will be given your rations, like the others and of course you will stay outside of society and will be allowed a certain amount of pay." Rudi nodded in silence, thankful that he was still alive.

Part of his rations as a 'prison of war', to make up for the lack of food, were daily cigarettes. Rudi's own father had died when he was only three years old from a lung infection, which they later told him was tuberculosis. He had also been told that his father was a heavy smoker. The Nazi government, likely because Hitler hated smoking, was the first to promote anti-smoking laws and did cancer research linking smoking with lung cancer. He had heard of the dangers associated with smoking since he became a teenager and had decided that he would never do it. This afforded him popularity with soldiers from his own unit and with the Americans after they were captured. He always had cigarettes to give away.

Recovering from his bullet wound quickly in his eighteen-year-old body, Rudi was assigned to his duties. Day after day passed as he put in his hours of work helping to rebuild the city on the polish border. Days turned to weeks, and weeks to months and before he knew it, almost two years had passed. His job was to drive a truck for the city's milk distribution center and in time his duties placed him into the hands of the British occupying soldiers. He noticed a huge difference in how he was treated, but his greatest reprieve of dignity came when he was in the hands and under the direction of the US soldiers. They even allowed him to attend some of their after-work parties. They seemed to like him because he was usually a cheerful and generous person and was quick to follow orders. Even so, he was reminded of his status day after day as he continued to work long hours with little pay for a bowl of mustard soup.

Germans, of course, were not legally able to acquire land, and couldn't do anything with the pittance they received for their labor. Not only that, but the Soviets who were occupying his part of Germany were surely tightening their grip with a communist agenda and the formation of the German Democratic Republic. The future seemed bleak, if you were willing to accept it, but Rudi was not. The blind courage of youth served him well again, as one day in the middle of the night, while everyone was enjoying a night of partying and dancing, himself included, Rudi simply stepped outside for a breath of fresh air and decided to make a break for it.

"I'm getting out." That was all that he could tell himself.

Introduction – Rudi

STANDING INFRONT OF THE HOUSE THAT HE had once considered home, twenty-one-year-old Rudolf Heinrich had never felt so bewildered and lost. After being drafted involuntarily and serving in the German army at the tender age of seventeen, he had seen enough in his short experience to make him feel as though he were three times his age.

"Hey! Kerl! There's no one here! They were evacuated like the rest of the filthy Germans on this street!" The Soviet soldier spat at him in passing. Rudi could tell he was getting ready to spit at him again, but he didn't move because he wanted to ask where his family was evacuated to.

"They're gone. They went to a hostel in the city." He leaned in closer to Rudi, no doubt taking pleasure in making him feel small. "No fixed address Nazi! They're gone, like all the rest of the Germans in Berlin! And they'll never come back. We'll make sure of that!" he said, placing his hand on the gun strapped over his shoulder.

Rudi was thankful the soldier walked away leaving him stranded. He had nowhere to go, and he didn't have a soul in the world to rely on, but he was no longer being subjected to humiliation just for being born German. He continued to stare at the house, remembering his childhood with his grandfather; the many lessons on the accordion and time spent telling stories and laughing. Unfortunately, he died while Rudi was serving in the army. Thoughts of denial for passage to visit him during his time of sickness brought up feelings of resentment. But unwilling to despair over the past, Rudi took a deep breath, releasing the guilt he was tempted to succumb to in a situation that he knew he had no control over. He also recalled happy times playing music with his best friend Gunther. His memories in this house would last him a lifetime, but Rudi started to realize that it was time he started moving or he would regret it. He walked briskly away from his childhood home in the opposite direction of the city as if he had a destination to go to. He didn't, but they didn't know that. He felt as though it was important, he pretended that he did. Ducking into the first alleyway he came to with no idea where it would lead, he ventured on, knowing he just needed to keep walking. He felt as though he were being watched. The alleyway led to another and then he travelled through several unknown back-alley streets, winding his way through to nowhere in a hurry. Finally, he could see some trees over the wire fence in the distance. 'Just keep walking along the fence...' he told himself, not knowing if anyone was following him. He calculated every move, even his breath. Having escaped from his assigned prison camp, he wasn't taking any chances. No one would 'capture' him again, charging him for forced labor in his own country, if he could prevent it. He travelled on foot towards the trees, his destination to anywhere but here. It was almost an hour when the fence turned into a concrete wall. It was high, but Rudi started getting excited. He didn't want to risk jumping the barbed wire fence, but a concrete wall; he could figure out a way to get himself over that. Still there was no stopping. He walked well into the dusk and on Into the night. Then, when it was completely dark and there were no lights at all and he could hardly see in front of himself to take the next step, he slowed his pace and found that the wall was indeed lower in some places than others. He walked into the pitch-black night and as soon as he came up on a tree that he could climb, he made quick work of it and jumped off on the other side of the wall. He knew he was risking his life; he had heard reports of people getting caught by border guards for trying to escape East Germany and being shot on the spot.

When he jumped out of the tree, it was a long way down, but his adrenaline kept him from feeling any pain from the landing or from the scratches he had acquired from scaling the tree like an animal. He ignored his physical condition and stood right back up. He walked further into the trees on the other side. He wished he could see where he was going on the one hand, but then he was also thankful he couldn't, not knowing what was lurking in the deep, mossy forest. He was forcing himself to travel through the night to be sure that no one was following him. He was scared enough to keep walking, his breath the only visible thing to light his silent, lone path.

At the first hint of dawn, he started to come out of the trees and saw in the distance an old barn at the end of a field. Once there, he easily opened the latched door and was met by a few curious cow eyes and an overwhelming stench of manure that brought water to his eyes. His first instinct was to hold his breath or run, but he was mindful that it was the perfect place to hide. He collapsed in the far corner by some cows in a mound of hay. He kept his eyes open, sheltered by a massive beast, focusing on the door when he found himself unable to stop sleep from overtaking him.

"Hey!" Rudi heard a faint voice. It was still morning, and he hadn't slept nearly long enough.

He stirred slightly in his sleep, unable to rouse himself because he was so exhausted.

"Hey!" The voice called again. This time the tone of voice was stern, and Rudi opened his eyes and sat up in place, still covered in hay. The cow had been moved out of the way and suddenly Rudi realized he had been discovered. The expression on his face gave away the panic that he had felt all night during his flight for life.

"Don't worry. I'm a farmer, not a soldier." The man said, looking down at Rudi in a solemn way.

"Why are you sleeping in my barn?"
Rudi tried to gather up his crumpled self and give an intelligent answer. He opened his mouth and realized he didn't know how to answer the question. Luckily the farmer was more filled with compassion than anger.

"Get up and I'll take you inside for some food. You can help me on the farm today to pay for your meal, but you can't stay here. I don't want any trouble for my family. You'll want to keep moving tonight, but for now you can come with me. I'll give you some clothes at the house."
Rudi didn't know how to thank this kind man for his help. He worked as hard as he could in the field that day and ate well, feeling a resurgence of his strength returning.

The farmer placed a sack full of homemade bread, cheese and a canteen of water on Rudi's back, sending him on his way when it became dark that night. He gave him instructions for the direction in which to travel to best avoid the soldiers on his way to the western border. At the edge of the man's property, they parted ways, knowing they wouldn't meet in this life again. Feeling thankful and hopeful, Rudi set out once again to trek his way through the dark forest in hopes of reaching his destination.

It was an easier night than the previous one, not because the forest was any less dark or mysterious, but for the sole fact that he finally felt like he was not being followed. Under normal circumstances, he was not comfortable with feeling alone, but in his present situation it was as welcome as the moonlight illuminating his path to freedom. Once again, he pressed forwards in all the strength he had left from having slept very little and worked very hard, his body wanting to rest from the exhaustion threatening to slow him down. He was so tempted to give up, but also knew that his odds of surviving this break for freedom were greater if he kept moving. Just because he felt like he was alone, didn't mean he was. He knew the soldiers were expert trackers. That thought kept his feet on the move through the night once again. How he managed to come out of the forest at first light and stumble into yet another farm, he didn't know, but for God's grace. Here he was again seeking solace amongst the farm animals. This time it was in the horse barn, and they weren't willing to share a stall. Rudi still found a corner where the hay was stored and leaning against the wall, sweet sleep came quickly.

"What is this? A bum in the barn?" A farm hand asked, poking Rudi with a pitchfork. It was sharp enough to rouse him at the first jab. Rudi stood up immediately, again with a horrified look on his face.

"This is not a place to sleep off your …. Oh!" The farm hand was caught off guard when he saw the cuts and bruises on Rudi's arms and hands, he had gotten from forcing his way through thorns and bushes in the forest. He recognized that Rudi was not drunk, nor was he a homeless man asking for a handout.

"I'll work for whatever food you can give me today. I'm on my way to the Western border. I'd like to reach Stuttgart actually." He explained. "I've come from Berlin." The man immediately understood and was willing to help.

"Wait here." He spoke. "I'll be right back." Rudi trusted that he was an honest man, leaving him in the barn only to procure provision; not to report him. The minutes seemed like hours and Rudi was almost ready to make a run for it when he saw the farm hand returning with food and fresh clothing and another man who he assumed was the owner of the farm.

"Krause. Mein Name ist Krause. Ich bin der Farmbesitzer." He was right. This man owned the farm. He was very forthright and welcoming, extending a handout to Rudi. He had apparently come at a good time; the man needed an extra hand on the farm and was pleased to pay with food as well as a fair wage.

"How do you have horses? I thought they were taken for the war." Rudi asked curiously.

Krause looked over his stalls which were filled with colts and a couple of fillies. "They didn't take the pregnant horses. I'm a breeder."

Rudi lifted his chin, understanding.

"Have you worked with horses?" the owner asked.

Rudi shook his head. Krause wasn't deterred. He simply handed Rudi a pitchfork and pointed to a wheelbarrow.

"You can start by mucking out the stalls. Peter here will show you how." He instructed, pointing to the farm hand and giving Rudi a roll of band-aids and a pair of gloves. "You'll want to take care of those hands first."

Rudi nodded. "Thank you!"

"See you at breakfast!" Krause answered walking back up to the main house.

Rudi stayed for two days against his better judgement. He could've stayed longer; even obtaining a job here, but he wanted to keep going.

"I have to get to Stuttgart." Rudi explained. "I'm a leather smith and I'd like to continue to work in my field of business, but I'm more than thankful for your help Mr. Krause."

The gracious older gentleman nodded, again reaching out to shake Rudi's hand.

"Well, if you ever change your mind Heinrich, you can have a job with me." He offered. "I think you're free from danger now. I don't think you have to worry about being caught anymore. We're all German you know."

Rudi smiled but having experienced the prison camps, he wasn't willing to trust his luck.

"I'm an East German soldier who has jumped the wall. I can't be sure that I'm safe until I'm settled in Stuttgart, under the French occupation and where there are lawyers and such. I just want to arrive safely in the city."

Krause nodded in understanding. "Well don't worry about us. We never met you." He placed Rudi's wages in his hand and an antique compass and sent him on his way once again.

Rudi was almost overcome with emotion because Krause had treated him so kindly. He had been brutally handled by some of the soldiers overseeing the Germans in enemy prison camps and being that he was so young, he was only doing what he was told from the time he was taken into service; usually unloading corpses covered in lice from the back of a flatbed truck to be thrown in the city center and burned. Before that, his own family was never demonstrative of affection, so this friendly farmer left a lasting impression on his heart. Still, with a strong desire to reach the security of a West

German city, Rudi continued his journey. He no longer wore his army uniform, having traded it out for farm clothes. He was much less conspicuous as an East German escapee and was prepared to blend in with the crowd as soon as he came to the city. Knowing there was no turning back because there was nothing to go back to, he had to keep going, his future a making of his own imagination.

The unknown forest was starting to seem less scary. He was no longer travelling at a hurried pace. With his precious compass guiding him, he stepped methodically over tree roots and vines, knowing that the end goal would be worth the battle to get there. He kept a tune in his head to keep from becoming fearful of what he might be running from or into and having had more sleep from staying with Krause and his farm hands for two days, he plunged onwards into the night with miles behind him and untold miles still ahead. Krause estimated that it would take him at least two days to reach his destination. Rudi lifted his chin and clenched his jaw with determination. He knew that in Stuttgart, he could obtain a job and a safe place to live. He had it in mind to start building a life for himself if he had anything to do with it. He kept up his courage until his body grew tired; his legs and feet warning him that they needed a break. Choosing a large tree to lean his back against, he slid down until he sat on the ground. The night air was cold, but his feet were burning, and he could hardly feel his legs. After ripping into some of the loaf of bread in his backpack and gulping down some water, sleep came swiftly, but it wasn't deep. His body was still on alert, as a mother with a new baby; for any sound of danger. He awoke a couple of hours later by the breaking of a branch. No animal appeared from the brush to threaten him, but still it was enough of a scare to cause him to resume walking. As day approached, Rudi realized that he was still in the thick of the forest and every direction he looked seemed alike. The only way he knew it was during the daytime, was by looking up, above the trees. The forest was still dark and there was no hint of a worn path which made him realize that he would be in trouble if it weren't for the compass that Krause had gifted him; probably an heirloom from a father or grandfather. Rudi suddenly realized that this was not just a useful trinket. Right now, he felt like it was a life saver. At that moment he looked up and said a prayer of thanks to the God he didn't know for this masterful provision.

Further he trudged, only stopping to relieve himself, keeping step with the song in his head. Before he knew it, the sky was starting to darken and somehow the forest became even darker. He was amazed that he hadn't encountered any wild creatures, sure that they would be as scared of him as he was of them. Needing another break, he sat against another tree and took some bread and cheese from his backpack and allowed himself to rest awhile. He listened for the unique sounds of the forest, but only heard birds and what he told himself were squirrels rustling the leaves on the ground. He felt like they were curious about this stranger in their midst. Aware that this was no time to give up, he forced himself onto his feet again, rehearsing the thought that he was almost there. Another hour into this game he started laughing, feeling somewhat like he might be going in circles like a hamster on a wheel. Then he told himself that this is how people go crazy. Inside his own mind, he was having a conversation with Rudi Heinrich. It passed the time and before he knew it, the night had come in like a bandit. Just as he was getting tired again, he spotted some light in the distance. He walked further on, and the light became brighter. He sped up his pace with the renewed energy of hope. Almost running, he came to a place in the forest where his hope was satisfied. The distant glow was indeed the flickering lights of a city at night.

Introduction – Maria

MACH'S SCHNELL MARIA! ÄHNE IS WAITING! We need to work together."

Nineteen-year-old Maria Riekert shifted her canister filled with forty liters of milk along the rocky ground. Her mother was sitting in their three-wheel truck waiting impatiently for her to finish loading the milk cans. Overseeing the area's daily milk distribution, she knew how people could get when they had to wait in line.

Maria stole a moment to straighten her posture. Sometimes she felt like an old workhorse that was pushed beyond its strength. Hoisting the canister onto the flatbed of the truck, she shoved it towards the back to make sure it wouldn't topple when they drove home.

"What took you so long?" her mother asked when she finally took her seat in the truck pulling the door closed. At first Maria didn't respond, thinking that the answer was obvious.

"I went as fast as I could Mama." She murmured, not daring to be disrespectful.

"We'll have to be extra fast getting the cans unloaded." Her mother instructed. "I'll set up the table and take care of the customers. You can unload the canisters. We'll have to tag team because there's a lot of work on the farm today and you need to help your grandfather in the fields before it gets dark."

Maria nodded, thankful that she had the strength to do it all. She loved her grandfather more than anything and since he had lost three of his four sons in the war, including her father, he needed help plowing his fields.

Maria's identical twin sister, Anneliese, was busy looking after their younger siblings, cooking the meals and cleaning the house. Maria would much rather be out of the house, and she loved working. She often thought of her father's words; taking them to heart. "It's a gift to truly enjoy your work and get satisfaction from knowing you put in your best effort." Not only that, but she was always mindful of her promise to him to look after their mother when he was away in the war and to do anything she asked. He had especially impressed it on his eldest twin daughters, not knowing that it would become a forever promise because he wouldn't be coming home again.

Once they were back at the 'milk store' across from their house, Maria started unloading the canisters from the truck. Her mother took the accounting books and a pen and set the cash box next to herself at the table. She turned back to Maria and let her know that time was running short.

"Once you finish unloading the last of those, you can just be on your way to the farm. I'll clean these up myself when the people have gone." Maria stopped and looked at her mother who was getting ready to open the doors for the line-up of customers waiting to get their milk ration for the day. She gave her a positive, obedient nod.

"Yes Mama. I'll be back on the six o'clock train. Hopefully I'll make it back in time for supper."

"We'll save you some in case you're late." Her mother assured her.

There was no extra 'thank you for your help today' acknowledgement. Maria's work in the business and on the farm was simply expected.

After an hour's train ride and a half hour walk from Reutlingen to Immenhausen, where her grandfather owned five fields of grain, Maria finally arrived at the farmhouse. She burst in the back door, almost breathless from her haste. She scoured the house in search of her Ähne, but instead she bumped into her grumpy Godmother.

"He's already left for the third field. He said you two had worked over the other ones earlier this week." Anna commented, turning to make herself busy in the kitchen behind Maria. "I thought it was you I heard coming in the back door."

"I got here as fast as I could." Maria sputtered. "We had a busy day at the Milk Centrale."

Anna was her father's only sister. She lived on the farm helping her dad run the household because, like so many other German women, she was left a widow during the war and her mother, Maria's grandmother, passed away shortly after Anna's birth. Maria's grandfather never remarried, raising four boys and Anna on his own. It was a choice he regretted in his old age, often complaining of loneliness.

"You can still catch him." Anna said, "he's been expecting you, but it was getting late. He told me to send you out to meet him when you arrived."

Maria turned on her heels and almost ran out to the third field knowing exactly where he would be.

It only took her a few minutes at her top speed before she spotted him in the distance trying to tell his stupid cows which way to walk to be able to plow a straight line. As soon as she reached him Maria almost stumbled through the middle of the plow to take the lead for the cows, guiding them by tugging their heads in the correct direction. She had a method that worked like a charm; pulling each beast forwards by putting her fingers in their wet nostrils. It was not pleasant, but she had experienced so many more disgusting things on the farm with the animals, that such a simple task did not faze her in the least. In fact, she felt quite proud that she was not afraid to do it and as such was most useful to her grandfather. His horses had all been taken from him to be used for war purposes, so he had nothing left with which to plow the fields. This was Maria's solution.

Maria almost fell into the back door of the farmhouse feeling tired and hungry from trudging through the mucky fields, leading the plow all afternoon. After washing up and changing her clothes, she left her grandfather's farm in time to board the six o'clock train to Reutlingen. She sniffed her sleeves and her blouse, just to check, not wanting to look or smell like she'd just come from the farm. Afterall, she didn't know who she may have the pleasure of meeting on the way home.

"I'll see you next time Maria! Be careful and say hello to your dear mother for me!" Her Ähne called after her, watching as she made her way down the lane towards the main street in Immenhausen. His gaze fixed steadfastly on her slim, youthful figure until she was out of sight. He felt so grateful for Maria's willingness to always come and help him with his work. She made it possible for him to stay on the farm; the life he'd always known. He silently wished he could express his deepest gratitude, knowing that if he tried, the flood of tears would come, and his pride couldn't stand it.

Maria slumped in the first seat available once she boarded the train. She was exhausted and happy, knowing that she had accomplished so much on this day. The ride from Immenhausen to Reutlingen gave her sweet time to rest and to steal a peek at her beloved novel. Normally she was instructed to put her books away during the working hours of the day. That was a tall order because reading was her favorite past time. Here, during this hour, she allowed herself to escape her own reality. She particularly enjoyed romance novels and mysteries, allowing herself to experience adventures she only dreamed of. It was a blessed relief, and she savored every minute.

Once she stepped into the front door of her home on Gerber Strasse, Maria understood that her mother had been swindled out of their own family's portion of milk for the day – again. She could tell because the glasses set at the table were filled with water. Her mother was always lenient with the people who inevitably had hard luck stories. When it was Maria's turn to oversee the ration allotment, they had milk in their glasses for dinner. She made sure of that.

"Next time I'll do the books Mama. I know you don't mean to shortchange us, but I'm stricter than you and we need our milk too." Her mother looked up and smiled at her oldest daughter. She knew it was true.

"As long as we are still in time to take care of Ähne for the day." Her mother agreed. It was a deal, at least for the next time. Maria was determined to have milk for their family, especially since they were the distributors for goodness' sake. It just meant getting to the Milk Centrale a little earlier, but so be it. In any case, it was the end of another day and they each had enough to eat and a nice house to call home, which was more than so many people she knew. But most importantly they had one another.

Chapter One

"YOU LOOK BEAUTIFUL!" RUDI SAID WITH THE same sparkle in his eye that he always had for his sweetheart. She half laughed at his admiration, after all she was celebrating her eighty-seventh birthday.

"How beautiful can I be? Here in this hospital bed?" Maria questioned, but judging from the way he looked at her, there was not one doubt that his words spoke the truth from his heart.

"Oh Rudi" she dismissed the compliment like it was silly. But he wouldn't have it. He wanted her to know how much he loved her.

"You are still as beautiful to me today as you were the day we met." She squeezed his hand, because looking into his eyes, she knew that he was expressing exactly how he felt. All their children and grandchildren watched, but Rudi was oblivious. His eyes and attention rested on the love of his life, even though he was a ninety-year-old man. Matthew, one of their grandsons, broke the silence.

"Still chasing your wife after all these years huh Opa?" Rudi nodded.

"Oh, I will never stop." He answered. Even with a tube in her nose to drain the blood clots from her lungs, Maria managed to laugh.

"Yup. He's always been fresh with me. Remember when we met Rudi?" she recalled as the family around her leaned in. They had heard the story before, but there was always something new to be learned. Rosie enjoyed watching her mother's eyes light up as she reminisced.

"Go ahead Mama." She encouraged. "The tale is so beautiful; it never gets old."

Maria looked at Rudi, a sparkle in her eyes. "Hallo Fräulein! You called to me!" They beamed as they recalled their first meeting. Then she looked at the interested loved ones gathered around, waiting to hear more.

"...and I thought – what a fresh young man!"

* * *

THEIR STORY BEGAN ON AN EARLY SPRING morning in Reutlingen, Germany 1950. The country was still recovering after the war and the East was still separated from the West, intently patrolled by foreign border guards. French occupying soldiers controlled passage from the West, and Soviet occupying soldiers controlled the East. Rudi had managed to get a job as a leather craftsman's apprentice in Stuttgart. His boss needed to travel to Reutlingen to acquire business from a certain tannery and on this day, his regular driver had called in sick.

"Is anyone here able to chauffeur me to Reutlingen?" he asked of his staff in the back room, who were busy crafting orders for the day. Rudi, being one of the apprentices, stepped up.

"I can drive." He said, eager to make a good impression.

His boss smiled, impressed by Rudi's enthusiasm. He walked over to his young apprentice and put a hand on Rudi's shoulder. "Get your wallet. You'll need your papers." He instructed. Rudi's task that day turned out entirely different than expected and it was a day that would change his life forever.

Rudi tapped his fingers on the steering wheel as he casually rested his elbow out the open window of the company car. His boss was inside the shop, and Rudi, pleased with himself having smoothly negotiated safe passage through the stringent check point, scanned his surroundings, waiting for his boss to return. He was suddenly stopped in his surveillance when his eyes laid hold of a beautiful young woman, wearing a dark green, belted spring coat and high heeled shoes. He had to seize the moment.

He whistled, "Hallo Fräulein!" The beautiful young lady looked in the direction of the whistle as did everyone else on the street. He was looking right at her.

She stood for a moment, dumbfounded. 'Could he be whistling at me', she wondered?

"Yes you!" the man spoke to her again.

'How bold! How very forward', she thought! He gestured for her to come over to his car. She hesitated, but then out of curiosity, she cautiously crossed the street.

"Are you whistling at me?" she asked, surprised.

"Yes", Rudi smiled, thinking on the spot. Suddenly, he came up with a random question, "I wonder where I can buy post cards around here. I'm from the East, and I'm just here to chauffeur my boss on a business trip". She stood a moment, taking it all in.

"Anyways", he repeated, fumbling to make sense. "I'd like to buy post cards."

Maria, catching on that this was an attempt at flirtation, smiled as she gestured down the street, "in the train station – there's a kiosk and they sell post cards." He was thinking of another question to ask her the whole time she was answering the first one. At a loss, he just decided to be honest.

"Okay. Thank you. Well, my name is Rudolf Heinrich by the way. I'm from Berlin." He rambled, confirming the fact that he was not from the area and trying to validate his request for postcards.

"Hello Rudolf", she said, "I'm Maria."

"Hello Maria. It's Rudi actually", he said quickly, wanting to explain before his boss came back. His heart pounding, he went on. "My boss is a leather smith and since I'm his apprentice, I am acting as his chauffeur today while he does business here." He pointed to the leather shop.

Her gaze followed his gesture to the tannery on the corner of the street. Then he immediately turned his attention back to her. "I don't know anyone here. I mean I've never been in this town, but I would sure like to go out with you sometime." Maria hesitated. "Please?" he asked with a twinkle in his eye, "We could exchange addresses and the next time I'm in town, maybe we could go on a date?" She smiled at him sideways, knowing that this sure was a bold come-on, right in the middle of the street.

"But you don't even know me." Maria protested.

"Yes, but I'd like to. Please?" Rudi pleaded again, quickly writing his name and address on a piece of paper. "In any case, I'm going to give you my address. You can decide later."

His confidence attracted her instantly, plus, he had a great smile and beautiful brown eyes, so she accepted the paper with his address, and then turned and went on her way, looking back to smile.

Just then Rudi's boss came out of the leather shop and got in the car. As they drove off, Rudi glimpsed Maria in the side mirror as she crossed back over the street and continued walking.

Bursting through the front door, Maria searched the front of the house for her mother, only to find her in the back, working in the kitchen. Maria was almost out of breath and pacing.

"You won't believe what just happened to me Mama". Her mother, also named Maria, looked at her daughter and noticed how flushed she was.

"Tell me. I'm curious". She said.

"I met a very fresh young man who whistled at me from his car. When I walked over to him, he asked me on a date right then and there." She prattled, hardly catching her breath. Her mother laughed.

"Well did you give him your address?"

"No. But he gave me his. I can hardly believe it; I took it. Look, here it is" she said, pulling out a piece of paper from her pocket. "He was so bold, so ....so bold." Her mother put her hands on her hips and had to laugh.

"And... what else? He didn't smell the cows from your having come from the farm, did he?"

"Well," Maria thought with a smile starting to come across her serious face. "I don't think so. I had changed into my spring dress and coat before I left Ähne's house. Anyway, he had a beautiful smile and nice eyes, I suppose." looking at her mother for a

35

reaction of some sort. This time her mother was amazed to see Maria's feathers ruffled but passed no judgement. The practical, independent daughter that she knew Maria to be, under normal circumstances, would have considered such frivolous flirtation as nonsense. She was intrigued to see Maria exasperated.

"Well anyway he said he wants to go dancing with me." Her mother nodded and smiled.

"Well, there's no harm in writing him. You might not see him again. He was probably just flirting."

"I know," Maria agreed, settling down a little. The incident had upset her otherwise calm and collected demeanor. None of the young men in their district would even think of being so forward. She turned and went up the stairs to tell her sister the story from the beginning.

"Well keep the address in a safe place." Her sister told her. "You never know when you might feel like going dancing with a stranger." They laughed together and then went about their chores for the day.

In the hustle of everyday life, the events of that fateful spring day faded into time, although periodically Maria had to smile when she thought of her admirer 'from Berlin.'

By the middle of the summer, the young adults in their district were starting to plan their get togethers where Anneliese, Maria and their twin cousins performed funny skits together. Two sets of twins in a who-done-it comedy always kept their audience laughing. Maria wrote the scripts, coming up with plot twists and funny characters from old men and women who couldn't remember one another, to bank robbers who confused the police when they were trying to accuse the correct person. The talented musicians in the group would play their instruments, giving the others an opportunity to dance. Sometimes Maria and Anneliese would sing in harmony to add even more entertainment and then everyone broke off into groups or couples and they spent the rest of the evening simply socializing. It was fun for a while, but Maria didn't always have the best time. Anneliese was usually the center of attention, laughing and flirting with the young men, and game for adventure if she was in the mood. Meanwhile Maria usually ended up going home by herself at the end of most of their social events. She was the opposite in personality of her twin; not a flirtatious teenager at all. She was looking for substance instead of a fleeting kiss now and again.

"None of the guys have the courage to ask for a dance anymore these days." Maria complained after they came home very late one Saturday evening. "How are you supposed to get to know them if they don't even ask?"

Anneliese shot her sister a knowing glance. "First of all, you don't give anyone the least bit of encouragement with your air of.... of aloof-ness."

37

"What?" Maria laughed. Then she shrugged. "I don't even care." She resolved. "I don't want a man who doesn't even have the courage to step up and ask me for a dance." Anneliese looked at her sister, wisely keeping her silence, only raising her eyebrows.

"Well, I had fun." She simply said.

"Of course you did." Maria mumbled.

"What?" Anneliese asked, having heard an unintelligible remark.

"All I'm saying is that if I was willing to flirt or even...kiss...anyone who showed the slightest interest, then I'm sure I'd have more suitors too." Anneliese simply nodded. She didn't want to argue.

"Why are you so closed off anyway?"

"I'm not. I'm just selective." Maria answered.

"Well, if that's the case." Anneliese answered, "then I suppose you may have to wait until a perfect stranger comes to sweep you off your feet. Like that guy from Berlin."

Maria was silent, but she was thoughtful about how that may've turned out.

* * *

RUDI DAYDREAMED ABOUT THE BEAUTIFUL Fräulein that he encountered in Reutlingen for a while, although he knew that his chances of seeing her again were slim to none because he hadn't gotten her address. In any case, work kept him busy and in the evenings he found himself at the local pub enjoying himself with a stein of beer.

Occasionally a young lady would catch his eye, but never anyone that he wanted to date seriously.

No sooner had the air turned nippy, than the leaves started falling off the trees and people started preparing for Christmas.

"You know what Maria," her sister, Anneliese proposed, "we should write our Christmas cards early this year and you should write that guy who gave you his address from his car!"

"Oh Anne! That was such a long time ago." Maria said, "at least six months. Why would I do that now?"

"Because it's perfect timing! It's normal to send Christmas cards and it's non-committal. And you did say he has nice eyes and a nice smile. If he doesn't write back, it's no big deal. It's only a Christmas card." She shrugged.

Maria considered her sister's suggestion, admitting with a twinge of disappointment, that she hadn't received any such attention from the local young men as of late, so she decided to go along with the idea.

"Genius." Maria said. "Okay, I'll do it! But what if he doesn't remember me?"

"But what if he does?" her sister said. "And this way he'll have your address too!"

Maria consented to doing as her sister suggested, trying not to place too much hope for a response. She did, however, make sure to send the card and the envelope and use her best handwriting and a sprinkle of perfume.

It had been a couple of weeks since she had mailed the letter and Maria was starting to feel somewhat discouraged that she hadn't received any response at all.

Suddenly Anneliese came running down the back pathway from the post office to their house.

"Maria!" she huffed, almost out of breath and holding an envelope out to her sister. "There's a letter for you from Stuttgart!" Maria stared at her in disbelief.

"Well open it!" Anneliese said giving it to her. They both sat on the bed, eager to see if Rudi responded positively.

"Dearest Maria," she read out loud,

"I was surprised to receive your beautiful Christmas card. I am very grateful that you kept my address and decided to send me a card. I wish you a very Merry Christmas too! Perhaps we can have our date that you promised me when I come to Reutlingen again? My boss said that he may do business there next month. Would you do me the honor of allowing me to take you out for a nice dinner and dancing?"

Yours,

Rudolf Heinrich.

The sisters looked at each other wide eyed and then burst out laughing.

"See?" Anneliese said, "It worked. You're welcome." Maria smirked, but then recognized that it was indeed because of her sister's encouragement that she was even bold enough to write the card.

"Thank you, Anneliese. We'll name our first daughter after you." They both burst out laughing again.

Chapter Two

DRESSED IN A DARK BLUE, PINSTRIPED SUIT with a long overcoat, Rudi hid behind a thick post on the landing platform in the train station. He was nervous that Maria would realize how short he was and be disappointed. When he recognized her standing alone, looking for him, he surmised that at least he was a little taller than she was. Slowly and with a mix of apprehension and charm, he leaned out from behind the post revealing his big smile. Maria caught sight of him and recognized him immediately. She flashed him a huge smile in return and they both made their way to greet one another. Rudi was quick to pull her hand in and turn a hearty handshake into a warm embrace.

After the initial first meeting jitters were overcome, they had what seemed like a full day of chatting and getting to know one another in person. They stopped by a local hotel so Rudi could unload his suitcase and freshen up for their date and in no time were making their way down Gerber Strasse to find Maria's mother looking out the window. She spied them, coming down the street, the young man with a small paper in hand, looking at the houses trying to locate the correct address that Maria had sent him.

'Oh, my goodness!' Maria's mother said to herself. 'Oh my gosh! It's him!'

Rudi's eyes lit up, having found the correct house. Turning to Maria, he came to the front door.

"It wouldn't have been that hard, you see?" he told her, "I would've found your address eventually."

"Uh huh." She answered, smiling.

"But now that I am sure of where you live, I'll not be needing anymore directions, paper or otherwise." He assured her, already assuming he would be coming again.

"You must be Maria's mother." Rudi confidently inquired, holding out his hand. "I'm Rudolf." They stood awkwardly shaking hands for a moment. "I'm the one who called Maria from the car...back when...we first met." He explained. "She probably told you about me. I know that it was a little –

43

forward." Looking back at Maria for assurance, he continued. "You can call me Rudi. It's nice to meet you." Maria's mother tried her best to be forthcoming.

"Hello Rudi. I'm Maria Riekert. My daughter and I have the same name. I mean Maria was named after me." She said a little flustered. "You can call me Frau Riekert." Maria's mother said, wanting to ease any anxiety he might be feeling in this first meeting.

Leaving Rudi and her mother to chat, Maria went up the stairs to get changed into appropriate clothes for their dinner date. Having just met one another after simply writing letters, she wasn't sure if Rudi was pleased by her appearance, but she was cautiously optimistic. She quickly put on a long blue dress with small white flowers and wore her soft brown hair down around her shoulders. Rudi had to catch his breath when he saw her again. He smiled at her, still somewhat speechless, but looking at her now, he was so thankful that he decided to make this trip and visit the pretty Fräulein from Reutlingen. He had a hard time hiding his delight in her appearance. Maria's mother noticed...

"Are you ready to go"? he asked as he stood up, reaching his hand to Maria. She smiled and looked at her mother.

"I suppose I am." She answered shyly, placing her hand in his. Rudi turned back on his way out the door.

"I'll have her back before midnight."

Appreciative that he was given this opportunity, especially because they had only just met, he was determined to make a good first impression. Once they had left the house, Maria's mother stood at the window watching her daughter walk down the street with a spring in her step. She was grateful for this occasion. Rudi seemed like a nice young man. She was sorry to admit that Maria had had a very hard life, and it was so good to see her happy. She was hopeful and blindly trusted that this could be a very good beginning for her serious daughter.

"On recommendation from the guy at the hotel, I was thinking we could go to the restaurant just three blocks from here if you don't mind walking. Apparently, they have a nice dance floor too. Do you like dancing?" Rudi asked Maria.

"Yes, I do like dancing! Although I can't say that I've had much opportunity around here, but yes, I do enjoy it."

Rudi was intrigued. "Why have you not had much opportunity?"

"Oh," Maria explained "I have to help my mother a lot with the family business, so by the time we can go out and do something fun, we're too tired I suppose."

Rudi was still intrigued. "Who's we? And you can't be tired all the time."

Maria giggled nervously, "I'm always saying we because I am a twin. We do everything together. We usually go on dates together. I mean double dates of course. And no, we're, I mean – I – am not tired all the time, but we've – I've – had to be dressed in black and behave like I am in mourning for so long, that it seems like - I - don't get to have fun like this very often. I am really looking forward to this tonight." This confession gave Rudi more incentive to show this darling young lady the best time he possibly could tonight.

"I hope that you fully enjoy this evening. I will certainly do my best." He promised her. Wishing that he could pull out every luxury to impress her and make her feel special, he resigned himself to doing the very most with what he had to work with. "I hope you're hungry. I think this restaurant has good food. At least I hope they do. I've never been here before either, obviously" he said nervously, "so let's hope we like it." He offered her his arm and they walked briskly down the street. Before they knew it, they had arrived, and it was much nicer than either of them expected. They were seated immediately, and they both remarked how lovely the atmosphere was. As soon as they received their menus the music started to play. It was uplifting and romantic, as if God himself had orchestrated this beautiful night for them. Rudi turned on the charm. He stood up and walked over to her chair, gallantly holding out his hand in a gesture for her to join him on the dance floor. Maria deftly placed her hand in his, allowing him to lead her. He placed his hand on the small of her back and gently swayed her to the music. It was enough to melt her defenses. She had never been romanced in such a chivalrous manner. Rudi, having guided a few young women around the dance floor in his day, was careful to be the perfect gentleman, letting her discover his leading rather than forcing it. While Rudi held her close during one of the slow dances, Maria turned her head towards him.

"This is impressive. It's so lovely here. I never knew." she admitted. Rudi looked at her with a special gleam in his eye, like he was just the one to show her a good time.

"You see, it was meant to be that you met me that day and now we enjoy this beautiful time together. Just think what we both could have missed." Maria listened while following his lead on the dance floor. She realized that this in fact was true. She could have chosen not to follow through with his invitation and simply sit at home again, with her mother and siblings and not have this amazing evening with a man who made her feel so special. He was right, it was worth taking the chance to go out with him.

"It's true. I am very glad I came. So grateful. Thank you, Rudi." She almost whispered. When the music stopped, they kept on dancing until they realized that they were the only ones left on the dance floor. They both laughed and then found their way to the table to sit down. Rudi walked her over to her chair and held it out for her. He was careful to make a good impression. These manners were something Maria had never experienced before. She had only imagined being treated this way because of the novels she read. And here she was, living out a fantasy. Having grown up in a farming community and then immediately plunged into the harsh survival activity of wartime, made it difficult for the youth to interact romantically. None of the young men she knew would act this way towards a young lady. They simply had no one to teach them. She couldn't imagine where Rudi had learned his behavior, but she was thankful to be experiencing this evening. She was flabbergasted and didn't quite know how to act. Just then, their waiter came, and Maria followed Rudi's lead, even in her restaurant etiquette, ordering the same dish of Rouladen and a glass of wine. They spent the evening on and off the dance floor, lost in each other's eyes. Time seemed to stand still just for them. When it was almost midnight, Rudi cautioned that it was time to take her home, remembering that he promised her mother.

As they were walking back to Maria's house, feeling confident that he had given Maria a good time, Rudi decided to ask if he could see her again.

"It won't be until two weekends from now because I will have to come from Stuttgart, but I would like to take you out again. Maybe we could go dancing again. Would you like that?" he asked, hopeful that she was having as much fun as he was.

"I would. Yes. I would like to see you again." She answered positively. "Thank you so much for tonight. I've never had a dance partner like you. Where did you learn to dance like that?"

Standing in front of Maria's house, he pulled her close to answer her question. "Oh, I just picked it up here and there. I love to dance." He told her. Then he twirled her around and drew her close again, "that's why I'm good at it, ha-ha." Then he became serious, as his brown eyes looked sincerely into her light blue/green eyes, "You are a lovely lady, Maria. Thank you for coming with me tonight. You have made this a wonderful trip for me." He leaned in to give her a small kiss. "I will see you next weekend!" And just as soon as he dropped her off at her door, he waltzed back to his hotel. He felt like he was dancing on a cloud because Maria was the girl of his dreams, and he knew it this first night.

Chapter Three

THEY WERE STILL HOLDING HANDS AS MARIA recalled her joy from their first evening as a couple. "I had never danced like that!" she told all the family gathered around her hospital bed. "It had been years that we were even allowed to go out and celebrate anything."

"Why?" asked Brittany, their youngest granddaughter, who was always so intrigued by their family history.

"Well, we had lost so many people during the war and for each one of my uncles, we needed to wear only black for a whole year. It was tradition. Three of my father's brothers, had died in the war. Luckily, my Mama didn't agree with that dress 'rule'. She was more – how you say – 'free' with that. She let us wear different clothes sometimes. A lot of the time actually." Everyone around the room listened in serious silence, but Maria lifted the gravity of the memory. "Well, you don't want to wear black all the time. It makes you even more sad. I was so thankful for my Mama. She was lenient in lots of ways – and – she was a very smart businesswoman." Maria was proud to say.

Melissa, her oldest granddaughter was interested in this family trait, "what do you mean, Oma?" she asked.

Maria did her best to explain. "Ja, Melissa, good business sense runs in the family. You have inherited that from her, and I think from me too." She gave her a wink and Melissa smiled. Maria went on to explain, "When my mother was very young, maybe seventeen, she worked in the 'Milk Centrale', which was the city's milk distribution center, before the grocery stores took the 'milkman's' job away. She oversaw the books. It happened that the mayor of the city noticed how smart she was at her job and asked her to keep the books for him. It was because of my mother's knowledge about the milk business, we were able to do quite well for ourselves just after the war, when other families were struggling. And she did that after my dad died in the war – she was without a husband. She was a smart woman," Maria reminisced "and she loved Rudi very much. When she realized that Rudi could only come every three

51

weeks because he had to stay in a hotel while he was visiting, she offered him my brother, Siegfried's, room." She explained. "Siegfried was only ten, so he was still young enough to sleep in her room. That way, Rudi could come every weekend from Stuttgart, and it would only cost him the train fare." She looked back at Rudi, and they seemed to go back in time again. "It was a big house too. She rented out four bedrooms and we each had a room – remember Rudi?"

***

"I DON'T CARE WHAT OTHER PEOPLE SAY RUDI. It is my house, and I can do whatever I want." Rudi almost said something, but Maria's mother shut down any doubts about his welcome. "It's what I want to do and so that settles it. It'll be nice to have a man around the house on the weekends. It's like you're one of the family when you're here anyway." She looked between Rudi and Maria. "You two better get going or you'll be late to give out the milk. Off you go!" Rudi gave Maria's mother a big hug.

"Thank you very much. Now I will be here every weekend. You're going to get sick of me." He warned.

"Nonsense! And you mind as well call me Mom. Now, you better put your suitcase upstairs and then drive over to the Milk Centrale. They'll be waiting for you." Rudi almost ran up the stairs with his suitcase, he was so happy, and he came bounding down again to swoop Maria up in his arms.

"Let's go slow poke." He joked.

He sat in the driver's seat of the milk truck. He was very confident behind the wheel because he had driven plenty of milk trucks before, although none of them were three-wheelers. Even so, he figured he was able to drive the fastest so they would not be late.

"Have you ever driven a three-wheel truck before? It is not easy to drive," Maria cautioned him, "The steering wheel doesn't automatically straighten out. You have to turn it back after you make a turn." Rudi saluted her, as if to say 'Roger that' while keeping his eyes on the road. He literally heard her words one minute, even acknowledging them, and forgot them the next. He was turning in to the Milk Centrale but went blank when the steering wheel seemed to get stuck. Luckily, just before they were about to roll, Maria dove into his driving space, taking the wheel in her hands. She brought it back around to straighten the vehicle just in time. Rudi stopped, his heart pounding. It was a moment of panic – averted.

"Now you know what I mean. It's not easy, is it?" Maria questioned.

Rudi caught his breath and recovering his pride, said "Well once you get the hang of it..." Maria just looked sideways at him.

"Uh huh. C'mon, we've got to get the milk cans from the back." They jumped out of the car and carried the big aluminum cans to the filling station. Their district was quite densely populated because it was central to a lot of farms and the small villages surrounding them. They sold just over 400 liters of milk every day. Maria was accustomed to pushing the filled milk cans along the floor to the truck because each can contained 40 liters of milk, or ten and a half gallons. She had to fill at least ten of them, sometimes more. With all her might, she lifted them into the back of the vehicle. Now that Rudi was there, he simply carried them from the warehouse to the flatbed of the truck. They were very heavy, but it was easy for him. Maria wished she could have the strength of a man, for even a day, just to know what it was like. Once they were loaded, they had to drive back to their place of business, which was across the street from the house on Gerber Strasse – a somewhat make-shift garage/store. Once their paperwork was signed and while they were walking back out to the truck, she gave him a playful shove. He stumbled and laughed and pulled her close for a quick kiss.

"Thank You", she said, "You've made my job so much easier. Normally it takes all my strength to hoist those cans full of milk into the truck.

"Hoist?" Rudi teased. Maria giggled, realizing it was an awkward expression.

"Yes. It's so heavy for me."

He picked her up and set her in the back of the truck. "Is that hoisting?" she giggled some more.

"Yes." She realized he was playfully egging her on. "I'm serious. It's very hard for me."

"And yet you always do it," Rudi remarked, making less of the help he was providing her, but she was very serious and extremely grateful.

"I have to. That's our business." She explained. "How else can my mother make money? You just made it so easy today. I'm trying to say thank you."

He kissed her again. "You're welcome." He lifted her back out of the truck and ran around the front "And now it's time to go sell some milk!"

Maria hesitated, "Are you sure you want to drive?"

"I'm sure. Get in. I got this," he boasted. Opening her side of the car door, Rudi gestured for her to take a seat. Then he ran behind the truck to his side of the car. As he got in, he slammed the door shut and, with his arm out the window, slapped the door a couple of times, giving the truck some instructions, "Hear me Gretel, you're going to behave this time!"

Maria laughed, "Gretel?"

"I want her to give us a smooth ride, so she needs a little love tap." He explained. Maria was entertained. She realized that Rudi liked to make every moment fun. The ride home went smoothly until the very end, when he nearly drove the truck into the side of the garage. Again, Maria leaned in forcefully, taking the wheel to steer it back.

"Rudi!" she screamed. When they stopped, they were both silent for a moment. Then Rudi burst out laughing.

Maria shook her head and had to laugh with him. "You nearly took me out!" she scolded.

"Oh my Gosh! We made it! We survived! I did better that time, right? Say Yes!" he leaned in close and searched her face for a positive answer, hoping she wouldn't be mad. Maria, still shaking her head, gave him some grace, "you'll get the hang of it, if you don't kill us first." He walked around to her side of the car and let her out. Maria walked behind the table and opened the ledger books as Rudi unloaded the milk cans. She walked over to the door and before opening it for their customers, she turned back to look at Rudi.

"Are we ready?" she asked.
He nodded with confidence. "Ready!"

"A lot of people came with their pots, or plastic containers, or whatever they had and flooded into the store, Rudi taking position next to his Fräulein protectively.

Because the distribution of milk was government regulated after the war, it was given out according to how many people lived in each household. Some tried to get more milk by saying they were allowed more, but Maria kept a strict watch over the books. Seeing Maria behind the table controlling the books

56

was disappointing for such people because when her mother oversaw the distribution, they were sometimes allotted more than their assigned portion. They knew they couldn't get away with any type of manipulation of Maria. She always gave the correct amount. After the customers left, Rudi helped her wash the milk cans out with soap and water, and hung them upside down, ready for the next day.

Walking back over to the house, she gave him another playful shove. He stepped back, still feeling a little sorry for his mishandling of the milk truck.

He tried to joke with her, "Hey Fräulein! Watch your step - Flirting on the job can cause car accidents!" She threw her head back laughing. He was testing the waters to see if his unintentional misadventures with the 'company car' were still annoying her. She had long since forgiven him, but he wanted to make sure.

As they came in the house, Maria's mother turned around, amused, "Fun day on the job, you two?"

"I'm either going to laugh or cry Mama. Rudi's getting used to driving the three-wheeler."

"Oh, I see. Well, I would've liked to have seen that." She laughed.

Rudi's eyes grew big. "Maybe you wouldn't have, "he said, "but we're both still alive."

Just then Maria's twelve-year-old brother, Siegfried, came bounding in the back door. He walked right over to Rudi and looked up at him with pleading eyes "I'm going out in the back to chop wood. Want to come help?"

"Let Rudi have something to eat first, Siegfried," Maria's mother said, "apparently he's earned it." She smiled to herself.

Maria fixed them a plate of food and then, as he was sitting down to eat, Rudi spied two little dark eyes peeking around the corner where the stairs were. It was Maria's little sister, Hildegard. She was a tiny figure of a thirteen-year-old teenager, curious and shy, until you got to know her. She had met Rudi the previous weekend when he came to see Maria, but she hadn't yet gotten to know him well enough to be herself in his presence just yet.

"Hello there sweet little pumpkin. I see you peeking around the corner. Why don't you come out and give me a proper hello?" asked Rudi as he boldly stood up and held out a hand to her. She was shy, but Hildegard was not meek. She had spunk and courage to call her own, a typical independent third child. She would not be scared away, but instead she responded with confidence and grace. "Hello Rudi. Nice to see you again." Rudi was instantly charmed by this delightful tiny creature.

"I think we need to give you a new nickname. Hildegard is too plain for someone as cute as you, and pumpkin, well, everyone uses that one."

Hildegard just stood in the kitchen against the stove, listening and smiling, wondering what he would come up with. Rudi only gave it a moment's thought and announced, "Hätele!" You are my little "Hätele!" which is a German term of endearment for a wispy girl.

"Alright then," Hildegard replied, "You are my Möpsle!" which is also a German term of endearment. It means jokester and a visual picture of someone with a round face. Maria and her mother threw their heads back laughing at these two going at it. Hildegard and Rudi hit it off instantly. Meanwhile Siegfried was getting impatient. Rudi noticed and quickly finished his lunch and went out to the woodshed with Maria's brother.

"You might want to get ready for tonight, Maria. We're going dancing, remember?" Rudi exclaimed on his way out the back door. Maria glanced at her mother and smiled.

"I suppose you're developing quite an attachment to our Mr. Berlin!" commented her mother. "He certainly does bring a lot of life to our house." Maria smiled as she comparatively thought about her twin sister secretly going on dates and staying out half the night.

"I am, I think I am Mama." She smiled.

"Well, do you think that's wise Maria? I mean how long have we known him really?" Her mother's comment immediately put Maria on the defensive.

"I would rather be with someone fun and someone who was kind to me and to my family, than someone who only 'looked' good, but whose character I could never trust." She decreed.

Maria's mother raised an eyebrow.

"I know you're talking about your sister's boyfriend." Continuing to wash her dishes in silence, she added her own opinion. "I think I must agree with you on that. He is very handsome, but he's always trying to get Anneliese away from all of us and who knows what they're doing so late?" she remarked, a little worried. "And as for trust? I don't think that ever came into play with Helmut as long as we've known him. There does come a time when you must take a chance, like we did with Rudi when we first met him, but it's easy to surmise the quality of someone's character after you've known them for a while. Mind you Maria, we must remember that we only see Rudi on weekends, and we don't know his family." She warned. "But still, he works hard, he's kind to all of us and he is very helpful. I think there's a lot to be said for the way he treats all of us."

Hildegard was still in the kitchen, listening to her mother and her sister, and decided to chime in. "I like him too. I like Rudi. He's nice to me, and he's a lot of fun!"

Maria's mother laughed. "Well, you got her vote!"

Chapter Four

ALMOST AS IF HE HAD HEARD HIS NAME mentioned, Rudi walked back into the house to get a glass of water from the kitchen. Before she knew it, Maria felt him sweeping her off her feet and into the living room all the while twirling her around and whistling one of his favorite tunes. Maria was trying to follow Rudi's lead but wanted to change her flat working shoes for a pair with little heels, so she could twirl. She excused herself for a minute and went into the bedroom to quickly find some different shoes, when suddenly, Anneliese came into the living room from the front door. She stood at the entrance to the living room and blankly stared at Rudi. Rudi stood still, absolutely confused as to how Maria could go out of the room one way and somehow go outside, circle the house, and enter again, in less than a minute. She was wearing the same clothes. Her hair looked the same. This was perplexing. He nearly had a heart attack when Maria, number one, came back into the living room from the entrance to the bedroom.

"What? Hold on! What?" His mind raced as he tried to configure the explanation. "You never told me you have a twin!"

Maria wrinkled her brow, "Yes I did!" she protested. Rudi was completely flabbergasted. Anneliese was already laughing.

"Allow me to introduce myself. I'm Anneliese."

Rudi shook her hand and turned to Maria, "If you did tell me, I forgot. Oh my Gosh! I thought for a minute that I lost my mind!" Maria laughed.

"I'm sure I told you on our first date." She assured him.

"Well, I've been here a few times now and I've never met the other you!" he reasoned. "Or have I?" The three of them had a good laugh together and Anneliese liked him instantly. When they stopped laughing Maria held up her shoes.

"I found my dancing shoes!"

"Ooh where are you going?" Anneliese asked.

"Dancing of course," Maria answered as she put her shoes on and put up her hands to resume dancing with Rudi. Rudi politely made an invitation.

"Do you want to come along?" he graciously asked Maria's twin. Anneliese smiled, but squirmed a little, giving an excuse.

"I think Helmut is taking me out on his motorcycle tonight. I don't know where we're going, but thanks anyway. Maybe another time."

"Hey — when are you coming out to finish the wood?" a little voice asked from the kitchen. "Coming right now Siegfried!" Rudi called back. Maria walked to the back door with him. "The sooner I finish with the wood, the sooner I can get ready for tonight." Maria gave him a smile and a kiss.

"Alright. I will go get ready now. Don't be too long!" she called to Rudi on his way out.

Anneliese stood in the doorway looking out after Maria's boyfriend. "What a nice guy." She smiled at Maria. "Not someone I would ever date, but nice."

Maria turned to her sister, "Yes, I know. If he isn't over six feet tall or has a pretty-boy face, you're not interested. I have got news for you sis — a guy like that rarely has a good personality. It's all about him and the way he looks. Never mind treating you with respect, or doing anything that makes you happy, or how about maybe being kind to your family?"

Anneliese put her hands on her hips. "Helmut is kind to my family. He's never been mean to you," she tried to engage her mother in the conversation. "Right Mama, he's been nice?"

Maria's mother answered, "He's nice enough when he comes around to take you out Anneliese. Maria is talking about spending time with us. All of us, as a family." She looked at Maria, gathering courage to confront her daughter, "and we just wonder where you are sometimes, so late into the night." Anneliese got defensive again, avoiding the question.

"Well, he's very kind to me and when it comes down to it, that's all that really matters. He's nice to all of you, I've seen it." Anneliese went to her room to get changed, leaving Maria and her mother still wondering where it was that they were always going. She was secretive, which left Maria to conclude that she was up to something that she knew was wrong. It made her love Rudi even more, contrasting his thoughtfulness to always bring her home on time so her mother wouldn't worry. He had an open, helpful, and cheery personality which she inevitably compared to Helmut who was a man that always seemed like he was on the take. She felt blessed to have found Rudi and she was thankful.

Maria walked into her bedroom thinking how fortunate she was. She knew that she was falling in love and felt like she was walking on a cloud. She danced over to her mirror where she had her hair combs and a perfume bottle that Rudi had given her. She put on a wine-colored dress that was tightly fitted at the waist with a long flowing skirt. She stood admiring how pretty she felt as she looked in her mirror. She was very slim and kept her petite figure in check mostly because she was always so busy working. It was so wonderful for her to have an evening to look forward to with Rudi. Her life had changed so much since she met him. She stared in the mirror, remembering how difficult it had been for her mother and all her siblings after their father died in the war. She remembered vividly a man dressed in army uniform, knocking on their door. Her mother's reaction when that man left, forever ingrained in her memory. She was like stone for weeks. She tried to console herself over her husband's death by rocking in a chair for days on end. Maria remembered begging her mother to snap out of it and come back to them because they needed her. One day her grandmother took matters in hand and gave her daughter a piece of her mind.

"Don't sit there and act like you're the only one who lost a loved one." She chided. "You lost a husband, but your children lost a father and you're letting them grieve alone. Is that right? Is that what you want him to see, watching you from heaven? You are sitting here in your rocking chair, feeling sorry for yourself, while your girls are working like dogs to take care of the family. They are grieving too, but you don't see them lying down and giving up. They are still alive. Their sister and brother are still alive and need to be taken care of – and so do they, for goodness' sake. They are only ten years old Maria. All of them are yours and Eugis' children and they need you. You are all they have now, so it's time for you to snap out of it and become their mother again! No more time for self-pity. It's time to live again!"

Maria's mother listened to the chastening of her mother. This time it was as if something clicked. She came out of what seemed like a trance. All her children were surrounding her, and they all gave her hugs. Everyone was crying, but it was like a cleansing.

The next chapter in their lives would be hard, not having a husband or a father, but they had each other, and they trusted God to see them through. Really there was nothing else they could do — God was all they had, but in time, they would come to realize, that He was enough.

Maria blinked at herself in the mirror again. She had come a long way since those sad days. But she had a lot of tough years in between too — like running the milk business with her mother and helping Ähne on the farm while Anneliese helped with the children and the cooking. She often wondered if life wasn't meant to be easy. Maybe the hardship developed strength of character and helped people to rely on God if they didn't become bitter. The hardship helped Maria to realize that she was not always in control of her life and sometimes that was a difficult thing to accept and sometimes it was a blessing. Thanks to her father's influence, even from his letters that he sent to her from wherever he was stationed in the war, Maria learned to lean on God. That knowledge comforted her and made her strong. She was not scared at all. Her mother knew that and understood that of anyone who could help her with the business and with the chores on the farm, it would have to be Maria. In her mind, she could do anything. She had come to fully rely on her in many ways, even as a young girl.

Her thoughts came back to how blessed she was now as she stared at herself in the mirror all dressed up and feeling like she was treasured by the man she loved. She thought, "what an amazing God I have!" Just then, Anneliese interrupted her thoughts.

"You smell nice. What is that?" Maria held up her perfume bottle.

"Rudi gave it to me. It's from Stuttgart. Would you like some?" Anneliese jumped at the offer.

"Yes, I would. Thank you." Maria looked at her sister's dress.

"Anne, you might need a sweater if you're going on the motorcycle. It'll get cold tonight."
Anneliese protested. "No, I can't wear a sweater on a motorcycle. It'll just get in the way. Besides, it'll also cover up my figure. I wouldn't want that."

Maria let out a sigh. Suit yourself. I'm taking one in case it's cold when I come home from dancing."
Anneliese half laughed at her sister.

"I'm sure you are." Anneliese took one last look at herself in the mirror. Turning towards her sister, she said "Enjoy your evening, Maria. I hope you have fun dancing." Maria came over and gave her a hug.

"You too." Maria whispered in her ear, "we smell nice." Laughing, Anneliese let go and left the room.

Maria called after her, "Be careful Anne!" She didn't hear a response, so she went back to her dresser and put the finishing touches of blush on her face and put up her hair. She was so happy, and content and she wished the same for her twin, but she understood that she had to let go and let her make her own decisions.

Chapter Five

SUDDENLY, THERE WAS A KNOCK ON HER bedroom door. She opened it and stepped back, catching her breath. Standing in her doorway was her best friend, her confidant and her man; Rudi. All dressed up. At that moment she wanted to tell her sister that she was thankful that she didn't find Rudi attractive because she wanted him all to herself. He wore a dark suit with a white shirt. His tie completed the look with blue and wine-colored stripes. He certainly knows how to dress, Maria mused. Rudi, although particular about his own appearance, suddenly forgot himself the minute he stepped into Maria's presence.

"You look beautiful Maria. I can hardly believe that you're my girl." His expression of approval melted her heart. She knew how happy he made her feel and hoped that she made Rudi feel the same. He held out his hand and together they walked down the stairs and found Maria's mother sitting and resting; a very rare sight indeed. She looked up at her daughter.

"You look beautiful Maria." Then she took a second look at the two love birds in front of her. "What a wonderful couple you two make." She was about to get up to walk them out.

"No, no mom. We can see ourselves out. You sit and rest tonight. You're always working," Rudi said. He walked over to her and gave her a hug goodnight. Hildegard was also downstairs sitting at the table with her mother, working on some hand-sewing. Siegfried was already in bed. Hilde, looking up, noticed Maria's 'glow' and how lovely they looked together.

"You two look like a fairytale. I wish I could go dancing too," she said blissfully. Rudi accepted that as an invitation and an opportunity to take 'Hätele' on a few swirls around the kitchen. Once again, he was whistling one of his favorite tunes and took Hilde by complete surprise. She was game and up for the challenge though. She kept up quite well with what she knew, and Rudi was such a good dancer that it was easy to catch on to the steps.

When he politely brought her back to her chair, he said, "thank you for the dance, 'Hätele.' I'm sure we will have many more opportunities to swing around the dance floor together. But for now, I bid you two lovely ladies good night. I am going to try and impress my sweetheart with a few dance moves of our own."

"Well, you just know how to charm everyone don't you?" Maria's mother said. Rudi winked at her and laughed. Maria gave her mother a kiss on the cheek.

"We will be back by midnight as usual Mama. You don't have to wait up. I'll be fine." She said.

"I know," Maria's mother waved them off. "Thank you, and good night."

"Good night Mama. Good night Hilde. Love you!" called Maria. And with that they were out the door and on their way to another night of dinner and dancing.

When they had been walking for half a minute, Maria let out a big sigh.

"What is it?" Rudi asked. She stopped and turned to face him.

"I just can't believe how you have managed to come into our lives and take everyone in my family into your confidence. We have experienced the most wonderful breath of fresh air, of new life, because of you. It's just you! You have a very big personality Rudi." Shocked by the compliment and not sure what to say, he just squeezed her hand as they continued walking. "I mean, I was just remembering as I was getting ready tonight, how sad, really, and difficult, times have been for all of

71

us. But you came along and it's not like the difficult times didn't happen, or that they somehow have disappeared, but you seem to make everything... just... easier. I wonder if we'll ever look back on this time as if it's even been hard after all."

They walked in silence for a few moments.

"Well, what else is there to do? I mean, we just do what we need to, so we mind as well enjoy ourselves. This is our life. This is what we have. And what we make of it, is what we live and what we will remember." He squeezed her hand again. "You've made my heart happy Maria. I feel at home with you. I've never felt so welcome, or so loved anywhere." She was silent, hoping he would elaborate because she wanted so much to learn more about his family and his past. He started to feel comfortable enough to share his life experiences, meager as they may be, with her trusting and open heart.

"My father died too when I was very young. Not in the war, but I never knew him. I was only three years old. He contracted tuberculosis and was not able to recover. Growing up, all I remember is spending time with my grandfather. He was the one who raised me because my mother and her new husband were businesspeople and didn't have much time to care for me." He told her.

"I'm very sorry Rudi. That must have been hard." She said.

Actually," he continued, "that's all I ever knew, so while it was a bit lonesome at times, I had never experienced anything different. As a matter of fact, I still don't know where my parents are. We lost contact when the war ended."

"What do you mean?" Maria asked. Rudi knew that she was sincerely trying to understand, so he backtracked his story a little to share a glimpse of his recent life with her.

"I was drafted in the army when I was seventeen," he began, "so that's six years ago now. Time flies. Anyway, at that point Hitler was losing the war and so they took all of the young men to fight. We had no choice."

"That I know." Maria said, understanding.

"That experience is a story for another day. But when the war was over, I was eighteen and I didn't even know where my parents were anymore because when the Soviet soldiers started to occupy East Germany, they took whatever houses they wanted and sent the people off to the labor camps to help clean up. To avoid that, my family moved, but I don't know where. They just picked up and left the house." He glanced down at Maria as she was trying to take it all in.

"At the time," he went on, "I was in the American and English occupied section, up north, by the Netherlands. There wasn't much communication, as you know, for quite a while. In order to get information to someone, it would have to be in person somehow and everyone was so separated. The wall went up and Berlin itself was divided into sections. So, while I was in forced labor for a while I went to work as a milk truck driver - with four wheels," he joked, pushing his shoulder into hers, "and then one day, I decided that since I had no family connections, no ties at all really, I could go where I chose." He confessed. Maria stopped and looked at him again.

"Oh, my goodness" Maria said, not knowing how to make him feel supported.

"That's right," he said, "Our part of the country is occupied by the Russian soldiers. You are lucky to have your district occupied by the French. I'm sure you've heard stories of people being shot for wanting to leave the East by jumping the wall. They know how restrictive it is for people and they will do anything to keep the young people inside."

"So how did you manage to escape?"

"I left at night and stayed with farmers during the day. I traveled again at night through the English occupied section and people helped me and fed me in return for work. I was determined to make it to the French section and that's where I stayed. And then I found a real job at a leather shop in Stuttgart."

"I see." Maria listened intently, shocked that he had such a hard time to get to the free side of Germany.

"Oddly enough, the day I met you, my boss' driver was sick and he needed someone who could drive him to Reutlingen. He came to the back of the store and asked if there was any of us who could drive and so for that one day, I had the privilege of driving him to your part of the country." Maria stood with her hands over her mouth, amazed both at his story and at the fact that it was by such slim circumstance that they even met.

"And that's the day we met..."

"Yes! The most important day of my life!" he said. Maria blushed.

"Did you find your family?" she asked, horrified at the thought of losing hers.

He understood her thought process and so he quickly assured her, "No. not yet. Hopefully I will soon. But now you understand why I feel so at home with your family. I love your family. You are all so warm and loving and caring. I've never had that. Even though you didn't grow up with a father, you are still a loving family. I love that and I love you." Maria stood there in the street with her eyes fixed on Rudi and wanted to share with him how much she loved him too. For a moment she was speechless, not sure if she heard the words correctly. It was unexpected, and she didn't know how to respond. After what seemed like too long of a break of silence, he wanted to retract his outburst of honesty.

"I'm sorry, I didn't mean to make you feel uncomfortable." He started.

"No. Not at all." Maria finally responded. "Well, it sounds like we've rescued each other because I love you too Rudi. With all my heart." she said, stopping to look at him sincerely. He leaned in and kissed her for a long time. They stood outside, with no one watching, just happy and content in each other's embrace. At that moment Maria knew that it could only be God who brought them together. What a beautiful mess they were together. And they were completely happy. When they stopped kissing, Rudi looked at her and smiled.

"How about we go dancing Fräulein? I think we have something to celebrate." Maria smiled back at him.

"Lead the way Rudi." She gleamed into his face, putting her hand in his. They happily walked a few streets further and found a new restaurant they hadn't tried before. Once again, they danced the night away, experiencing the joy of discovery and love in each other's eyes. They realized for the first time that they would stay together, each feeling that they had found their life partner. It was a wonderful feeling, Maria thought. A wonderful, warm, fulfilling feeling. She was truly happy again for the first time since she learned that her father died. She didn't even realize that anything was missing, but it was a sense of belonging, a sense of being protected, a sense of peace. And because it was Rudi, it was also a sense of excitement. He made her forget that she and her family had to work so hard just to make a living. He made her forget that she had to give up her own ambitions to go to school and become a teacher because she was needed at home to work. All she knew was that she was exactly where she wanted to be in the present moment. She hoped Rudi felt the same. She searched his eyes for evidence and found her answer in his loving gaze. She knew that he didn't have much money, having only started working in Stuttgart recently and not having any family connections, but it didn't matter to her because she felt confident that theirs was a love that would stand the test of time. Even if time was all they had to spend on each other, she knew it was enough. And hearing his expression of love tonight gave Maria confidence. Knowing each other's heart made everything easier. They could sincerely and unashamedly plan for their future.

The stars seemed to shine extra brightly on this clear, cool night as they walked home. Rudi could see his breath as he spoke. "Now that I know I've won your heart, I will work to keep it for the rest of my life." Maria was taken by surprise. Again, she didn't know how to respond, but she finally broke the silence,

"Will you?" she asked, wanting him to affirm his declaration. He pulled her in and held her tight.

"No matter what happens," he vowed, "as long as I have two hands to work, I will always do my best to take care of you." She smiled up at him and he gave her a long lover's kiss. When he let her go, he held her hand all the way home, swinging and twirling her around along the way.

Sunday morning Maria and Rudi had to spend two hours in the milk store, but they were happy to do it. It didn't matter what they had to do; they were just happy to be together. It was Rudi's last day before he had to go back to Stuttgart to work in the leather shop for another week between visits to Maria. She wanted to take him on a trip to her grandfather's farm, but Rudi protested.

"I just want to spend my last few precious hours with you before I have to go back to work in Stuttgart. Can't we just go for an ice cream?" he pleaded.

Before they knew it, time had gotten away on them, so once Rudi had departed for Stuttgart again, Maria went to visit her grandfather without him.

Her Ähne had suffered a hernia and wasn't able to look after the animals let alone plow the fields, so Maria helped a hired hand with both of those chores, but on Sundays all she had to do was feed the animals. After a night like she had with Rudi, her grandfather was one of the first people that she wanted to introduce him to. She loved her grandfather dearly. He had taught her all about faith and she held his approval and love in high esteem.

"Ähne and Anna, I have a new boyfriend that I want you to meet." They both looked around but saw no one.

"Well not today. He had to leave back to the city, so he wasn't able to come with me." She stated sadly. "His name is Rudolf Heinrich." They nodded. "We call him Rudi. He's from Berlin, but he's got a job in a leather store in Stuttgart now, so he visits us every weekend!" Maria's grandfather was quite surprised.

"Every weekend?" he questioned.

Maria quickly answered in defense, "Well Mama is letting him stay in Siegfried's room because it's such a long trip." Her grandfather was silent for a moment, taking in all the information.

Maria wanted to let him know that Rudi wasn't freeloading, so she explained further. "He helps me with the milk business and around the house whatever needs to be done. Otherwise, he could only come every three weeks, because he'd have to save money for a hotel. Mama is kind enough to let him stay with us while he visits." Taking it all in, her grandfather understood.

"Well, I'm sure that your mother is happy to have a man around the house sometimes. Then he looked between his granddaughter and Anna. "I hope you and this new boyfriend of yours are behaving yourselves." Maria laughed and assured him. Anna was quiet. She didn't say a word.

"Yes Ähne. Rudi has been a perfect gentleman towards me." Her grandfather nodded.

"Well, if you want to bring him here to meet me, you must be somewhat serious about this fellow?" Maria smiled because she figured that her grandfather would cut right to the chase. As they were talking, her Godmother, Anna, excused herself to get something from the kitchen. Maria stood up to follow her down the stairs and help her, but she suddenly overheard Anna speaking to a neighbor about Rudi. She could hardly believe her ears. "Ja, Berlin. He probably has a funny dialect that is hard to understand, and you know how Berliners are, stuck up and good for..."

"Anna!" Maria yelled. "If I hear you saying one more bad word about Rudi, I'm leaving. Yes, he's from Berlin and yes, he does have a different dialect, but as a matter of fact, he speaks the highest German there is! It's us you should be making fun of, not him!" Anna had no idea that Maria was standing at the top of the stairs, and she immediately turned red-faced with embarrassment and apologized prophetically, promising that it would never happen again. "I wanted to bring him here to meet you because I trusted you to treat him with kindness and respect," chided Maria.

"Oh please, Maria. I am sorry. You are right. You know us farmers get carried away with foreigners."

Maria took offense to that statement as well, "well he's not a foreigner. He's German. And if you can stop being prideful for a minute, you might learn something because he comes from a part of the country that we all call home, where they speak our language properly. I want you to get to know him if you can set aside your prejudice." Anna was instantly remorseful and didn't even realize that she was being prejudiced in any way.

"I would like to get to know him, Maria. Give me another chance. I won't make fun of him again." Maria had to let herself calm down before she could go back to visiting with her grandfather, but it was important to her that they get along, so she lovingly forgave her Godmother and helped her carry up the coffee tray with the pieces of cake while the neighbor quickly took her exit, hearing Maria lose her temper.

"I know you would like Rudi." Maria started telling her grandfather when she went back upstairs to continue her visit. "He gets along with everyone."

Maria's grandfather had learned the lesson of not being judgmental about someone before getting to know them. His teacher was Maria's mother. Long ago he refused to let his own son marry Maria's mother because he thought that she was too poor and therefore not good enough for his son. It took him three long years to finally consent to their marriage. Now, he was extremely grateful to have the help of his son's children that Maria's mother was raising on her own. He learned to love his daughter-in-law as much as he did his own daughter.

When they had visited a little while, Maria hugged him goodbye and had a word with her Godmother.

"Don't worry Anna, I don't hold grudges. It's a waste of time." She said, giving her a hug as well. "You're just going to have to meet Rudi yourself. I know that you'll love him, just like everyone else does."

"Thank you Maria. I hope to meet him soon. See you next time!" she said waving. Maria went out to the barn to feed the animals, mindful of completing all her chores before she left.

The following Sunday when they had another chance to visit Maria's grandfather together, Rudi persuaded her that they should take advantage of the beautiful weather and hike the Schwäbische Alps.

The closest climbing mountain was called the Achalm. There was a café halfway up where people could rest and purchase refreshments. Rudi bought them each an ice cream cone and they took a little break to enjoy the view. What may've seemed like quite a climb to some, was nothing to the two lovebirds. They laughed at people who were just as young as they were and who seemed to have sturdier physiques but were huffing and puffing to finish the trail. Granted they were both walking on air because of their new-found love. They dispelled an energy that was contagious to people around them, but they didn't notice; no one else in the world existed. They were lost in the bliss of their love for each other. Occasionally, Rudi would stop on the way up the trail to give Maria a little kiss, but neither of them was tired nor out of breath. As she looked out over the scenery, Maria marveled at the beauty of this creation. Well-known for its grazing lambs, especially in the springtime, the baby sheep were scattered over the Achalm hills, not bothered by the people stopping to take pictures of them. They were unafraid of humans.

"It's beautiful up here Rudi." She said as they laid down under a shady tree. She held out her hand to touch one of the sheep. "The lambs are so sweet, so tame." Her eyes were drinking in her surroundings, and its beauty filled her soul. "It's so peaceful." Rudi had to agree, but his eyes were not focused on the lambs. He only had eyes for Maria. Noticing that a lot of people were making their way back down the mountain, she sat up and looked at her watch.

"Oh Rudi, we're going to have to leave now if you're going to make your train back to Stuttgart." Reluctantly he agreed. It was as if they were in their own little world on this mountain, no awareness of time. It was such a beautiful day to remember.

On the train ride home, Rudi reminisced over the weekend he just spent with Maria. The whole family was wonderful, but his mind and his heart were centered on one sweet, innocent, and loving woman who he knew one day would be his wife. The joy in his heart was so big that he wanted to stand up and shout right there on the train. It felt like he couldn't keep his feelings all to himself. He remembered that he did have some paper and a pen, so he took it out and began to write a letter to Maria. He wrote to her every day that he was not with her because it made him feel like he was in her presence. He never thought he'd feel this way about anyone. He loved her so much, he never wanted to be apart from her.

Chapter Six

A S HAD BECOME THE NORM FOR THE RIEKERT household, the focus was starting to become weekend visits from Rudi. The talk around the table was easily centered on Maria's boyfriend. He brought life into the house, and they all waited to see him again on his next weekend visit, almost as much as he waited to see them, Maria in particular. As they were sitting around the table gushing about how much fun they all had when Rudi was around, Maria's mother informed them that they all needed to be seriously obedient to the soldiers that occupied their district of Southwest Germany.

"I heard that a farmer in Endingen, was very upset with a foreign soldier in his village and it turns out that they fought, and the soldier was killed. You know they are not all nice. They pretend to be nice sometimes to lure young girls and then they do terrible things. I've heard of some girls being very hurt, even raped." Maria's mother warned. The girls were silent, and Maria instinctively put her arm around Hildegard. "It's true." Maria's mother continued. "I will tell you of something terrible that happened that day in Endingen. – not long ago. I'm not sure of the reason for the famer's anger," explained Maria's mother, "but he went out and well, when the other soldiers realized that one of their own was killed, they came and got seven people from that village, because they didn't know who did it, and you can bet they didn't care why. Anyway, they got seven people and shot them in the middle of the village square, in front of everyone. To make an example. The mayor of the village was included in one of the seven." Maria and her siblings gasped.

"What are we supposed to do?" Anneliese asked.

"Well just be smart." Her mother answered. "Follow the rules and keep to yourself. Don't look them in the eye." And looking specifically at Anneliese, "And for goodness' sake, never try to flirt with them!"

Anneliese protested "I wouldn't flirt with a French soldier!"

"You'd flirt with a tree if it …" Maria was saying when their mother interjected.

"That's enough girls!" she held up her finger to demonstrate the gravity of the situation. "Be extra careful and watch out for each other. We are in serious times. Just because we lost the war doesn't mean it's all over for us. We are still occupied by foreign countries." She let up a little. "Luckily, the soldier overseeing our village is a good one – apparently. But please don't put him to the test. We must quietly go about our own business." They all looked at each other and gave a group hug.

"Well, I'm going to bed." Anneliese said, as she hugged her mother good night.

"Me too." Maria yawned and hugged her mother and her little siblings on the way to her room. When they were snuggled under their covers in bed, Anneliese asked how Maria's night of dancing went. They hadn't been together since Saturday night.

"Rudi and I are so in love. I'm going to marry him one day." she confided to her twin.

"Marry him?" Anneliese asked, surprised. "You know that already?"

Maria smiled confidently. "I know. I know that I know. He told me that he loves me. He also loves my family, which I think is evident. He loves spending time with all of us." Anneliese was strangely quiet.

"What about you? What's going on with Helmut?" Suddenly she became defensive. She was also a little less than confident, but she wasn't about to let that show.

"Helmut's not the same kind of personality as Rudi. He doesn't have a friendly disposition. He is the youngest of thirteen children." She explained.

"Wow!" Maria exclaimed.

"Yes. And I don't think that his mother particularly cares too much for Helmut." she said sadly. Maria looked at Anneliese with concern.

"That's sad. I'm sorry Anne." Anneliese always had a big heart, easy to forgive, but also easily taken advantage of.

"Actually, Rudi's mother didn't have much time for him either." Maria added.

Not being able to use his upbringing as an excuse for his behavior, she continued to explain away Helmut's lack of ownership or expression of love in their relationship.

"Well, he may not be as outgoing and openhearted as Rudi, but he does love me. He doesn't have to say it. I know from the way he kisses me and touches me." Maria didn't want to hear more.

"Okay Anne, you don't have to tell me." She said quickly so that she didn't have to know things that she already guessed.

"Well, it sounds like you already do know." Anneliese continued. Maria didn't want her to confess what she already suspected. "Yes, we are. And yes, we did. And I liked it. Sorry Maria. I know you wouldn't do that. But I'm not you." Maria was suddenly very sad and ultimately disappointed in her sister. Still, she wanted to give Anneliese the benefit of the doubt.

"I'd like to get to know him then Anneliese if you two are that serious. You know Rudi, but maybe we could do something together, so I can get to know Helmut a little better. We could go on a double date, like we used to with Gerhardt and your first Helmut ha-ha. Why do you always choose guys with the name Helmut?" They both laughed. "Remember that? Only I wouldn't want to play any tricks on Rudi like that!"

Recollection of their youthful dating days lightened the atmosphere between them. They laughed reminiscing about all their antics as teenagers. Gerhardt was Maria's boyfriend and Anneliese was dating another young man named Helmut. Both boys were confident that they knew their girlfriends well enough that they could tell them apart. One day Maria and Anneliese schemed a switch of identities to test them.

"The only way they can tell us apart," said Maria, "is by our birthmarks. So, you keep your left cheek turned away from Gerhardt so he doesn't see your birthmark and I will keep my dimply chin down a little so Helmut doesn't notice." Anneliese agreed. She liked to scheme occasionally. It was fun.

"And I will be a little more of a chatterbox, like you," she said.

"Yes, I know. That is true." Maria conceded. Anneliese continued, "and you have to remember to be a little quieter today." That would be difficult for Maria, she admitted. She loved to talk, but it was just for one date. She held out her pinky to her sister. Anneliese responded, "Operation switcheroo!" They both laughed until their sides hurt. When their boyfriends arrived, they didn't suspect a thing, not even for a moment. They spent the whole day hiking the mountains together and when they came home in the evening, it was time for the big reveal. Just as they were about to say good night at the door, Maria exposed their secret.

"You said it would never happen, couldn't be done! You" – and she was gesturing to both guys – "have thought this whole day that you were on a date with your girlfriend." Gerhardt and Helmut looked at one another, puzzled. "You have both been with the wrong girl – all day!" she triumphantly announced. Instantly Helmut stepped towards who he thought was Anneliese, took her chin, and turned her face to the left. Gasping, he stepped back, realizing that the birthmark was not there. He indeed had been hoodwinked.

Gerhardt, eyes popping, threw his head back, laughing. Then he stuck out his hand to shake Maria's hand and offered her kudos. "Congratulations! You proved us wrong." He gave her a big hug and reached out his hand in congratulations to Anneliese as well. All four of them laughed.

"Oh yes, I remember," said Anneliese. "I think Helmut would have been upset if it weren't for Gerhardt. He was so 'game' for the whole thing. You could have done anything with that guy. He really loved you, Maria." Remembering, Maria agreed.

"Yes, he did. But now that I've met Rudi, I'm so glad that I didn't agree to marry Gerhardt. He was a wonderful friend, but I didn't have anywhere near the kind of deep loving feelings that I do for Rudi." Anneliese nodded her head in understanding.

"Rudi's the one for you." She turned out her light, "and honestly Maria, I think Helmut is the one for me."

"Okay Anne. I hope he makes you happy."

Anneliese turned over in her bed as if to say good night. "Thank you." She whispered.

The next few days Maria and her mother were busy with the milk business again. It was a hard job physically, but Maria was so happy that she didn't even mind. She received a love letter from Rudi every single day which she kept tucked away in her apron pocket so if she ever started to feel sad or homesick for him, she only needed to look into her pocket to remember how loved she was. She wrote Rudi back too, but sometimes she only had enough time to write him a card because she was working so hard between the milk business and helping her grandfather on the farm. Some days she came home and could hardly eat, she was so tired.

Anneliese spent her days at home cooking and taking care of Hildegard and Siegfried whenever Maria and her mother were working. She simply didn't have the stamina to work in the field like Maria. Even though Anneliese was born first and seemed to have a stouter and more muscular frame, it was always Maria that was the healthier one of the two. Maria's mother told them that even though Maria was slighter in build, she came out kicking and punching. She was a fighter from birth and wondered if one day she would need that spirit to face whatever circumstance life would throw her way. It was as though her temperament was divinely designed to suit her purpose. In any case, Maria much preferred to be out and working the business with her mother, rather than being cooped up in the kitchen all day, although she was a good cook as well. She just preferred to be busy outside of the house whereas Anneliese much preferred to be inside, close to home. She was the more timid one of the twins and had always seemed to lack the strength that Maria possessed in droves. It was fine with her when she was chosen to babysit her siblings. There were times when Anneliese needed to rest because she became tired easily; not seeming to have a lot of energy. Some days she had more strength than others. She didn't have an explanation, but she simply learned to cope.

Like the rest of the family, it wasn't long before Anneliese was also looking forward to the weekends when Rudi would visit because they usually had something fun planned. This weekend there was a wedding in the family, so there would be lots of dancing and celebrating. Maria was thankful because it was a great opportunity for her to introduce her boyfriend to a lot of her extended family without having to travel and visit everyone in different villages. It would also possibly be a good opportunity to get to know Helmut better. She loved all her siblings so very much, but most especially her identical twin. It was so important for her to be on good terms with the man that Anneliese wanted to marry.

Maria was looking forward to the wedding on Saturday night as well, but she was just happy that Friday had arrived, the day Rudi was coming 'home'. She eagerly waited in the station for the train from Stuttgart. Looking down at the tracks, she didn't see anything. She looked around at the others waiting to receive their loved ones. Everyone was looking at their watches, growing impatient. Finally, she spotted a gleam of light far off in the tunnel. She wasn't sure at first, but then as the light got bigger, she knew it was finally the train from Stuttgart. Rudi had arrived. He was one of the first passengers off the train. Glancing around, it only took a moment before he found Maria. She ran towards him as he dropped his bag and opened his arms to receive her embrace. People around them did a double take because of how happy they were to see each other, and they whistled, some even clapped in encouragement. They giggled under Rudi's fedora, and it gave them even more license not to shy away from their public display of affection for each other. On their way home Maria stopped Rudi to show him the letters he had written to her that were stuffed in her pockets. Rudi was pleased to see that she treasured them; even carrying them on her person.

"I enjoyed the letters you sent me too – even the cards" he explained "but there were a couple days that I didn't receive anything." He faked a pouty lip.

Maria sighed, "If only you could see how busy I am everyday Rudi." He waved the complaint away, "Never mind that. I know how busy you are and how hard you work to help your mom. I'm not really complaining, I'm just so excited to get something in the mail from you that I miss it when nothing comes. But I know I'll see you in a few days anyway, which is my great consolation." She gave him a great big smile and squeezed his hand even tighter. Once they arrived home, everyone was so happy to see Rudi. Even Maria's mother gave him a warm welcome 'home' and made sure that she sat him down promptly to have a hot meal after his travels. He felt so appreciated. "What a wonderful welcome I get, coming 'home' to all of you. It's such a treasure to me. I look forward to it all week."

Hildegard marched right up to him and announced, "we've been looking forward to you coming this week too." Rudi could barely get his question of "Why?" in before she blurted out "we're going to a family wedding! You'll get to dance with me!" Rudi looked at Maria who was thoroughly enjoying the excitement on her sister's face.

"My cousin is getting married." Maria's mother explained. "All of us are invited if you are up to it. Hopefully you haven't made other plans because it will be a lot of fun and you'll have a chance to meet more of the family. The only thing is, you'll have to work the milk centrale with me tomorrow because Maria is needed on the farm to help Ähne plow the fields during the day."

"Okay. That's fine." Rudi said. "I can do that. Plus, I do love a good wedding."
He turned to Hildegard. "We'll have to practice a little Hätele. Maybe in the living room after dinner with the radio?" She nodded and looked at her mother for reassurance.

"Well, you can stay up for a little while. I think it'll be fun to watch you two practicing." She laughed.

After supper that evening, all the girls helped in the kitchen cleaning away the dishes of the day.

Rudi went upstairs to get settled in his room, Siegfried trailing close behind.

"How do you like my room Rudi?" Siegfried asked. Rudi sat down on the bed right next to him.

"I think you have a great room. I'm very glad that you let me use it while I'm visiting on weekends. As a matter of fact, I don't think that I properly thanked you for that. I think that I should take you out to get some ice cream every time I come just so that you always know how thankful I am to you for your sacrifice. Sound good to you?" Hmm Siegfried thought for a minute.

"I'll probably need to ask Mama for that. She would probably say yes, but I should ask." Rudi agreed.

Siegfried came bounding down the stairs with so much excitement, Maria wondered if something was wrong. He was nearly out of breath, "Mama, can Rudi take me for an ice cream when he comes to town? He said he always wants me to know how thankful he is that I am giving him my room to use when he stays here."

"Hmm..." Maria's mother had to think about this one. "I think it's nice to do it once Siegfried, but I don't think that Rudi should be expected to take you out every time on top of taking Maria out."

Siegfried looked at his sister, "we can take turns then."

His mother's first instinct was to say no but then she realized that Maria and Rudi were going to go somewhere anyway, and it was such a sweet gesture to always give Siegfried something to look forward to, being stuck in a house full of only girls. "Okay okay..." his mother answered, "You certainly know how to get your way." She chuckled.

Rudi came down the stairs and Siegfried gave him the thumbs up. Being treated to ice cream was so special. It was a big treat, especially to have it every other weekend. The prospect of such a gift was unimaginable, which made Siegfried so much the happier. And once again it gave him a special time with Rudi, his father figure, that he so craved. Rudi noted the joy on Siegfried's face and made a promise to himself to always make good on his agreement.

"Alright Hätele. You ready?" Rudi looked at Siegfried. "Maestro – music please." Siegfried went to the radio and put on some nice dance music. Hildegard jumped up and held out her hands confidently. Rudi laughed. He enjoyed her enthusiasm. Anneliese and Maria sat side by side watching Rudi lead Hilde in a simple waltz. It didn't take her long to catch on. She was also a very good dancer. Maria's mother decided it was a perfect time to teach Siegfried a few dance steps, so the twins sat and watched the two couples cutting up the dance floor. Maria grabbed hold of Anneliese's hand. She noticed it was a little clammy.

"Are you feeling okay Anne? You look a little pale." Maria didn't miss much when it came to her sister. She may not always agree with her ways and decisions and vice versa, but the twins were always watching out for one another.

"I'll be fine," Anneliese said. "I'm just a little tired. It's been a long week. I love watching Hilde and Rudi dance! And look at little Siegfried!"

Maria smiled. "Ja, he's not so little anymore." She said as she watched her brother move across the dance floor with Rudi giving him pointers now and again on how to lead like a gentleman. "We're so blessed to have each other aren't we Anneliese?" she squeezed her sister's hand.

"We sure are!" she agreed. Just then they watched as the couples backed into each other and everyone had a good laugh.

Chapter Seven

A S THE EVENING WORE ON, IT BECAME evident that it was time for Hildegard and Siegfried to go to bed. Rudi, Maria, Anneliese, and their mother stayed up a while longer talking with Rudi about Stuttgart and even about his time in the war. They were curious because what they knew of it, the experience of it, of their dad, was only what he shared with them when he came home on furlough when the twins were twelve. That was the last time they saw him. Of course, he played down the horrors of what he lived through, not wanting them to worry, but they longed to have a better understanding somehow. When their father wrote letters home, they were full of love and prayers. He always told them that he was praying for them every day. The only thing that was important to him, was that his children would know the love of Jesus as much as he did. Facing death every day made him take his faith very seriously. He didn't choose to fight in the war, he was forced to. Unfortunately, many people had developed a true hatred for German people, especially those who fought in the war, but Maria and her family, along with thousands of other German families, had suffered the tragedy of losing many loved ones including their father, and were left to fend for themselves. Non-German people didn't believe or want to understand that many German people were caught in the political crossfire of their leaders and had little choice but to obey their government. Rudi shared a little about not having much to eat and of how he had to hold his best friend while he was dying. It was a memory that he wished he didn't have. It was hard to let go of, even though he hated talking about it. "It's good for you to talk about it." Maria's mother assured him. "We are your family, and we are safe for you. If you talk about it, it will be easier to deal with. The memories won't haunt you as much because they won't be hidden." Rudi listened and had such a lump in his throat that he couldn't say a word. They were all silent and he knew that this time it could not be stopped; he did cry a little.

"I just couldn't stop the bleeding." Rudi said, through his stiff upper lip. "I didn't know how.

There was so much, and it just flowed from him. All I could do was to hold him as I watched him in agony. And then he just went limp in my arms." He recalled. "I was helpless. I had nothing to give. I didn't know what to do. What to say…" He was silent and he trembled recalling the horror of that day.

"There were so many." he finally said, as he lifted his eyes and seemed to look out as he shook his head. "So many. So many. And we were ordered to move on. I had to leave him right there. And they were all left." Rudi came back to his present surroundings. He looked at all of them, listening, and he felt the tears on his cheek. They were all supportive and gave him encouragement, Maria especially. He took out his handkerchief and wiped it under his eyes. "Sorry." He apologized, "I got lost in the memory."

"No sorries required." Maria's mother said, through her own hoarse voice. She thought of her husband and what he must have experienced, but never talked about. "We are always here for you Rudi. It is good and even important that you talk about your experience during those days. Without that, your own spirit would carry the dark memory alone and it will fester. You need to feel secure enough in our love for you, that we understand you were called, forced even, to serve in such a terrible circumstance. You must trust us to always support you." Rudi nodded but couldn't lift his gaze to look anyone in the eye. After a silence, Maria's mother had a confession of her own.

"Well since we're being honest..." she started. Everyone's ears perked up to listen to the patriarch speak in a hushed voice. "I'm going to tell you something that I hope will not change the way that you feel about Maria and all of us."
Rudi wrinkled his brow and looked at Maria questioningly. Maria shrugged her shoulders not knowing what her mother was about to say. "This is a secret that we must all keep, at least for now." Maria and Anneliese looked at each other in silence, neither one guessing what was about to be divulged.

"It was before the war, that I found out the truth and I've kept it very close to my heart ever since. I expect you to do the same." She looked at Rudi, who nodded in silent consent. Suddenly, the twins understood what she was about to say, but kept quiet. Knowing how you feel about the war and about the communist regime and mostly your aversion to the Nazi agenda, I feel safe in sharing this story with you." Again, Rudi nodded in silence. Maria's mother took a deep breath and started to explain, hoping and praying in trust that Rudi would be faithful to keep their secret.

"My mother, whose name was also Maria, had a boyfriend when she was a young lady of eighteen. That detail is insignificant." she went on, waving her hand, dismissing impertinent information. "Her boyfriend was beloved by our whole family, apparently, and they dated for a couple of years. But as time went on everyone wondered why these two didn't get married. Then one day my mother had to confess that she was pregnant." Rudi lowered his chin but continued listening. He knew this situation would bring her mother shame, but he was not judgmental.

"In those days, that was shameful enough, but if you can believe it, all her relatives were saying that 'finally they'll have to marry.'" She explained. Rudi cracked a smile as she continued speaking in earnest. "Then the real reason for him not proposing for all that time came to light. He couldn't ask her to marry him because he was already married." Rudi's eyes grew big. "Yes! He had a wife and five children in a village about an hour's carriage ride away from my mother." Maria's mother said. "Now the secret that we've kept for so long, and I'm expecting you to do it as well - is that this man was fully Jewish." Suddenly Rudi's eyes grew huge. He shot Maria a quick glance. It occurred to him that she had never mentioned this, but at the same moment that he questioned it, he understood the level of trust required with this information.

"I see." Rudi said. "Well, you don't have any worries with me. That's not important to me, but what happened to your mother?"

"Well, she bore the child obviously." She laughed, gesturing with her hands over her own body, seated on the chair in front of him. Rudi shook his head, smiling. "Yes, of course, but then what?"

"Well get ready for this." She shared, leaning in. "He divorced his wife and asked my mother to marry him." Again, Rudi's eyes were huge with surprise. "But" she went on, "my mother didn't want anything to do with him from that time on. Or any man. She was so hurt and angry. She did eventually marry a man with seven children who had lost his wife, and the two of them fell in love after all, but I could write a book about that. That's a story for another day. All of this to let you know that not only is it unlikely that you and Maria came together because you are from what is now East Germany and she is a farm girl from the West, but the kicker is that you are, I should say were, a German soldier and she is partly Jewish." She nodded. "Which, like I said, is our secret." Rudi nodded in agreement. "And honestly, while they were growing up, Anneliese and Maria had blond hair and blue eyes, like me, and even Siegfried, so there was no problem when the soldiers came to the door."

Rudi listened intently, nodding his head in understanding and then shaking it and laughing.

"Well congratulations for keeping that secret in plain sight and surviving the craziness of the anti-

Jewish forces in this country. You had some kind of luck with your blond children, didn't you? What about Hildegard?"

"She was instructed to let them see her, but to pretend to be shy and hide behind my skirt keeping her head down. We practiced."

"Good job!" he said. "That is an amazing story!"

"Well true life is sometimes more interesting than fiction. It certainly is in our family." She said. There was a moment of dead silence, but Rudi was quick to dispel any fear.

"I can't imagine anything that would change my mind about Maria or any of you. Certainly not what family or race you were born into. Actually, I applaud you for the genius cover up."

"Oh, that was all God." Maria's mother admitted. "He's the one who gave me the blond-haired, blue-eyed children."

"Nevertheless," Rudi quickly added, "I agree that we should all tuck it away and not speak of it again for many years. Why invite trouble?"

"Yes, exactly." Maria's mother said. "Besides which, it's getting late and it's time to go to bed." Everyone stood up. Maria's mother turned around as she was headed to her room.

"Thank you for sharing about your experience in the war Rudi. I know that was hard for you, but we have to trust each other, don't we, with all our past, especially if we want to have a future." she said, looking at him and Maria standing next to each other hand in hand. Rudi embraced her, feeling like he was truly a part of the family. When she turned and went to bed, Rudi held Maria back as Anneliese made her way up the stairs. Then he turned and whispered to Maria.

"I'm sorry all of that came out just then. I've never talked about it before. With anyone. It just came pouring out once we started talking about the war." Maria was very supportive.

"It's not good that you've never talked about it before. I'm glad you finally did and why would you be sorry? That would have been a very traumatic experience. It's not something that should get swept into your subconscious. I'm very glad you shared it. Thank you for sharing it. We've always been a little curious about what it was really like for Papa. I can understand better now why he didn't share any details with us, especially as children. It sounds like it was a horrific experience and honestly," she said putting a hand on his heart, "I'm also glad you cried about it. I think I'd be more worried if you didn't cry about that." Rudi just looked at her and had no words about how happy he was to have her. To have her love. She knew his thoughts and reassured him. "Rudi you are home now. I am your home. You can share anything with me, and we can work through it together. Anything." He was so grateful. He wanted to give her the same security.

106

"And the same is true for me. Even though, I was a little surprised that you've never mentioned that part of your history before."

"I honestly didn't think of it. The war's been over for a few years now and yes, it was a big secret then, but we don't have any contact with that side of the family, so it doesn't come to mind." She said.

"Okay, well that makes sense. What a story though! It would make a good book one day." Maria smiled and gave him a very long kiss good night.

Chapter Eight

EVEN THOUGH IT HAD BEEN A LONG DAY of work at the Milk Centrale and now as she was finishing with the animals on the farm, Maria did not feel tired. Instead, she was excited to go to the family
wedding celebration in a few hours.

"How exactly are you getting there?" Maria's grandfather asked.

"We're taking the three-wheeler, of course. That's what we always do." Maria answered. Her grandfather stopped for a minute and looked at her from underneath his glasses.

"You better be careful. That buggy has a mind of its own." He warned.

"Oh, I know. I know. Trust me, I've learned." She replied. "Rudi is having some challenges learning about that." Instantly he knew that they had probably come close to some near-death experiences in that car. He thought about chastising her for letting him drive, but then he pictured what it would look like to see Maria teaching her boyfriend how to drive a three-wheeler. Instead, they started laughing. Not wanting to miss being in on a joke, Anna came bursting into the room.

"What are you all laughing at? What's so funny?" She asked. Her incessant need to know just made them laugh a little more.

"Oh, it's nothing Anna, we were just talking about Rudi's driving. Anna just looked at them, satisfied that they weren't laughing behind her back and left the room again.

"Maria thank you so much for coming. It is always so nice to visit with you." Her grandfather said. "I don't know what I would do without all your help. You know if something ever happened to me, and I had to lose my farm – tell your mother – (he lowered his voice to a whisper) – I want to come and live with her. I would want to live with her, not Anna. I can't follow all of Anna's rules. I would rather be free to do as I please and say what I want to say, and to fart once in a while." They chuckled again, but Maria's grandfather wanted her to know that he was serious. "You have a warm-hearted mother, Maria." He looked down, in what seemed like embarrassment. "I misjudged her once you know." He held up his finger as old people do sometimes to make a point, "but I learned" he explained, "She is a giver. She gives of herself to her children, her family and anyone she can help. And now I love her. See how love can change you?!" He winked at Maria. "Tell that Rudi of yours to stick with you, Maria. You come from a good family. Smart. Hardworking. Giving. Kind. Oh yes, I could go on." Maria loved her grandfather so much. He was a joy to visit with and she loved helping him on the farm, even though it was hard work. But on this day, she had in mind that she wanted to get going to her cousin's wedding. He hugged her sincerely. "Dankeschön for the nice visit. Have a great time tonight! And be careful – especially with Rudi behind the wheel now." They both laughed, and Maria went on her way.

Once she had settled into her seat on the train ride back home, Maria thought, 'I'll have just enough time to change and go. I'm going to have to wait to eat until we get to the wedding. I'm sure the food will be good. Weddings are always a smorgasbord! And even if I don't like some of it, I'm sure I'll find more than enough to satisfy my appetite'. She knew Rudi would be game for a night of eating and dancing and meeting new family. This was his element. He had a gregarious personality and he tended to engage people's goodwill easily.

As soon as she arrived home, Anneliese was coming down the stairs all dressed and ready to go. "Oh Anne, you look so beautiful." Maria exclaimed. Anneliese smiled.

"Well thank you, but you better get ready. Pronto! Maria, I've already laid out the matching dress to mine, on your bed. Mama made them. She worked on them last week, late at night, when you went dancing." Maria almost ran up the stairs, she was so excited. She saw the beautiful light blue dress on her bed and squealed with delight. "Thank you, Mama. It's gorgeous! Thank you so much!" she yelled down the stairs. Then she stopped for a minute. She forgot to ask Anneliese which shoes to wear. She yelled down the stairs again, "Anne, which shoes?"

"...heels." Anne yelled up to her. She tried to ask again, but Anneliese exclaimed, "Helmut just pulled up. I will see you all there."

Maria, shocked, yelled down the stairs again, "Wait, what? You're going on the motorcycle in that dress?" But it was too late. Anneliese was already out the door. Maria went back into her room, shaking her head. She marveled at how different her personality was from Anneliese's. They looked identical but were worlds apart in their thinking – at this point in their lives anyway.

As it turned out, the ride to Endingen was a little on the rough side. Rudi and Maria's mother had finished with the milk business just in time to get ready for the wedding, but they were in a rush. Rudi tried very hard to follow all the rules of driving a three-wheel truck and amazingly he did not need help with the steering wheel. Afterall he was driving with Maria's mother and siblings in the car, so he was extra conscious of what he was doing. They arrived just in time to see the wedding ceremony and then find their way to the reception. The tables were decorated with beautiful summer wildflowers around a candle as a centerpiece on white linen tablecloths. The food was laid out in a buffet style and Rudi's eyes were already feasting because he was so hungry. Maria had also arrived ravenous for food, but when her beloved family members caught her eye, the hunger dissipated. Her attention had suddenly been diverted. In any case, people were still getting themselves to the right tables, and the line for the buffet had barely started."

"I haven't even had time to give you a proper hello." Maria said, turning to face Rudi. He wrapped her in his arms and gave her a wonderful kiss, but not wanting to draw too much attention at a wedding, they kept their public affection in check.

"How was the train ride in?" Maria asked.

"Long." Rudi answered in short. "How was your day?" he asked her.

"I wish you could've been there to meet my Ähne. He means the world to me." She said.

"Well, there's plenty of time for that." Rudi reasoned. "First things first. We have a wedding to celebrate!" Maria nodded but made a mental note that she would be sure to introduce them soon.

"At least I won't be the first one." Rudi whispered, pointing Maria's attention to the people already in line for the buffet. "Not to be rude, but if you don't mind, I'm going to go and get a plate of food. I can get you a plate too if you want?" Maria gave him a big smile.

"Oh no Rudi. That's fine. You go on ahead. I can wait a little while. I am going to greet some people I haven't seen in a long time." Rudi was thankful. As he made his way over to the trough, he told himself that there would be plenty of time to meet relatives after his appetite was satisfied. He was so hungry, he felt like he could eat everything on the table. It all looked so good. All his favorites – and more. He was also thankful that not too many people were in line yet because he wasn't shy about loading up. He was making his way over to a table and looking forward to digging into his plate of food, when he spotted Maria across the room talking and laughing with a young, good-looking guy. Then he noticed how the young fellow put his arm around her and gave her a kiss. He nearly threw his plate down. "Oh no you didn't!" Rudi exclaimed, scrambling his way over to where Maria was standing, almost leaping over chairs and forcing himself between them. At this point the young man had Maria in a full-on

113

embrace. It was all Rudi could do to keep himself from punching this guy, which it looked like he was about to do. "Wait a minute!" Maria proclaimed. "This is my cousin!" Rudi looked at her wide-eyed. He was in the throes of jealousy and had to immediately cool his jets and realize that he made a mistake. It could have been a disaster, but the young man immediately stepped in, "Hello. Rudi, I presume." Looking at Maria, he offered Rudi his hand.

"I'm Albert, Maria's cousin. I haven't seen her for a very long time, and we used to be so close. We grew up in the same house, so we were together a lot as youngsters. Oh look, here comes my brother Ernst." As Ernst made his way over, Rudi marveled – he was equally as good looking as Albert, of course, because they were twins. Rudi could hardly believe his eyes.

"Okay, Wow. Okay..." Rudi was trying to take it all in. He started to chuckle, realizing how ludicrous his attitude had been to these obviously jovial young guys. "I'm so sorry Albert. I thought you were trying to move in on my beautiful Maria." Maria looked a little embarrassed, but she took it all in stride.

"I understand. " Albert said. "This is my girlfriend, Irmschen." He put his arm around a very tall, slim young lady standing close by. He was doing all he could to make Rudi feel comfortable.

"So... two sets of twins?" Rudi asked.

"Oh yes!" Albert explained. "We have had quite a lot of fun, the four of us, confusing people. But like I said, we grew up together, so we've been pranksters together all our lives." Albert's eyes scanned the room. "I haven't found Anneliese though, Maria. Have you seen her?"

"I did see her earlier. She must be here somewhere." Maria answered, scanning the room.

"Good" said Albert, "we'll have to have a dance, the pair of us twins!" he beamed.

"Yes, we will" Maria said. "If I find her, I'll let her know." She turned to Rudi and led him over to their table. "Okay Rudi. I'm going to get my plate of food now. I'll be right back. If you see Anneliese, keep her here." Rudi agreed. "Wait. How many cousins do you have?"

"A lot" Maria answered, "and everyone is friendly with one another." She said, laughing. "Just so you know." Rudi smirked to himself as she walked over to the buffet table. Maria quickly got herself a plate full of food and realized her eyes may have been bigger than her stomach. She felt so hungry, but suddenly, she realized that her plate was piled high, and she would likely not be able to finish all the food. When she got to the table, Anneliese was already there sitting one seat away from Rudi. Next to her sat Helmut.

"I can't believe I got this much food" Maria said as she put her plate down.

"Don't worry, nothing will go to waste." Rudi answered between gulps. "This food is delicious!" Maria laughed. Before she sat down, she reached a hand over to Helmut.

"Hello Helmut! How are you?" she asked, wanting Anneliese to see that she was trying to get to know her boyfriend.

"I'm fine Maria. It's a wonderful wedding. I must agree with Rudi – this food is amazing!" Maria felt so happy as she sat down between the man she loved and the sister who would forever be her other half.

"Anneliese, I was talking to Albert. Actually, Rudi and I were talking to him and Ernst. They want us to have a dance with them tonight – like old times." Anneliese looked at Rudi, who was gorging himself on his food.

"So... you've met the other twins?" she asked, amused.

Maria laughed. "He did indeed, but that's another story. So how about when we're done eating, we look for them?" she asked. Anneliese looked at Helmut.

"Okay with you Helmut – if I have a dance with my cousin?" Helmut was also happily chomping on his food.

"Oh yes, of course. Rudi and I will occupy ourselves with the buffet and get better acquainted." Rudi nodded in agreement, just as the bride and groom stopped by to meet the "new boyfriends". They offered everyone a little bag of mints as a thank you for coming to celebrate their wedding day. Maria and Rudi stood up as Maria introduced him, along with Helmut, because she knew that Anneliese was too shy.

"It's such a wonderful wedding and I must say the food is amazing Carmen! Thank you for having us." Maria declared.

"Well thank you, I'm glad you are enjoying it." She spoke. "I wish I had more time to stop and get to know Rudi and Helmut. Weddings can be so busy, especially in our big family." She commented. "But please help yourself to the food and I hope to see you all on the dance floor." Turning around, she said, "I just saw your mother with Wilma and Siegfried" gesturing towards their table. "I think those two are ready to do a little dancing."

Maria nodded. "Yes, they have been practicing for this Carmen. We are looking forward to it."

"Well, the band assured us that they will play for three hours tonight so I think they will have plenty of opportunity to show their new dance moves!" Carmen looked in the direction of the "other twins." "I saw Albert and Ernst here too – will you all be dancing together, I hope. At least once?" Maria looked at Rudi, who was still feeling a little embarrassed about his earlier behavior.

"Yes, that's the plan Carmen. We've already talked about that." Maria replied.

"That's nice. People always love to see the twins together." Carmen said. Maria and Anneliese smiled at each other. "You two ladies look lovely by the way." Carmen commented, hoping to engage Anneliese.

"Thank you, Carmen." Anneliese responded. "You look absolutely beautiful tonight."

"Thank you, Anneliese." Carmen said.

Maria whispered to her sister, "normally, I'd say we should go over there and help Mama out a little, but I think our little sister and brother are doing just fine. Hilde is entertaining Siegfried quite nicely and I think Mama is okay. Let's just stay here and enjoy the evening with our men." Anneliese looked surprised.

"The thought never occurred to me to do any differently." Once again, Maria noticed the difference in their thinking, nevertheless, she agreed with Anneliese's outlook this time. "I'm sure our siblings will find their way over here sooner or later. Let's just give it some time."

"Agreed." said Maria with her arm around Anneliese, laughing. Suddenly, music started to play, getting everyone's attention, but then stopped suddenly for an announcement.

"I'd like to call the bride and groom to the dance floor for the first dance." Carmen and her new husband made their way through the crowd, and everyone stared and admired her beautiful dress and everything that was lovely about the newlywed couple. It was a wonderful waltz and Rudi, having finished his plate of food, was eager to take a turn on the dance floor as well.

"Do you love to dance Helmut?" Maria asked.

"I can dance." He answered honestly. "I do enjoy it when I dance, but it's not something that I love, no." Maria was trying to get to know him a little better, so she asked another question.

"Well then, what do you love to do?" Helmut looked down at her with a quizzical gaze and then wrestled with the question.

"I love riding on my motorcycle. I love being with Anneliese..." As he finished saying exactly that, as if perfectly timed, Anneliese walked over to him, and he planted a long kiss on her lips and then looked at Maria to prove his point. Maria wasn't exactly sure how she was supposed to respond to that. She just thought to say. "I love Anneliese too."

Just then the first dance was over, and people started moving onto the dance floor to join in the fun. Maria and Rudi were amongst them. First was another waltz and then the band livened things up with more upbeat music. People started to realize what an excellent dancer Rudi was, and because Maria had grown so accustomed to being his dance partner, she was getting quite a lot of attention as well. When they stopped to get a drink, Albert and Ernst made their way over to Maria and Anneliese. They were sure to bring their girlfriends with them, so that Rudi and Helmut wouldn't feel awkward.

119

They all twirled around the dance floor, switching partners from time to time. Rudi had a wonderful time dancing with Irmschen, even though she was too tall of a partner for him. Halfway through, he made the move to switch partners with Helmut so that the awkward discrepancy of their height didn't last too long. As soon as the set was over Hildegard had found her way to Rudi and pulled him away to make him promise to pick her for his next partner. This suited Albert and Ernst just fine. They could stay another while on the dance floor with their beloved cousins. Their girlfriends took their turns with Siegfried, so everyone was happy. Maria's mother sat back and watched all her children having a great time and her heart was full. She had a twinge of regret about not having a partner for herself because she was still so very young, only in her late thirties, but she felt that her life was too busy. At least for now. Maybe things would change when her youngest two children were a little older. When she started to feel a little lonely, she looked at her family and reminded herself how fortunate she was. One thing that did catch her eye was how Hilde was quickly becoming the center of attention with a lot of the teenage boys. She was full of life and a great dancer and Hilde was always game for fun. Plus, she was very pretty. She was everyone's darling and she knew it. On the one hand, her mother felt proud to have such a sweet, pretty, and vibrant young lady. On the other hand, she was a little unnerved. There was already a lineup of boys waiting to dance with her. Right now, amongst so much family, she felt completely safe, but she wondered if that was about to change.

"I wish we could have a wedding to go to every weekend!" said Hilde Sunday afternoon when everyone rested in the living room.

"You were in your element, huh Schatz?" her mother remarked. "You had a line of beaus waiting to dance with you!"

Hildegard threw her head back laughing.

"That's why it was so fun!" She quipped. Everyone laughed.

"I wonder", her mother mused, "what is in store for me with this up-and-coming whirlwind of a personality in my little Hilde. Your teenage years are upon us and so far, so good. I just hope that you are smart enough to keep it that way."

"The key", Rudi advised, "is not to let your heart get wrapped up in anyone yet. You're too young. You are right to have a little fun with your admirers, Hätele. Just make sure you don't make anyone feel like he's got you." She looked at him with a raised eyebrow. "A broken heart is hard to mend." Rudi explained. "It's never good. So – just keep it light-hearted and you'll be fine." Hilde raised her chin.

"Exactly!" she said as she danced around the living room, still vying for everyone's attention. Siegfried had plenty of dance partners at the wedding as well, but he was generally shy, so he didn't seek to be in the limelight. He was three years younger than Hildegard and still very much a boy. He just watched her entertain everyone and was content to sit next to Rudi while he could.

"Come sit in front of me, Hilde. I'll do your hair." Anneliese offered. Squealing with delight, she ran upstairs to get clips and bows. She loved having her hair brushed and trying different styles. Rudi sat down for a rest next to Maria and put his arm around her. Siegfried leaned on Rudi, as they talked about last night's party. It became a quiet, comfortable evening in the Riekert household before it was time for Maria to walk Rudi back to the train station for his trip back to Stuttgart.

Chapter Nine

RUDI LOOKED AS THOUGH HE WERE RELIVING the events in his mind that Maria described so beautifully to her guests. But the day was soon becoming evening.

"Na, Rudi." Maria said. "It's time to say goodbye to everyone for tonight. We've certainly reminisced long enough." Rudi looked like he was in a dream, but he had been sitting a long time, which was not good for his back.

"Ja. I think you're right. I do need to go lie down." He looked up and nodded to Rosie, his youngest daughter, to take him back to his own room. She happily agreed, wishing to spend every possible moment with her dad. She had come from North Carolina to look after her aging parents, particularly

Rudi, having fallen and broken his hip. She had moved away because the government of Canada couldn't afford the socialized healthcare system twenty years earlier. At the time, her husband had just graduated nursing college and couldn't find a job because the hospitals were having to shut down beds, even some facing closure. She followed her husband to Raleigh, North Carolina where he found a nursing job in a big hospital. They moved south with their two-year-old daughter, Melissa, when she was thirty-nine weeks pregnant with her second baby. That was twenty years ago. Looking at her dad and suddenly realizing all the years of togetherness missed, Rosie could only wish she had not stayed away from home for so long. But regret is a hard taskmaster, so she turned her thoughts to what could be done presently. Knowing that Maria would soon be released from the hospital because she was getting better, she coveted the time she had left with her dad. So, after Rudi said good night to everyone, Rosie told her family that she would meet them back at the house in Port Dover. She wanted to spend a little more time saying good night to her dad after the nurses got him lifted into his bed. To Rosie, her dad seemed to be in a lot of pain, although he never complained. She could tell by the way he clenched his teeth as the chair lift was letting him down into position above his bed.

Rudi looked at Rosie, half shutting his eyes. He imagined what she must be thinking. He wished that she didn't have to witness him in such a helpless state. His back was very sensitive because of several broken vertebrae, and it was all Rosie could do to watch this procedure night after night and morning after morning. This man, once strong and vibrant, able to carry her and even her children on his broad shoulders, now having to be mechanically lifted into his bed was a hard sight to witness. Rosie often relied on his strength to carry anything heavy or to do any work that would have been backbreaking for any man. She remembered watching as he built the patio in the backyard at the house she grew up in. He lifted stone after concrete stone and placed them perfectly in a beautiful pattern of red and white checkers. He built huge cedar benches lining either side of that patio and many times used his strong physical abilities to help neighbors in need. It was hard to watch him in his limited physical capacity with pain that made it difficult to sit up for long periods of time, let alone try to stand.

But he was ninety and he was tired. And his back was literally broken.

And Rosie still didn't get it. She did, but she didn't want to. She wasn't ready – yet. Once he was in his bed again and ready for the night, she pulled out a book that Maria wrote.

"Do you want to hear more of Mom's book, Dad?" she asked, hopeful that he wanted her to stay. Rudi was glad to have the company. He was glad that Rosie wanted to spend her time with him. He listened to her read and enjoyed the story that his beautiful wife wrote when she was young. It was an intriguing tale, full of romance and heartbreak. He liked it because it was well written.

"Now this is good German!" he smiled as Rosie happily did her best to read it for him. Rarely would she stumble through having to sound out a word she didn't know, but even then, Rudi helped her along, his mind still as sharp as ever. Occasionally when he dozed off, he would talk in his sleep as if he were re-living past experiences in Germany.

"It's amazing how you remember so much of your life when you're young." Rudi told Rosie when he awakened. "I can see my old room and my grandfather. It's funny what comes up in your mind when you have a lifetime of memories." He said. Rosie was smiling, listening to his musings.

"I suppose childhood is very... impactful." She acknowledged. "I'm grateful I had such a good one. Thanks to you Dad. Actually, I do have really good memories. Lots with Tante Helga and Onkel Frank." Rudi smiled and nodded.

"You have some not good ones too when I was drinking. It would have been helpful to see the end of my choices and how they affected others before I made them." He regretfully admitted. Rosie bobbed her head from side to side. "I guess. That's true. But that's not how it works and besides it was all so long ago. Mom forgave you. God forgave you.

Who am I to not forgive you? Love forgives, right?"
She smiled at him.

Rudi nodded, smiling back. "I'm very selective with my memories. Did you have good memories of your childhood?" Rosie asked.

Rudi's smile faded a little. Then he shrugged. "Well, it's funny. You can be selective in your mind sometimes, like you said. I do remember mostly good things." He answered without elaborating. He was always happy to share his past after the time that he had met Maria, but no one was privy to much of his childhood and youth. Rosie often wondered if he tried to forget certain things with the numbing effects of alcohol when she was younger. She nodded her head, happy that her father seemed at peace. Another thing that she noticed was that surprisingly, the texture of Rudi's skin didn't change much. He had beautifully smooth olive skin.

"To this day," Rosie randomly evaluated, "you do not have a wrinkle to speak of – very strange. I hope my skin stands the test of time like yours, Dad." Rudi had to laugh.

"I just use Nivea in the morning and at night. That's all."

'That's his secret.' Rosie thought. So of course, she would do the same, hoping for the same results. Genetics, she hoped. Only time would tell. It was getting late, and Rudi needed to sleep. Rosie could tell it was time to say good night, so she closed the book.

"Are you okay here tonight, Dad?" she asked, leaving his room while he was lying on his side, facing the window.

Rudi was still in pain, but he didn't want her to know. "I'm fine." He answered. "Good night." When Rosie left the hospital to drive back to the house in Port Dover, Rudi called for a nurse to bring him some medicine.

Chapter Ten

MARIA WAS ALREADY OUT OF HER HOSPITAL bed the next morning.

"Mom! What are you doing wandering the hall?" Rosie asked, shocked to find her mother walking around with her IV's attached.

"I'm not wandering." Maria calmly answered. "I'm exercising, like I'm supposed to." Rosie spun on her heels and purposefully inquired at the nearest nursing station.

"Is Maria Heinrich supposed to be out of bed?" The nurse's smile was so big, Rosie thought that even her eyes looked as though they were smiling.

"Yes and isn't she a trooper?" the nurse answered. "If she can prove to us that she's capable of mobility, she can be released soon. We still have her hooked up for now because she has a lot of fluid to replenish and we are still monitoring her but at the rate she's going, she'll be able to go home in the next couple of days.

Shocked, Rosie walked back to her mother. "Okay, well it looks like you win patient of the year! Way to go mom! You can go home in a couple of days if you keep this up!" Maria smiled at her youngest child out of the corner of her eye.

"See, I told you." She giggled.

Rosie laughed to herself shaking her head and Maria picked up her pace as she finished the walk back to her room. Rudi's case, however, was not as easy. His will to get better and his determination were impressive according to his physical therapy team who visited him every day. If possible, they were trying to help him become sufficiently mobile enough to earn his ticket home again as well.

Rosie and her sister Christine had a meeting with the hospital staff responsible for placing long-term patients. They were looking for answers as to what the family wanted to do with Rudi.

"We need to set a deadline for a decision." The long-term care coordinator argued. "We are not able to keep him on a medical floor when he is not sick. We would have to move Rudi to the fourth floor, where our long-term patients are, while they wait for placement in a nursing facility." Placing her dad, or either of her parents, in a long-term care facility, was not an option in Rosie's mind.

"We can set a deadline, and then we'll discuss it again." She told the administrators. They accepted a date that was ten days from the time the meeting took place. There was a restriction on new patients and all visitors on the fourth floor due to an outbreak of the C-diff virus. The gastro-intestinal 'bug' was very dangerous to anyone with a compromised immune system or the elderly. And it was very contagious. This situation, although not good for those infected, worked in their favor. At least it gave them time to focus on bringing Maria home and at the same time keeping Rudi and Maria on the same floor so that they could still visit one another.

"I need some help with this shaving." Rudi said to his nurse. He wasn't quite able to reach the faucet in the bathroom from his wheelchair.

"I've got you covered." His nurse smiled, assisting him while he shaved and brushed his teeth for the day.

"It looks like you're going to visit the queen." She joked. Checking his face for any nicks from the razor or missed shaving cream.

He nodded. "I am. I'm going to see my wife." His nurse smiled, checking him over to make sure that he was presentable before she wheeled him to Maria's room.

"They certainly don't make men like you anymore Sir." His nurse commented, turning his chair into the room where his daughters were already at Maria's bedside, arranging her many flower vases on her windowsill from all of her well-wishers.

Rudi turned his head to thank his nurse.

"Not true." He answered. "She should have left me a long time ago." His nurse stepped back and looked to Maria who had overheard him.

"I married him for life. But he's right, it wasn't easy." The nurse backed away laughing.

"I'll have to find out about that another time." She said.

Rosie stepped up and turned the conversation back to their happy times. She was always the one who was hungry to hear more of their love story and so she urged her mother to continue to give her more details of what it was like for them when they were young.

"Well, it had been a bit of a search to even find Rudi's family. " Maria told her. "The German government made people register their names and their new addresses once they had found a place to settle because so many people were 'lost' so-to-speak. The war had literally separated so many families. We had to inquire with the consulate and wait until they could match the request with their new address. Many German people were suddenly chased from their homes during the war," she explained, "so they had a lot of names to search. But one day, they were finally able to give us a solid answer." Rudi's eyes looked serious as he remembered that time.

"Oh, Rudi" Maria probed for his memory of their earlier days "– was it fall? Ja, it was October when Mutti came to visit us. And your stepfather too. And Rosi! Oh, that was difficult for me, but oh how I loved your sister. Right from the start." She looked at Rudi. He nodded and their eyes sparkled once again.

Chapter Eleven

I HAVE ASKED MY FAMILY IF THEY COULD MAKE a trip to West Germany to meet you. What do you think? Do you like that idea?" Rudi asked Maria while they were waiting at the station for the train to arrive. Maria was instantly in favor of meeting his family. She knew so little about them, other than they were businesspeople and not particularly close to Rudi. Nevertheless, she was hoping that once she got to know them better, she would get to know Rudi on an even deeper level.

"Of course, I would be so happy to meet your family." She answered, excited that they were moving into a new phase of their relationship.

"I told my mother about how much I love you and that we are serious about each other." he explained, squeezing her hand and looking deep into her hazel eyes. "She said, 'if that is the case, they would make every effort to visit us and look forward to understanding why my heart has settled on you.'" he told her. "It will be the first time that I've seen them since I left for the war! So much has changed for me, and I am excited to introduce you to them." Maria smiled and looked amused.

"And why has your heart settled on me Rudi?" she induced.

"Oh, that's easy. Because you're crazy enough to put up with me!"

She made a smirk that let him know she was not satisfied with that answer.

"If I'm being serious," he said looking playfully into her eyes, "I would tell you that – you're kind of a cutie and you are so loving, and did I say kind? Yes, okay, well I suppose I fell for you at first because I think you're beautiful, but now I know how smart you are, - like I said – kind, loving, sincere and really, well, I have come to trust you Maria." He explained, as though he were also explaining it to himself. " I know that a lot of people rely on you. Your mother, your siblings, even your grandfather. But I suppose that I rely on you too. I rely on your honesty, I guess. There may be other girls who are pretty, but no one is as pretty as you. There may be other girls who are fun, but I have the most fun with you. You are a gem and I know it. A diamond in fact! I have found my treasure and wouldn't let you go for all the world!"

"Well thank you. That's certainly a lot to live up to." Maria said, flattered.

"You don't have to live up to it, my dearest Maria. It's simply who you are." Rudi stated matter-of- factly as he pulled her close to give her a kiss.

"Well, I'm not going to think about that." Maria stated practically, fearing that she couldn't possibly be as wonderful of a person as he described, but since he thought so, she didn't want to blow it. "But I am looking forward to meeting your parents and your little sister. When can they come?" she asked.

"Well, she's my half-sister because he's just my stepfather, but I'm hoping they can all come in a couple of weeks. That way we don't have to worry about the winter weather, and I think that their business takes a slower turn at this time of year."

"Perfect!" declared Maria. She would have time to talk to her mother about it. She wanted her whole family to meet Rudi's family. After all, she thought, and hoped, that one day, through the two of them, their families would forever be united. Two weeks would give them all plenty of time to prepare for the visit. She kissed Rudi one more time before she bid him goodbye for another long work week in the big city.

Chapter Twelve

THE TRAIN WHISTLED LOUDLY AS IT PULLED into the station at Stuttgart. Maria accompanied Rudi to greet his family as they got off the train. They had government issued passes from Berlin to visit West Germany for one week. Marla was fidgety and her palms were a little sweaty as she waited on the platform with him.

"Nervous?" Rudi inquired. Maria shrugged, trying to shake off her anxious thoughts. She just squeezed his hand and smiled. He squeezed hers back and they smiled at one another in silence. He was feeling a little nervous himself. They both took care to wear something nice, Rudi in dress pants and a nice shirt and overcoat, and Maria wore a blue dress and her fall coat. They were both full of anticipation. Rudi, because it had been a long time since he'd seen them and Maria, because it was the first time that Rudi would present her as his girlfriend, and she so much wanted to make a good first impression. They both stood a little straighter than usual, but full of happiness to share the love they had found in each other with those who were most important to them. The train finally stopped and let out its steam. The doors were opened. As the passengers flooded out, Rudi hadn't yet caught sight of his family.

Suddenly, a tiny voice cried out, "Rudi! Mein Bruder!" Halfway down the long train, Rosi peeked her little head out from behind her mother's cloak. She came running towards Rudi with her arms wide. She was so excited to see her big brother. She was a beautiful nine-year-old girl with blonde braids down to her waist, blue eyes, and freckles all over. Behind her, with a stiffness of demeanor that comes from an heir of high German sophistication, Rudi's mother greeted her son with a rigid hug and his stepfather, offered a handshake. Rudi reacted on the spot with a tinge of disappointment from the cold greeting and therefore also a little embarrassment. He held out his hand to introduce his parents and Rosi to Maria. Rosi immediately stepped forward to give Maria a warm, hearty hug, which worked wonders to break the ice that apparently needed a little chipping. Rudi's mother gave Maria a very business-like greeting as did his stepfather, but Rosi quickly bridged the gap as she gushed about how beautiful Maria's dress was and how she wished she could have one as pretty as hers.

"We aren't able to buy nice things like that in East Germany. Everything is controlled by the communist government occupying our eastern section." Rudi's mother explained. "I'm afraid that Rosi has a keen eye for pretty things, so she will notice everything that attracts her in the least."

"Oh, I don't mind at all." Maria said. "I notice nice things too." She remarked as she looked down at Rudi's sister. Rosi held Maria's hand and they became instant friends despite their age discrepancy. Rudi led them, talking all the way, as they walked to his small apartment, not far from the Bahnhof. He explained how he came to work for the leather smith and how his employment led him to his chance meeting with Maria, even though she lived in Reutlingen. He was so excited to finally see them, especially his mother. His eagerness to have them accept Maria as a part of the family also made him share more information than they could possibly absorb in a first meeting. He talked a mile a minute. Even Maria, who was a talker by nature, felt like he was rambling.

When they arrived at his apartment, Rudi felt another hint of cool reservation from them. Although it was small, with only one bedroom, he was proud to have it and kept it clean and very presentable. There was a small table in the kitchen/dining area and a small living room. It was very comfortable for a bachelor and quite adequate for Rudi's purposes. He put on a pot of coffee, and they had their afternoon 'café' together. Maria had shared a wonderful apple streusel cake that she baked herself. No one said a word.

"Of course, we know that this is too small for all of you to sleep here," Maria began, "so we have arranged to have you stay in Reutlingen in my mother's house." She looked at all of them excitedly and once again received somewhat of a cold response from Rudi's mother and stepfather. Rosi, in blissful ignorance, looked up at Maria and pushed her way through to link arms with her and then she laid her head on Maria's shoulder. She could not be sweeter, Maria thought. "My mother's house is big enough and we thought it would be the best arrangement because we all want to get to know each other's family." Maria was hopeful as she looked for a positive response to her generous offer but was met with only a sideways glance as Rudi's mother looked down her nose at what she felt was a groveling young lady from a poor family.

"Well Rudi," his mother stated "this is a nice enough apartment while you work here in the city. But don't you remember how nice it is at home in Potsdam? Our house is much better than this and it's very convenient to the Straßenbahn into Berlin. Since you've been working in Stuttgart for a tanner

140

all this time, I'm quite sure it would be easy enough for you to get a job doing the same kind of work in Berlin. You'd probably even get a higher wage because it's Berlin!" It was the most talking Maria had heard from Rudi's family since they arrived, however not a single word was meant to include her in the conversation. It was as if Rudi's mother had an agenda for this visit and it had nothing to do with meeting her, let alone her family. She quickly surmised the purpose for his parents' visit. They wanted to take Rudi away from her and move him back to East Germany. Rosi of course was oblivious to the divisive atmosphere that her mother was trying to create between Rudi and Maria. Apparently, she didn't think Maria was good enough for her son. Considering this realization, Maria had a hard time keeping her thoughts to herself as the afternoon went on. She had tried to welcome Rudi's parents with open hands and an open heart and yet, before they even set foot in her mother's home, they had the nerve to patronize her with their condescending attitude. Rudi was caught between trying to make an impression on his parents, sharing the details of his new life, and at the same time, trying to keep favor with Maria. It was a game that couldn't be played for long.

"I think we better go back to the train station so that we can still make the four o'clock train to Reutlingen." Rudi cautioned.

'Or we could send you on the first train back to Berlin.' Maria mused in her mind, somehow managing not to vocalize her thoughts.

"I know the schedule well. I've been travelling to see Maria every week since we started dating. We don't want to be late, or we'll miss it." Rudi continued. Maria smiled and kept silent.

His stepfather quickly noted "That's a lot of train fare Rudi. Every week?"

"Yes!" he answered happily. "Maria's mother kindly allows me to stay in her brother's room while I visit. That way I don't have to spend money on food or anything else. She has been very gracious to me. I am excited for you to meet her." Rudi's parents walked behind them the whole way to the Bahnhof. The atmosphere was strained, and it didn't change much during the entire trip to Reutlingen. As they walked down the street to Maria's home, Rudi's mother, Luise, changed her demeanor. She was impressed with her surroundings.

"This is the street you live on Maria? Your mother has a house on this street?"

"Yes." Maria answered, somewhat annoyed at this point because of how this prideful and somewhat prejudiced woman had been treating her. "My mother owns the house and the business across the street from her house. We have a milk distribution business. She rents out four of the rooms in her three-story house to single people, but she has plenty of room left to accommodate you for your visit. She has been expecting you for a couple of weeks." Once they entered the house and Luise was introduced to Maria's mother, her entire demeanor changed.

"Lovely to meet you, Frau Riekert." She glanced at Rudi with a look of approval, but still didn't give the time of day to Maria. "I must say, I wasn't expecting to find you, a single mother, in such a big house. How do you manage it?"

Maria's mother laughed, "Well it certainly doesn't come from nothing. I have to work hard for everything and if I didn't have Maria to help me, I simply could not do it. Anneliese helps me at home with Hildegard and Siegfried when he isn't staying with my mother. And she does the cooking as well. We all work together. You could say it's a family business." Maria looked around her living room and realized that it was indeed quite a comfortable home. She hadn't thought much about it up until now.

"I must say that I am very grateful to both of my girls. They've had to give up a lot to keep this family going, but you are right to say that it's a lot for a single mother." She looked at Maria with a twinge of regret in her eyes, "You see Maria always dreamed of going to the University to become a teacher. She was definitely smart enough, but unfortunately for her, I have always needed her help since their father died. I had to keep her home to help run the business." Maria's face was saddened, but she understood the situation and made the best of it. Her mother continued to give Rudi's parents a small glimpse of how she came to be in this house. "We started out on a farm. My husband ran the business, and I stayed home with the children and cooked and kept the house. When we lost him to the war, we tried to keep the business going on our own, but it was too far to travel into the city and back every day. We lived in Immenhausen, which is more than an hour away. On the farm, we had a horse, four cows, a goat, 2 swine and about 400 chickens. We milked the cows and gathered the eggs every day and brought it all to the city to sell to the Milk Centrale. In exchange they provided us with 40-liter bottles of milk, already prepared, for us to sell. Some whole milk, for the babies, and some reduced fat for everyone else. We sold it to our customers in the city and some in the rural areas where we lived. That gave us a good start in our business. But driving back and forth made for a very long day away from home. Like I said, it was almost impossible when my husband died in the war. That's when I decided to move to the city to make it easier for us to carry on the business." Luise nodded, taking in the hard effort that was required to have such a nice house.

"I have accepted some boarders in four of the suites upstairs. They pay me enough rent to take care of the mortgage so we can live comfortably."

She finished, looking around at their faces. "Ja, but it hasn't been easy. And it's still a lot of work every day." Luise and Rudi's stepfather seemed very tuned in and attentive. "I don't think our lives were meant to be easy," she went on to explain. Rudi's parents looked puzzled. "Well how else would we know that we need to rely on God. We always think that we are self-sufficient when things are too easy, or we have amassed too much wealth. It's rare to find a person who is wealthy and still knows that even their money and intelligence that they have been given to achieve it, is all a gift from God. As if we are capable of anything without Him." She chuckled, but they weren't laughing. They had never heard anyone talking about God in that way and they weren't quite sure what to make of it.

"Well hard work is always required if we want to achieve wealth." Luise finally said.

"For most people," Maria's mother agreed, "unless you have a wonderful inheritance. Then hard work is just a matter of character and integrity, isn't it?" she went on. "As far as we are concerned, it's a part of life."

Luise agreed. "That is something we have in common. Yes, I've had to work very hard as well for our business. We buy what we can very cheaply on the market and sell it again at a higher price. We've done well, but it takes a lot of time. We sent Rudi out on his bike when he was a youth to work his own little corner. He did okay, but it wasn't something that he wanted to continue into adulthood." She looked away, somewhat thoughtful of what her success had cost her. "I must confess, I didn't have much time for him. We were always so concerned about the business. There is always a sacrifice isn't there Maria?" She was directing her conversation to Maria's mother, who without contemplation had to agree.

"Yes. I think there is." The two ladies were able to see eye to eye in some ways and Maria's mother was always very jovial and a very generous host. She did her best to make Rudi's parents feel welcome. She even slept in Maria and Anneliese's room so that she could give them her bedroom while they stayed with her. During their visit, Maria and Rudi still had to work in the milk business, but they tried to provide Rudi's parents and Rosi with lots of entertainment when they had finished working for the day. They visited the Black Forest and had dinner in the quaint little town of Heidelberg.

Thankfully, everyone in the two families seemed to get along. Rosi especially liked Hildegard, who was just four years older than her. Everyone liked Hilde because she had a way of always bringing the sunshine with her dancing and her light-hearted, warm personality. It became a friendly atmosphere after all, but to Maria, it seemed as if once Rudi's parents noticed that she didn't come from the poorest of circumstances, that her union with their son was approved. Although not completely. They wanted to give him one more chance to return to Berlin with them.

"Rudi, if you want to follow them and return to East Germany, that is up to you." Maria said. "I am certainly not going to hold you here, only to have you wonder later in life what could have happened if you would've taken them up on their offer. But know this – I am not going to continue a relationship with you from that far away. So, if you leave with them, you also leave our relationship."

Rudi didn't even have to think about it. "I've never entertained the idea of going back to East Germany. For what? First, I'm in love with you. Secondly, I have a job here – well Stuttgart, but I mean West Germany. Why would I go willingly to a place I worked so hard to flee? It's controlled by the communist GDR in Berlin. There's no way I'd go back, even just to be in closer proximity to my family. And to be honest," he finished in a whisper, "your mom has been more of a mother to me in the short time that I've known her than my own mother. Not that it was entirely her fault. I believe that she has always needed to work very hard to support our family. Whatever the case, I am happy to stay here. I choose you. If you'll still have me?"

Rudi's humble answer made Maria soften a little. She had been on her guard the entire visit. She recognized that there was an air of contention breeding in her future relationship with Rudi's mother. But Maria was very sorry for her attitude and for not being able to rise above the nonsense. Originally, she was so excited about getting to know Rudi's family, which made all the fake heirs of superiority they cast over her seem like such a deep disappointment. She was hoping for open conversations and sharing family stories when all she seemed to be left with was a feeling of having been scrutinized for position and wealth. The first moment she realized this was the case was the moment she decided that she didn't care whether she measured up for their acceptance. She was ultimately disappointed in what she thought was proven to be a lack of integrity on their part. And yet she loved Rudi and she also fell in love with Rosi. Someone with as shallow of a character as she was judging Luise to have, somehow managed to turn out two amazing children with very sweet dispositions. She knew that she may've been unfair in her own estimation of Rudi's mother, but at this point she was glad to have the whole visit behind them.

Her own deduction of Luise's character made her even more thankful for her own mother's easy-going personality. Her mother didn't take offense to anyone or entertain presuppositions. She just accepted people as they were and made the best of everything. It was a wise example to follow, but first Maria realized that she would need to deal with some of her own pride before she could learn to be forgiving and hopefully less judgmental.

"There's always a reason people are the way they are. We just do not know what circumstances in life have formed someone's thinking. Either way, we should always take the higher road of forgiveness and try to make peace." her mother wisely advised. She had plenty of life experience to back up her own realizations. She was literally prevented from marrying Maria's father for three years because his father deliberately withheld his blessing. It was for the same reason. He thought she came from a poor background with no dowry to speak of. And now, years later he loved her as if she were his own daughter. "Sometimes it takes years for God to chip away at a person's character. Just because someone is older than you, doesn't mean they are wiser." Her mother counselled. Maria hoped she would have many years to grow a different perspective on Luise. For now, she was pleased to know how much Rudi loved her and happy that indeed their relationship was most important to him because he chose to stay with her.

Chapter Thirteen

ONCE THEIR VISTIORS LEFT, THE RIEKERT household returned to its own rhythm and Rudi and Maria's growing love story did as well. Rudi approached Maria's mother one day in the kitchen while Maria was upstairs getting dressed.

"Mama, I have a question to ask you." She stopped what she was doing because Rudi wasn't usually this formal with her.

"You know you can ask me anything Rudi, go ahead." He started to look a little sheepish, but humbly put his hand on hers.

"I want to ask Maria to marry me. Is that okay with you?" He was so relieved, first - because he was able to get the words out. For some strange reason he was nervous about it, and second - because of her reaction.

"Oh, for goodness sakes Rudi, I thought something was wrong. Of course you have my approval! I have been expecting this for a while now. It's very nice of you to ask me though. I feel honored that you did that, but you have my full blessing and I'm sure of agreement on that from every person in this house and in the whole family for that matter. We've all come to love you! Every one of us." Rudi beamed like a ray of sunshine, but he made her promise not to say anything to Maria until he asked her. Which again, was simply understood.

Not long after, during one of his visits, just before Christmas on a cold, crisp evening when it was already dark outside because of it being so late in the year, Rudi suggested that he and Maria go on a stroll to the city center. It was exceptionally beautiful and peaceful because the snowflakes were gently falling, and the city was alight with Christmas decorations. The whole atmosphere was very festive. Rudi made sure that they brought some warm blankets and Maria had put some hot cocoa in a thermos-type flask for the two of them. At the city center, they sat on a bench and Rudi put his arm around his sweetheart.

"Right now, I feel pretty nearly perfectly happy." Maria said. "Just sitting here with the man I love. We don't even have to keep up a conversation. I just like to relax with you Rudi. I am at peace." They were full of contentment in each other's presence. The winter air was making it difficult to venture out like they so enjoyed doing, but Rudi had something special in mind on the way home that would make it even more memorable. Since the beginning of December, he started to look at engagement rings. They had been dating since the spring and almost from the beginning they each knew that they had found their life's mate. Now that any opposition from his family was dealt with, engagement was sure to happen; it was just a matter of when. They had both talked about how nice it would be to have a wedding the following summer, so Rudi went ahead and bought Maria a beautiful ring and kept it with him, on his person, the way she did his letters that he still wrote to her daily when he was in Stuttgart. That way, if there was ever a very romantic moment, he would be prepared. He wanted it that way, so that it would be like a gift to both of them, rather than rehearsed. He already knew that he had won her heart, so he didn't need to impress her in order to get her to agree to marry him. They were more confident than that in one another's affections.

Rudi had in mind to ask her to marry him in front of her house, because that's where he realized that he wanted to have her for his wife, the night he dropped her off after their first date. But as they sat on the bench together and the mood was so romantic because of the lights and the peaceful feeling, he decided that he couldn't wait any longer and this was one of the most romantic evenings that they had ever had. What was so special was that they were not doing anything extraordinary. That's what made it even more magical. So right there, sitting on the bench in front of the city square in Reutlingen, turning to Maria, he took her hands into his.

"Darling. I want to ask you a serious question." Maria was almost scared the way he started.

"What is it Rudi?" He took out the ring box with one hand and held onto Maria's hand with the other.

"I want to ask you to be my wife, Maria. I love you more than I ever thought I could love anyone. I can't imagine my life without you. I never want to lose you. I would do anything for you. Would you do me the honor of becoming Mrs. Heinrich?"

Maria had no idea this was coming tonight. She was surprised and excited all at the same time. She held out her hand for him, having to laugh.

"Why am I shaking?" she giggled, looking up into his sincere, soft brown eyes.

"No need, my darling. I will not hurt you and I will never leave you. No need to fear. Now, will you marry me?"

"Yes darling. Of course, I will marry you and cherish you as long as we live. You are and always will be the love of my life." Rudi opened the box, took out the ring and slid it onto Maria's finger. She looked at the ring and then leaned in to give Rudi the longest kiss they had ever had as if to seal their engagement. They were so happy on this night. It was as if nothing could possibly ruin their happiness. They sat on the bench a while longer listening to the Christmas music playing in the square and watching as people were walking by. They sipped on their hot cocoa and occasionally stole a kiss and just rested. It was a regular day, but suddenly everything was made new. Nothing would ever be the same again. They weren't just boyfriend and girlfriend anymore. Now they were engaged and looked forward to spending a lifetime together. They sat there and basked in the glow of their love for a long time, neither one of them wanting this night to ever end.

In the morning, coming into the kitchen where the family was gathered for Sunday breakfast, Rudi, suddenly, put his arm around Maria and cleared his throat as if to get attention. "Maria and I want to tell all of you first; before we tell anyone else... We got engaged last night." There was a moment of silence as everyone looked at each other not knowing what to say.

"What does this mean?" Siegfried asked.

"It simply means that we are going to get married Siegfried." Maria explained. "So, for you it means that Rudi will be your brother-in-law."

Siegfried smiled, excited that Rudi would be a permanent part of the family, not that he ever doubted. He hugged them sincerely and stood next to Rudi as if he were already his own brother.

"Congratulations!" Maria's mother said. "It's about time!"

"What?" Maria asked, turning around to her mother.

"Well, he asked my permission a few weeks ago. I have been wondering what was taking so long."

Rudi laughed. "I wanted it to be romantic. I was waiting for a special time and when we went for a walk last night, it just seemed so right." He looked at Maria and they smiled at each other and kissed.

"Wow. Okay. Are you guys going to keep doing that all over the place now?" Hilde asked, "Because I'm really happy that you're getting married, but – ugh! Not ready for all of that."

"Just wait until you get engaged." Maria defended herself.

Anneliese stood up from her chair and gave Maria a big hug. "I am so happy for you Maria. Rudi is a wonderful guy. I know you'll be very happy together." She also gave Rudi a big hug. "And you take care of my twin. She means all the world to me."

"I will Anneliese. She means all the world to me too." Rudi said.

"Well, this has been an eventful day, even before it really gets started." Maria's mother said. "I think we should celebrate. Just our family. I know there's a lot of celebrating to come, but just us, here tonight - before Rudi goes back to Stuttgart. Let's have a nice dinner and Anneliese, maybe you can make a cake. We should celebrate a little." Maria was so happy that her whole family loved Rudi so much. Even her extended family welcomed him with open arms and always treated 'Maria's Berliner' with respect. This evening they would feast and party, celebrating the blessedness of a close-knit family, which meant all the world to both of them. They knew that was something they would strive for in the family they would create for themselves wherever their lives would take them.

Chapter Fourteen

A S THE SNOW BEGAN TO MELT AND THE flowers poked their way through the frozen ground, Maria started looking forward to her future with her husband-to-be. She started to get ideas for their upcoming wedding and was eager to get her plans underway. First on the agenda was to set a date so that she could plan everything around that. She knew it would be sometime in the summer because they had already talked about that, but she still wanted to make sure that Rudi had a say in the decision. They were sitting around the kitchen table one day in early spring when the planning got underway in earnest.

"I was thinking maybe June, but then Anne and I have our birthday in June. But July is already so hot.

What about May Rudi? What do you think of May?" Maria questioned.

"That's only a couple of months away. I mean we could, but I know my family won't be able to get papers that quickly." He answered. Maria thought about it and then said, "Well maybe we could do it at the end of June then."

Just then Anneliese came bursting through the front door and went straight upstairs. They were all silent for a minute.

"Give it a few minutes. Something probably happened with Helmut." Maria's mother guessed. Before they realized it, a few minutes had turned into an hour and then, being patient, they waited even longer, all the while tossing around ideas for Maria and Rudi's wedding. Time got away on them and by the time they thought of it again, they realized that Anneliese had been in her room for the better part of the afternoon.

"I'm going to check on Anne." Maria said as she stood to go upstairs. Coming closer to the bedroom door, she could hear crying. She turned the doorknob carefully and quietly pushed the door open to find Anneliese lying on her bed with a handkerchief in her hand. Maria walked over and sat next to her sister.

"Oh Maria!" Anneliese exclaimed as she fell into her arms. First Maria just let her cry. After a couple of minutes, she pushed Anneliese back so she could see her puffy, tear-streaked face.

"Anne, what's wrong? What happened? Did you and Helmut break up?" Anneliese shook her head. Maria was confused. What could be making her cry like this? "Anne, you have to tell me. You've been up here a long time." Maria took her own handkerchief and wiped away Anneliese's tears. "Now, whatever it is, you can tell me."

With an almost panic-stricken expression of worry, she pleaded with Maria. "Don't tell Mama. You can't tell her – at least not yet." Maria looked suspicious. "I'm pregnant." Anneliese blurted. "I wasn't sure why I was feeling so strange lately, so I went to the doctor. Now I know." Her eyes got big. "But you can't tell anyone. Promise." She begged.

"Anneliese what are you talking about? People are going to know soon enough. And why are you so worried about telling Mama. She was in the same situation. If anyone will understand you it's her." She looked at her sister with compassion in her eyes and gave her a supportive hug. "What did Helmut say?" Anneliese pulled herself up to look at Maria.

"It wasn't all bad. He was surprised, but then he put his arm around me and said that we'd make the best of it." Maria nodded and started to smile.

"Well, that's good. I'm glad he's not leaving you over this."

Anneliese shook her head. "I think you underestimate him, Maria. He's not as bad as you think. He's a decent guy."

"Oh Anne. I hope so. For your sake. I hope I am so wrong about him." She looked down, hiding her disappointment in the timing of her twin's impromptu wedding. She had just come up the stairs from making her own wedding plans. "So, I suppose you'll be getting married?"

Anneliese nodded. "Yes, we will. But of course, I don't want an engagement celebration or a big wedding party or anything like that." Maria nodded, understanding, but also knowing how much her sister had to give up because she had made some bad choices. She got up to get Anneliese a wet cloth to wipe away her tears.

"Don't worry Anne. Everything happens for a reason. You know what Mama says, "if everyone waited to have sex after marriage, half the people in this world wouldn't be here. Honestly. So many people have made that same mistake. And all our mistakes, God somehow turns into something beautiful now or in the future. It helps us, doesn't it Anne, to draw closer to Him when we really need Him? I mean when we're looking for a miracle. Like you need right now when you tell Mama." She looked at her sister and waited for a laugh. Anneliese didn't even crack a smile.

"Okay, so what I mean is that sometimes God lets us make our own mistakes and walk down a dangerous path of our own making so that He can teach us obedience. It's a hard lesson to learn and sometimes the consequences can last a lifetime.

But I do think that you need to ask God for help. And you know that Mama might be mad at first, but God can soften her heart and she will come around. You'll see. It's strange how some people who have sex before marriage, don't get pregnant." They were both silent for a moment. "Even so, we know it's not His way and He always wants to protect us but Anneliese, God doesn't make mistakes. Don't cry so hard. This baby will be a blessing to you, you'll see." She held her sister's hand. "We will stick together like we always do. It'll be okay." She hugged her again. "Sooner or later, you'll have to tell Mama. Don't be scared. I'm here for you." Anneliese took a deep breath and tried to pull herself together.

"Just tell them I don't feel well, which is kind of the truth. I'll be down later." Maria got up from the bed. "Okay" she said, giving her a gentle smile. "And try to stop crying – it's not good for the baby."

Chapter Fifteen

IT WASN'T LONG BEFORE ANNELIESE HAD TO tell her mother because she was starting to feel sick and needed to go to the bathroom too frequently to call it normal. Maria wondered if their mother might already be suspicious of Anneliese's pregnancy because of all the signs, but she promised her sister not to say anything. She would let Anneliese do it when she was ready.

It was getting towards the end of spring when one day, standing in the kitchen and feeling rather brave, even confident, which presented as a false air of sassiness, Anneliese turned to her mother and announced, "I have something to tell you Mama."

Turning to her daughter, thinking it would be something involving Helmut, she listened as Anneliese abruptly sprung the news on her. "I am pregnant. I'm having a baby Mama. It's due in November. I'm pregnant with Helmut's baby." Maria's mother stood in shock. It took a couple of minutes for her to absorb the information and then the emotions kicked in. She was flooded with fear and anger all at the same time. Her immediate reaction was to slap Anneliese in the face, which she was instantly sorry for. Anneliese in turn, was mortified at her mother's response. "Why are you hitting me?" she cried.

"I told you not to do that! I told you not to have sex before marriage and now look!" Her mother yelled. Anneliese fired right back.

"Mama, why are you so mad at me? You did the same thing!" Her mother looked so hurt, so disappointed.

"That was so different, and you know that. I told you many times that I was overwhelmed with the grief of losing my grandmother and your dad was trying to comfort me. We only had sex that one night and then miracle of miracles, I was pregnant. You and Helmut have been carrying on for quite some time, I'm pretty sure. Staying out so late riding around on his motorcycle... Can you imagine what people think of you – us for that matter, because of you? Oh, I know Anneliese; your happiness is all that matters. But think of it, if I told you not to have sex before marriage because I knew how hard it would make your life, don't you think I wanted to spare you all that hardship, not to mention shame?" She looked at Anneliese with a mixture of anger and love. Now, she didn't know what she felt. "Well, it's done. We will have to deal with it." She turned around and started to busy herself at the sink. She turned around again to further question Anneliese. "Why did you wait so long to tell me?" Anneliese was silent and just looked at her mother who then turned to Maria for answers, but Maria also kept her silence. She wanted to say "Because Anneliese was scared you would react this way," but she held her tongue. Maria's mother guessed what they were thinking, but still she couldn't help what she was feeling. Hildegard hid behind Maria's skirt and Siegfried left the room altogether when Anneliese got a slap in the face.

The news was a shock to everyone in the extended family simply because there was no wedding, not even prior talk of an engagement. And no one really knew Helmut. He was just known as Anneliese's good-looking boyfriend, but he was not really welcomed in the family as Rudi was because he was never around. He was an entirely different character. He seemed to keep himself aloof on purpose.

Ever since Helmut found out he would become a dad, he spent most of his weekends at the sports complex. Certainly, he did not concern himself with the welfare of his baby's future mother. He was just trying to hang on to his own freedom as long as possible. Luckily, it didn't bother Anneliese very much. She was content to be at home when she wasn't with Helmut. And she was not the jealous type. It wouldn't be long before she would be far too busy chasing after a little one, then to worry about where Helmut was every moment that he wasn't with her. In any case, for the time being, she was concentrating on getting through the pregnancy. She did not feel good and yet, she still tried to keep up with her regular chores around the house. And for the most part, things started to settle down at home as well.

It wasn't long before their mother became used to the idea of her daughter being pregnant. She even kept a watchful eye on Anneliese's health, making sure that she didn't overwork herself and in turn possibly harm the baby. She even found herself growing somewhat excited about having a new baby in the house. But with the prospect of Anneliese having to focus on her newborn and Maria wanting to get married in the summer, and possibly moving out, she worried about the family business. How would she keep things going for herself and Hildegard and Siegfried. Hilde was only thirteen and Siegfried was ten years old. Somehow, she knew that their level of maturity was nowhere near that of Maria and Anneliese at that same age.

The twins were indeed thirteen years old when they started pitching in just before their dad died.

She had not realized at the time, the burden that she let her twins help her to bear. And they did it with happy hearts, ready to serve her in any way that she needed them. And here she was again, wishing she could ask Maria to sacrifice another year. But there's no way she would, knowing that Maria and Rudi had already given her so much of their time. Little did she know that the thought had already occurred to them. If it wasn't for the fact that Maria wanted so badly to start a life with Rudi, she would've already offered to stay so Hildegard could have another year to mature and be able to handle the responsibility that she herself had shouldered for so many years.

Siegfried, although the only boy, was the baby of the family and was always treated as such. He would not have been able to step into the role of helping to run the business at such a young age and all that Hilde was interested in at this point, was making herself pretty, dancing around the house and getting attention from anyone she smiled at; typical thirteen-year-old bliss. So, the unspoken solution rested on Maria and Rudi to wait another year before they married.

"I come on the weekends anyway. It won't be a problem. It will give us plenty of time to plan our wedding and we can even get in a trip of our own, to visit East Germany, where I'm from, before we settle in Stuttgart. That way no one feels rushed and it will be easier on everyone." Rudi conceded.

"Except for us." Maria pouted.

"Your mother has been so good to us, letting me stay in the house and everything. I think we owe it to her to make it easier on her. You know Hildegard isn't ready to work the business yet and even next year, she'll be a handful. She is not as 'responsible' as you." Rudi stated.

"Ja, she is always looking for ways to have a good time and she knows how pretty she is." Maria said, not entirely willing to sacrifice her own plans for the sake of others.

"Your mother knows it would be best, for herself and Hilde and Siegried if we stayed another year." Rudi said. "She probably just doesn't want to ask us."

Maria was so thankful to have such a kind and giving man for her fiancée. She was relieved that he was so considerate of her whole family. He clearly saw the need and was willing to give up his own desires for their sake. At least for now.

"Okay" Maria reluctantly agreed. Putting their own plans on hold seemed to be the only solution to this sudden dilemma. "Let's tell Mama that we will wait to get married until next summer. First things first – Anneliese is having a baby." She turned to Rudi "Thank you for being you. I am the luckiest girl in the world."

He smiled and teased, "I'll remind you that you said that one day. And you're welcome. Although I think I'm the lucky one." He put his arm around her, and they walked inside the house to find Maria's mother and give her the news.

* * *

ANNELIESE'S NEXT HURDLE WAS TO inform Helmut's mother that she would soon be a grandmother. It was the most awkward conversation that Anneliese could remember, and she'd had quite a few as of late.

"I know that you're happy to be in love sweetie," Helmut's mother said to her, "but can I give you some advice?" Anneliese leaned in. She was eager to please Helmut and to have a good relationship with his family. "This won't sound very motherly, but it is the truth, and you are young, so I want to help you. Of course, I love Helmut, he's my son. But he's not who you think he is. He is just like his father. His only concern is his own happiness, not anyone else's. Oh, he can put up a pretty good show. He's good looking, but that is where the beauty ends. He's selfish and inconsistent. I can't even imagine him being faithful to anyone. He drinks too much and all he wants to do is have fun. I am warning you because his father is the same. You would think that they would grow up and be responsible, but no. They are egocentric and controlling, even to the point of abusive. You may not get bruised on the outside, but he doesn't have it in him to make anyone happy but himself. You seem like a very sweet, decent young lady, so I want to be upfront with you."

Anneliese stood stunned, only having listened to the first part of this speech. No wonder Helmut is not able to show love to my family, she thought. He never received it from his own. She didn't consider that Rudi had grown up without receiving much love and affection from his parents either, yet somehow, he overcame that deficit and decided to be different.

"We all have choices to make. I know I can give him what he needs. I love him so much. All he needs is unconditional love and that's how I love him." Anneliese responded, not wanting to hear any more negative accusations against her beloved Helmut. His mother, saddened, nodded her head.

"Don't say I never warned you honey. Love is blind in the beginning. That much is true." She looked Anneliese over and then stood up from her seat in her living room. "Good luck to you. At least you don't have kids. That's one good thing." She left Anneliese in the room alone. After sitting there for a few minutes debating whether to say anything about the pregnancy, she decidedly followed her out to the kitchen.

"I wanted to tell you..." Anneliese began, when suddenly, she heard the low rumble of Helmut's motorcycle outside. She breathed a sigh of relief. She had not intended to give his mother the news all by herself. Helmut was supposed to meet her there, but he was at the Sportsplex playing soccer. He was late once again. He came in sweaty and very athletic looking, which appealed to Anneliese as usual. Just the sight of him swept her off her feet every time. She felt as if she couldn't live without him. He went straight to Anneliese and gave her a kiss. It was understandable why he was late, she thought. Obviously, he had been playing a game of soccer that went longer than expected. She didn't question him. She just trusted him. Blindly. He didn't offer an explanation.

He was about to go and shower when Anneliese explained, "I was just going to share our news with your mother." That was enough said, as Helmut's mother turned around with a look of shock, which Anneliese met with confusion. Helmut gave Anneliese a hug from behind and gently rubbed her belly.

"We are going to have a baby. Aren't you happy for us Mom?" She softened a little and forced a smile to congratulate her son and Anneliese. "I thought you were supposed to wait until after a wedding." She chided. "That's how I grew up anyway." No one said a word. There was an awkward silence. Satisfied, Helmut left the kitchen to have a shower. He was simply informing his mother of the pregnancy after the fact. He wasn't looking for her approval. His mother's expression turned to pity as she looked back at Anneliese. She saw all the signs of an unhealthy relationship at its beginning. She tried to warn her, but Anneliese was more stubborn than she was wise at this point. She wouldn't listen to anyone regarding Helmut. She loved him. And she was having his baby for goodness sakes. In her mind there was no turning back. And she didn't want to, but one thing she did want, was to get married.

It was a crisp, early spring morning when Anneliese, in a beautiful blue dress with a white collar, holding a bouquet of roses and carnations, and Helmut, in a dark suit with a white shirt and navy tie, stood before the judge at the courthouse. Maria stood with her sister as a witness to their union, and Helmut's mother stood for him, all be it reluctantly. She had already expressed concerns about their future; mainly for Anneliese's welfare. Be that as it may, Anneliese was sure that this was the right course of action for herself and her growing baby. At this point she hoped and trusted for the best, despite all the warnings and all the signs.

"I'm so happy right now, Maria." She smiled at her twin. "I know you will grow to love Helmut too. Just give it time. You'll see. I can't believe I'm here getting married." She felt the usual pre-wedding jitters, but it never entered her mind to delay or stop the wedding because of her uneasiness or last-minute doubts. "I'm sure it's completely normal to feel anxious before you get married."

Maria smiled back at her, speechless for a response.

"I wish Mama could celebrate with us, but I know that it's best just to do this quick, given my situation." She looked down at her belly. "At any rate, I'm thankful that I have you." She whispered to Maria.

"You'll always have me, Anneliese." Maria smiled back.

Chapter Sixteen

HEARING OF RUDI'S OFFICIAL PLANS TO MARRY Maria, his mother asked that they travel to East Germany to celebrate with his aunts, uncles, and cousins. She wanted to host a celebration of their own for the happy couple. Maria was a little leery because of how things went when they first met, but this time would be different because she was more confident and secure in her relationship with Rudi.

On the train ride to Berlin, Rudi was feeling grateful to be visiting with his mother before embarking on this new chapter of life. Even if it wasn't the strongest of family ties for him, it was the only one he had so it was no less important.

The train whistle blew, jolting them out of her thoughts and signaling that it was time to pick up their bags and disembark the train. As the door opened Maria spotted Rosi with her long blonde braids and big smile. She was hard to miss because she was literally jumping up and down, frantically waving her arms for them to notice her. Her joy was contagious, instantly putting Maria in a happy mood. There was no doubting your welcome around Rosi. Withing minutes, Maria found that Rudi's step-father had picked up her bags and led them to a small automobile. He exuded an air of aloofness that made Maria feel like he certainly was not going out of his way to make a big deal of their arrival, but she found the general atmosphere less hostile than when she had first met Rudi's family in Stuttgart. When they arrived at the house, Rudi's mother greeted them with a very warm smile and even a handshake.

"Welcome son." She even gave Rudi a hug, but Maria still felt the cold shoulder when it was her turn. It seemed odd in contrast to her very openly affectionate family. "Welcome Maria!" She beamed as she earnestly put her best foot forward with her future daughter-in-law. This was remarkable. Maria was moved at how hard they tried. It was positive and at the same time, sad to understand that their affections were so reserved. Not the wild bear hugs Rudi received from her mother, brother, and sisters just upon arriving for

174

his regular weekend visits. 'We're so different' she thought, and yet love is the universal language that breaks all barriers. They did truly love Rudi. Their deliberate attempts at outward displays of affection, however awkward, were a testament to that. Maybe they had never received such unreserved demonstrative love themselves. That must be it, she thought. No one can be so calculated in showing emotion otherwise. Suddenly, she understood how rich she was. She held out her hand to her future mother-in-law. She was trying to be as genuinely affectionate as possible, if for nothing else than to show them how it's done. It was obvious that they were a little startled and somewhat unnerved. Her mother-in-law's back stiffened when Maria leaned in to give her a slight hug. It was uncomfortable. Maria decided not to try so hard. She would just have to learn that this is how Rudi's family operates and to make the best of it.

When she thought about it, she realized what was missing. It was the unconditional love of God that according to Rudi, they knew nothing about. She felt excited that she may have the opportunity to share her faith. It was so important to her that she get along well with Rudi's family, she wasn't sure how she would proceed, but she knew if she prayed about it, sooner or later, God would give her a window.

Her opportunity seemed to present itself the following afternoon in her future mother-in-law's kitchen when they were amicable with one another over sharing a recipe for chicken fricassee.

"Mutti, I wanted to ask you if you would take me to church with you on Sunday? Maybe we can all go together?" Knowing, of course, that she did not regularly attend church, she was simply hoping that if they could go together while she and Rudi were here, even one visit might spark a small interest in them to attend again on their own. Luise was not playing any games. She gave Maria a blank stare and then changed the subject, as if to ignore the discussion entirely.

"You know in our part of the country we cook more with potatoes, rather than spätzle. Rudi will probably prefer that in most dishes if you want my opinion." She simply stated. How on earth Luise could jump from a question about church to Rudi's palate preferences, she didn't know, other than to assume that religion was a discussion she wished to avoid.

However, on the off chance that she didn't hear or understand, Maria decided to bring it up one more time.

This time it was later in the evening when there was a distinctive lull in the conversation around the dinner table. She looked directly at Rosi.

"Have you ever gone to Sunday School Rosi? I bet you'd like to take me! I would sure like to visit

176

your local church with you one Sunday." Rosi looked up and smiled at Maria. Then she looked at her mother.

"I would like to go to church." Rosi answered. "As a matter of fact, I've never been. I think it would be interesting." Luise's eyes grew wide and then narrowed, looking across the table at her husband. He took a deep breath and stood up to offer his guests more wine. Rudi gave Maria a swift kick under the table.

"You would enjoy the music from the choir and probably the preaching too." Maria continued, ignoring the obvious signal from Rudi to back off. "You'll learn about Jesus and how much He loves us and died for us so that we can all live together with Him in heaven one day."

Rosi's eyes brightened, and she leaned in to learn more. Luise intervened with a hand on Rosi's shoulder. Looking up, she distinctly understood that her mother was excusing her from the table.

"We simply don't fill her head with such talk." Luise directed towards Maria. "I find church very... theatrical."

"Maybe you need to go to a better church." Maria said. Rudi nearly fell off his chair. "God is not interested in theatrics." She informed her future mother-in-law. "He wants sincere hearts that seek after Him. He does, after all, offer us everlasting life, despite all our failures."

"Failures?" Rudi's stepfather asked.

"Despite our failures to be holy. Our sins." Maria answered. "He wants us to seek His forgiveness and His love. That's the whole reason He came from heaven to carry the punishment of our sins for us. And after He died, He rose again to everlasting life three days later, leading the way for us to do the same if we believe in His sacrificing Himself in our place."

Luise wasn't receptive at all. She stood up to gather the plates. "Like I said, we don't entertain such nonsense." There was silence all around the table and Rudi was lost for what to do to smooth things over.

All of a sudden, a scripture verse came to Maria's thoughts, which she mumbled to herself. "But God chose the foolish things of the world to shame the wise. He chose the weak things of the world to shame the strong."

Rudi immediately stood up to help clear the table. On the way to the kitchen, he passed his mother and gave her a playful shoulder bump. She smiled at him, assuring him that all was well. Maria, sitting with her eyes looking down, was feeling alone. Just then, Rosi popped back in the room, going straight to Maria to give her a hug. How did this child know that she felt starved for genuine friendship, a relationship built on trust and love within the fold of Rudi's family members? So far, no one could come close to giving that much of themselves, other than Rudi himself, and this very sweet little girl.

* * *

THE FOLLOWING EVENING THE FAMILY gathered in the formal room for visitors; the special party that Luise had planned to celebrate Rudi's engagement.

"Mutti – shau mal, wie ich tanzen kann mit meinem Bruder!" All eyes were on Rosi and her beloved brother Rudi as they danced their way across the living room. There she is, thought Maria, the only amicable creature in this bunch. Too bad she's only nine years old, she thought sadly. Rosi, in her buoyant nature, was truly a charmer. She had a big personality that stole everyone's attention in her presence. Paired with Rudi's cheerful and gregarious disposition, these two were a force to behold and they truly enjoyed one another's company. But as brief as their visit to Rudi's family would be and as young as Rosi was, Maria hoped that she would forever remember this time of love and friendship between them, and that it would grow in years to come.

"Look at my two children!" Rudi's mother boasted with pride, as she leaned toward her sister, Lotte. "I wish Rudi could stay with us," she sighed "but he has a good life with Maria's family. Her mother has done very well for herself." She turned her gaze towards Lotte, who was absorbing any morsel of information she could about Rudi's future wife and family."

Lotte mused, playing the devil's advocate, only for conversation. "Maria seems so...simple."

"Yes", Luise agreed, "but her mother is quite a businesswoman. She runs the milk business for their district and Maria is her right hand. She's very smart. I saw for myself. Otherwise, this marriage wouldn't work of course. So ja, I am pleased with Maria, as different as she presents herself to be. Rudi is completely in love with her, and I have come around to accepting it. She has my blessing." Lotte scrutinized Maria with a keen eye.

"Good, Luise. Very good indeed." She conceded. As though Maria could sense they were talking about her and her family, she chose to remain on the other side of the room. Rudi's family was completely given to enjoying the lifestyle of drinking and dancing and talking amongst themselves, many times about each other in a less than flattering way, most of which Maria felt was beyond her liking and even sometimes understanding. The area of Germany where she grew up was so different. She was a farm girl. She worked hard in the fields and family was everything. They had a lot of fun together and on Sunday they went to church. They had family parties too, where people drank and danced, but they celebrated each other and shared a genuine love for one another, that was not contingent on status or income. She truly felt like she belonged. Here, Maria felt judged and out of place. She couldn't wait to get home. Rudi, on the other hand, could enjoy himself fully in any atmosphere. He was loving towards his own family and Maria's family.

Everyone seemed preoccupied enough that Maria felt as though she could stealthily slip out the door for a walk in the fresh air. Quickly stealing away to her room to grab her overcoat, she walked carefully down the steps to the sidewalk in front of the house. She stood and took a deep breath. Looking up at the stars, she felt pressure lifting from her shoulders. Putting one foot in front of the other, she walked down the street aimlessly. 'Why am I feeling so sad at my own engagement party?' she asked herself. 'I'm not sure how I'm supposed to feel, but I'm pretty sure, this isn't it. Where is the love?' she asked in her mind. 'How can anyone function without it?' she wondered. Having grown up with the innate knowledge of the love of Christ, she felt desperately sorry for those who lacked it. Where is the meaning? And where is the love?' She wandered a little further down the street contemplating these thoughts when she felt instinctively that it was time she turned around. Upon getting closer to the house, she saw Rudi outside without a jacket and looking frazzled.

"I was about to blow the whistle on you and ask for a search party. What are you doing out here by yourself?" he asked.

"Oh, I was just getting some fresh air, Rudi. Nothing to worry about." He nodded, searching her face for signs that would tell him otherwise.

"Are you sure nothing is wrong. You've been gone a long time." He stated.

"Not really. You were just busy dancing. I've only been out here a few minutes." He looked at her sideways but didn't argue.

"Well are you coming in now?" he urged. Maria smiled and slid under his protective arm.

"Yes. I feel better now." She said.

The party was still in full swing, and Maria only slid away a second time, when the serious drinking got underway, of which Rudi was happy to partake. When she excused herself this time no one was surprised or protested. And this time she went straight to bed.

This was a part of her future husband, Maria was learning, that he grew up with. The late-night partying and the city life was ingrained in Rudi as much as the hard work and church on Sundays was in her. She understood that. At least she was starting to, and she decided that he was worth it.

Although he admitted to Maria that he felt her family was more giving with their affections toward him, he knew his own mother's limitations and loved her for everything that she was able to give from what she had in her own heart. It was the beautiful part of Rudi's personality that Maria fell in love with. He was not judgmental of anyone even though he was aware of their shortcomings. And even though it seemed like the visit was inconsequential at first, Maria was thankful for the time spent in sincere conversations with Rudi's mother. She began to see a deeper side of Luise.

She admitted to Maria that she was always busy making money. Unfortunately, all the money that she spent so much time away from her own son trying to earn was worthless once the war broke out. Soldiers took all their valuables and burned them. Luise often looked at Rudi regretfully. So much time wasted, chasing what was not important. She wished she could turn the clock back, but then she realized that it was past, and she had learned in her lifetime that dwelling on the past didn't help anyone. So, looking forward, she could give Rudi as much love as she was capable of and even show how giving she was learning to become by accepting his fiancé with open arms. Hosting a nice engagement party of their own was her way of demonstrating her love and good wishes.

Maria was also happy to learn a little history that only Luise was able to share. According to her, Rudi was very similar to his dad in personality. His father, apparently, had a very cheerful disposition and could make a friend anywhere he went. Unfortunately, he became sick with a lung infection, which they later determined was tuberculosis and he died when Rudi was merely three years old. By the time Rudi was six, Luise had met and remarried his stepfather, Max. He was the only dad Rudi ever knew, which Maria surmised was unfortunate having observed the aloofness with which he treated Rudi.

Fortunately for Rudi, and for Max, they all remained in the house, which was owned by Rudi's paternal grandfather. It was him who took Rudi under his wing from the time his son died, when Rudi was only a toddler. The two of them slept in the front room of the house, having separate beds of course, but sharing a bedroom, nonetheless. It was all the space they had since Luise and her new husband occupied the master suite and were in charge of the household. Spending most of their time alone together, Rudi and his grandfather became very close.

Luise explained to Maria that once he was a little older and could ride a bicycle, Rudi was employed by herself and Max - for free of course. At the age of ten, he rode from store to store in Potsdam, inquiring from each merchant if they would like to sell anything to a vendor in the big city. He would then take his list home, and they would in turn, purchase the goods the following day and then sell them at a higher price at the open market in Berlin. Luise was a shrewd businesswoman, but she, along with her new husband, were always travelling on the train to Berlin and back. They made a good living that way, but Rudi, in his free time, was always left in the care of hired help or his grandfather. He once told Maria that when he was away from home with the German army, he became aware that his grandfather had become ill. He asked his superiors for leave but was denied. Unfortunately, his grandfather died before he could visit him again. He always felt very sorry about it because his grandfather raised him and all they really had for close family was each other.

Rudi's mother absorbed the inheritance, but Rudi inherited something that no one could take away and that is his gift for music. It was his grandfather who taught him how to play the harmonica and the accordion, which he became quite good at. Never having had formal music lessons, he could play anything by ear. As a teenager he travelled to parks and outdoor venues, where he was one of five guys in a band, including Gunther. They regularly played the local circuit, but never took it seriously. It was just fun for them, but for Rudi, it all started with his grandfather, which he never forgot. He spent his childhood and his youth joyfully surrounded by music and love thanks to his grandfather and the time he willingly gave to Rudi.

Maria knew that whatever she learned about how Rudi was treated or dealt with in the past, it was his deepest wish to keep the peace in the present and show unconditional love. So, according to his wishes, she kept an open mind to give her future mother-in-law respect just for who she was.

Chapter Seventeen

WITHIN A WEEK OF THEIR RETURN TO WEST Germany, it became time for Anneliese to go into labor.

"You're squeezing too hard Anne! My hand is numb!" As soon as Anneliese could catch a breath between contractions, she let go of the iron grip she had on Maria's hand.

"I'm sorry Maria. I'm trying." She was breathing short and fast breaths as she tried to keep up her strength. "This is not as easy as it looks." She remarked sarcastically with a sideways smile to her sister.

"Oh, trust me Anne, you are not making this look easy." Maria said honestly. Anneliese started to squeeze her hand again as she felt another contraction coming. "Oh no," Maria whispered to herself under her breath, "I'm never having kids." The contractions started to come more frequently and more intensely. Maria was witnessing this process for the first time, but at least she stayed in the room. Helmut had already bailed out of his wife's circumstance and escaped the moment of truth by heading to the Sportsplex.

They hired a midwife to help with the birth, who was proving to be very skilled, and of course now that Maria and Rudi had come home from East Germany, Maria would not leave Anneliese's side. She had promised from the beginning that she wouldn't let her do this alone. Their mother was still running the business two floors down as customers continued to come in and out for their daily milk.

Rudi, attempting to make himself useful during this critical time, was constantly running between helping Maria's mother and running up to the third floor to check on how things were progressing. Hildegard and Siegfried stayed downstairs, busying themselves with simple chores, passing the time, expectant of a new baby in the house at any moment. Everyone waited, full of anticipation. It was getting to the point where Maria found herself overwhelmed, like Helmut, and looked for an escape.

"Anneliese, I have to go. I need a break." She ran out of the room and into Rudi's arms who had just made his way up the stairs to check on everyone. Maria found herself holding onto Rudi very tightly and when she pulled herself away, she emphatically stated, "I'm not having kids, just so you know. I'm not going through that!" Rudi held her at arm's length to see if she was serious, but he couldn't help the corners of his mouth from turning up. He was trying hard to stifle his laugh. They had already expressed to each other how they felt about kids. Rudi was on the fence and was willing to please Maria in this area, but Maria was adamant about how important it was that they have children. Even if it meant that they needed to adopt. Her doctor had once told her that due to her strenuous work with the lifting of heavy milk cans all through her youth, that her vaginal muscles had become so tight it would be next to impossible for her to give birth. This sudden outburst in the middle of her sister's labor trauma was a little surreal and Rudi knew it.

"Is it over? Is the baby here?" Rudi asked.

"No. But I had to leave. It's too hard. I can't do this anymore." Maria sighed as though she was exhausted. Rudi held his thoughts and comments to himself. He dared not utter a word.

Suddenly, Anneliese let out another cry of anguish as she tried to get through another contraction. Rudi and Maria stared into each other's eyes. Maria groaned in frustration with a wrinkled expression on her face. She knew she had to go back in the room to help, even though she desperately wanted to run. Instead, she accepted her duty, turned away from Rudi and went back into the room. As she picked up Anneliese's hand, Rudi signaled to the midwife for a word with her.

Just outside the room, he asked in a hushed tone, "Is everything okay? Is there a problem?"

"Oh fine", the midwife reassured him, "it's a normal birth. She is doing fine. It won't be long now before we see the head. The contractions are getting close." Rudi nodded and then turned to go back down the stairs with a good report.

"Oh Maria – it's so hard! I don't want to do this anymore!" Anneliese cried.

"I know Anne. I know. You can do it. Squeeze my hand. I'm right here." As Anneliese was staring into Maria's eyes, she heard the command.

"Push!" the midwife interjected, "I see the head! Push!" Anneliese bore down and did the best she could. "Keep pushing!" the midwife coached. As she gave another push, the head came out and the baby lay there almost delivered. "Another push Anneliese. Come on – we need the rest of him!" Anneliese bore down again and gave all she had left and finally Dietmar was fully delivered.

"You did great!" the midwife said as she quickly cut the cord. "You have a beautiful baby boy." She took him to the side and cleaned his nose and mouth and then the baby let out a loud cry. "There you go darling. All good. Everything is fine." The midwife did a quick check on him as she cleaned him up and wrapped him in a little blanket. Maria congratulated and comforted her sister who was completely exhausted. As Anneliese took a moment to catch her breath, she waited patiently for the midwife to finish her assessment and hand her the baby. "Here is your perfect baby boy. I will let you hold him for a moment, but then I need you to give him to Maria. We need one more push to get out the placenta.

Anneliese looked at the midwife, confused. "I have to keep pushing?"

"It's just routine. The important thing is that you have your baby." She promptly took little Dietmar out of Anneliese's arms and placed him in Maria's waiting arms, even though she seemed a little apprehensive.

Turning back to Anneliese, "Okay Mama, one more time, push!"

Maria sat mesmerized as she softly cradled this perfect baby in her loving arms. Just then Rudi was at the door and opened it a crack to see what was going on. He stood in awe of what he saw – his future wife cradling a newborn baby. His heart swelled more than he ever imagined it could. Maria was a vision of beauty. He simply adored her. Just then she lifted her eyes, somehow feeling his fixation on her. They held one another's gaze for a long moment. Then slowly and quietly Maria stood up to bring the baby over to Rudi to see.

All the while the midwife was still working on Anneliese so that she could be cleaned up and ready to receive her family and her son again. Rudi looked into the bundle all wrapped up in Maria's arms. He could hardly believe his eyes as this perfect little baby boy lay peacefully sleeping. He put his arm around Maria and just smiled deep into her eyes. They both knew that one day the baby they would be holding would be their very own.

"Okay", the midwife announced, "She is ready to hold her baby." Maria walked over to her sister to give Dietmar into his mother's arms. Anneliese held her breath as she saw her baby boy and lovingly held his perfect little body. The midwife stayed to assist with the breast feeding for the first time as Rudi and Maria made their way downstairs to share the good news with everyone.

"It's a strapping baby boy!" Rudi announced as he and Maria stepped into the kitchen where Maria's mother, Hilde and Siegfried were making themselves busy while awaiting the news.

"When can we see her?" her mother asked.

"The midwife finished cleaning her up and right now she's just helping her with the breast feeding. She should be ready for visitors in about ten minutes." Maria guessed. "So just so you know Mama – you will have to get all your grandchildren from your other children. I'm never having a baby." Maria proclaimed. Her mother laughed and turned to look at Rudi, who smiled and winked at his future mother-in-law. "Why we choose to put ourselves through this, is beyond me. No Siree!" Maria contested.

"You should try having twins!" her mother joked laughingly. "Now that's hard! That's why it's called labor. But, when the child is placed in your arms, the pain is forgotten, or at least we seem to feel the pain was worth the reward. Why else would women have lots of children? Ja, but like with so many other things, 'the pain lasts for a night, but joy comes in the morning'. Sometimes your greatest challenge turns into your greatest joy."

Maria's eyes grew big. "Yeah, well that was enough for me!"
Maria's mother let out a big belly laugh.

Just then Helmut came through the front door. He looked at them expectantly.

Maria piped up, "Go see your wife Helmut. She's fine. She's just feeding the baby." Helmut did not say a word. He practically flew up the stairs. When he almost reached the top, the door was open, and he could see Anneliese peacefully holding a little bundle while nursing. It was such a holy moment; he treaded lightly so he wouldn't disturb what was happening. Suddenly, his heart was filled with love and a divine sense of honor for his wife. He almost tiptoed to her side to behold his beautiful first-born son. Anneliese, pleased and tired, looked up at Helmut to see his reaction. He was caught in the awe of the moment.

"Beautiful." That was all he could say. Somehow that one word was enough to satisfy Anneliese who had worked so hard to bring about their little treasure.

"Dietmar, meet your Daddy." Anneliese said as she took him off her breast and handed him up to Helmut. Helmut seemed a little awkward, but he was visibly eager to connect with his baby boy.

"Hello Dietmar. I'm your daddy." He spoke. Maria was at the door, walking into the room to join them followed by her mother and two siblings. Rudi stayed downstairs in case there were any customers. "Nah Helmut. What do you have to say?" his mother-in-law inquired.

Helmut shook his head in disbelief. "I have nothing. I am undone. He is so beautiful." he repeated over and over. Anneliese smiled and blushed. Dietmar was handed around the room and then back to Anneliese. She looked up at Maria pleadingly.

"I am so tired Maria. Can you hold him for a little? I'm just so tired." she admitted. Maria held out her hands to receive Dietmar. She sat in a comfortable chair next to her sister's bed.

"Alright everyone – Let's let Anneliese get some rest." Everyone followed the direct orders from the midwife. They were all trying to help by being compliant. Even Helmut was eager to follow orders. He put his arm around Anneliese, "I'll be back soon." He assured her. Anneliese, beyond exhaustion, closed her eyes and fell fast asleep.

Chapter Eighteen

Four more days until Christmas!" Hildegard exclaimed as she bounded down the stairs. "Our tree is so beautiful. I can't wait to see it every day I wake up!" Maria was always amazed at the energy her little sister exuded.

"I'm thankful that Siegfried and Rudi already put it up. Hopefully it stays looking fresh until Christmas." Maria commented. "And I love the glow from the lit candles on it in the evening. It makes it look so peaceful and holy somehow."

"I know", answered Hilde, "but I just like the way it makes me feel so Christmassy to have it in the house." She explained, dancing around the living room.

"I'm glad you like Christmas so much", Maria said. All of a sudden, her thoughts went to the gifts that she would be able to present to her mother, which she usually prepared with her twin.

"Hilde, how about we make Mama something special for Christmas? Anneliese is obviously consumed with Dietmar. She won't have time to help make gifts this year, but we can make something ourselves."

"Did I hear my name?" their mother inquired as she poked her head around the corner. Maria turned on her heels, fearful that she had been overheard. "We were just discussing our Christmas party this year." Maria answered, quickly glancing at Hilde. It was a half-truth. They were discussing what to get her. "Who do you think will be coming?" she asked. Their mother stood for a moment contemplating.

"Well, I can tell you who's been invited, but I guess we'll have to wait and see who actually comes."

"Ooh I can hardly wait to hear," exclaimed Hilde as she hooked her mother's arm into her own and looked back at Maria. 'Oh, she's good, Maria thought. Leaving no thought in their mother's mind that they were discussing her gift. She's very good. Hilde led her out to the kitchen.

"Please tell me." She pleaded.

Maria followed close behind. She was eager to hear the guest list as well. Every Christmas they planned a big party which most of their relatives knew about. Maria's mother always had boarders, which was extra income and helped cover her mortgage, but when the family came to visit, they always offered extra space, even if Maria and Anneliese had to share their room with their mother for a night or two. And she was always the perfect hostess. Maria thought her mother had the gift of hospitality because she never turned anyone away. And she taught her children how to welcome people simply by making them live it. It was a family code that was never questioned. You simply do not leave people out in the street if they are asking you for help. She had the room and she used it to bless others.

So, on Christmas Eve the family, along with their guests, would first feast on a delicious dinner and then go to church together. After they walked home, the plan was usually to exchange gifts, talk and laugh the night away playing games, telling stories, and sometimes even listening to music and dancing. That's when the children would usually get tired enough to go to bed, allowing the grownups to have a night cap and have more adult conversation.

"I've been informed," their mother started, "that Albert and Ernst were wanting to come this year." She was beaming because she knew that the prospect of their twin cousins visiting would cheer her own twins. Then she turned to Hildegard, "and

I've also heard that Onkel Gottlieb and Walter are planning on joining us." Hilde's face lit up instantly. She really hit it off with Walter at the wedding in Immenhausen.

"And of course, your Dote will come for a while, even though she won't stay too long because of Ähne, but everyone else will probably spend at least one night." She looked at Maria and promptly added, "and Rudi of course."

"Does Anneliese know?" Maria asked.

"Not yet" replied her mother. At that, Maria turned and almost ran up the stairs to give Anneliese the news.

"Our cousins are coming!" she announced swinging into the open door of Anneliese's suite on the third floor. Albert and Ernst were more like brothers than cousins, since they were raised in the same house and lived together until they were ten years old until. They cherished the times when family events would bring them together again. This Christmas would be very special, giving everyone the opportunity to see Dietmar for the first time.

"Don't worry Anne," Maria explained, "I'll help you with everything. Hilde and Rudi can help Mama with the business, and Siegfried can go between all of us. We'll manage. It will be so good to see them. Aren't you excited?" Maria asked, full of anticipation and joy.

"Yes, I'm excited Maria. Of course. It's just going to be a little awkward at first." Anneliese looked down at Dietmar while he slept.

Maria brushed her sister's hair from her face soothing her fears. "I am right beside you. And Rudi too. No one will say a bad word about you. Albert and Ernst love you so much. It will all be so special." Anneliese kept silent. "I'm so glad Mama has such a big house." Maria continued.

This time Anneliese responded. "Me too. What would me and Helmut do without her generosity. We've really needed her, and she always comes through."

Maria nodded in agreement. She put her hand on Anneliese's shoulder. "I'm going down to help with dinner. I'll see you later Anne. Be happy. It's going to be a wonderful Christmas!"

Rudi was finishing up work in Stuttgart. It was Friday afternoon, and he was anxious to get his pay and get out of the shop in time to pick up the gold necklace that he spotted in the window of the jewelry store down the street. He needed to make one more payment before he could take it and give it to Maria for Christmas. He put up his leather tool belt and turned to put on his overcoat. Then he stood outside of his boss' office, hoping to get paid before leaving for the day.

"You're off to see that Fräulein of yours in Reutlingen I suppose? For Christmas?" he asked.

Rudi smiled, "Yes Sir," he answered. "I sure am."

"Well, I appreciate all the extra work you've put in for me these last couple of weeks Rudi. I think you'll like your pay this week. Merry Christmas to you." Rudi was very surprised.

"Thank you, Sir. I appreciate it very much." Rudi was eager to get to the store before it closed for the day.

"You're welcome Rudi. Get that Fräulein of yours something nice for Christmas." His boss called after him.

"Yes sir, I will. That's exactly what I'll do. Merry Christmas to you too!" Rudi called back. His boss smiled and went back into his office. Rudi quickly darted out the door and briskly walked down the street only to find the jewelry store had just closed. He stood outside for the longest time contemplating what to do because he was so disappointed. The owner finally came out from the back of the store. He saw Rudi standing in the front, looking dismayed. He walked over to him, as Rudi was peering in the window.

"Did you come to make the final payment on your necklace?"

"Yes Sir I did. I have the money right here." Rudi reached in his pocket. When he did, he realized how much extra his boss had given him. It was an extra week's wage.

"Since you've already paid for most of it, I'll let you in, even though I am closed now." The store owner said.

"Thank you so much," Rudi said, "it's very important to me." The store owner looked at Rudi and recognized the glow on his face.

"You have a special Fräulein." The store owner mused. It was not a question.

"Yes." Rudi answered. "We are engaged. I'd like this to be her Christmas gift."

He nodded in understanding. As he carefully brought out the necklace, he explained, "Someone else came by and wanted that necklace today. He was willing to pay for it, plus a little extra, but I told him I couldn't let it go because you only had one more payment to make. I thought it was something special to you. Here you go."

"Thank you so much for keeping it for me. I really appreciate it!" Rudi said, thinking that it was the luckiest day for him to have extra money and being allowed to purchase this special necklace for Maria. He took the little box, put it in his pocket and almost ran to the train station to make it on time. He stepped onto the platform, just as the train pulled into the station and was loading. Within a few seconds, the doors closed. Rudi sat down, catching his breath. He was on his way "home" for Christmas. He leaned back and breathed a sigh of relief knowing that he would be holding Maria in his arms in a couple of hours. The longest two hours of his week – every week. And now that it was almost Christmas it was time for their engagement party. They decided to celebrate Christmas and their engagement at the same time so that family members could come for both events and then of course this year was also the first time everyone would welcome the newest member of the family, Anneliese's son, Dietmar.

Rudi knew how much Maria and her mother counted on him. He was the man of the household, and he took that responsibility very seriously. He had done a lot to prepare them for this year's Christmas celebration. He had taken Siegfried out to help with cutting the Christmas tree down and putting it in the living room, which was no easy feat. He also made sure that they were stocked with enough chopped wood for their fireplace, and all their tenants, and he helped to take care of the needs for the business and whatever else was needed around the house. He did it all because he loved Maria so much from the very first day and then he quickly fell in love with the whole family. He felt like he struck gold, and he was not going anywhere. But most of all his responsibility was to Maria as her future husband, which was his favorite and most important preoccupation. And even though he was all about getting the daily tasks accomplished, he was also excited about celebrating at any and every opportunity. And what better opportunity than Christmas!

Maria was standing on the train platform when the door to Rudi's seating area opened. He stepped out of the train, and she instantly saw him and ran into his arms. Rudi was so happy. He swung her around and they giggled with glee as he set her down. He held his embrace and gave her a long, lover's kiss, giving rise to applause from the small crowd that had gathered on the platform to witness this young love in action.

"Let them look." Rudi said in her ear. He kissed her again. When he finally let her breathe, she whispered "Merry Christmas Herr Heinrich" in his ear.

"Merry Christmas Frau Heinrich," he answered.

"I like the sound of that." Maria told him as he put his arm around her and faced his audience. "Thank you. Thank you. Ha-ha. Everyone needs a little love in their life." He quipped. Walking past their admirers, he lifted his hat in acknowledgment of their applause and well wishes.

Once outside, she asked, "Did you have a good train ride?"

Rudi looked down at her, "I thought of you the whole way in, so yes, of course." Maria giggled, squeezing Rudi's hand as they walked outside the train station. "How's your Ähne?" Rudi asked, concerned.

"He's okay. We need to visit him though. He is expecting a Christmas visit, since he won't be able to travel to Mama's house and join us for Christmas dinner." Rudi nodded.

"And Siegfried? And Hilde? All okay?" Maria loved how interested he was in everyone's wellbeing.

"Siegfried has been with Oma most of the time. No doubt he will cling to you through the holidays and Hilde, well, she and I have managed to sew Mama a new dress at our dressmaker's shop. She let us use her needles and we picked out a beautiful light blue fabric to go with her eyes. I can't wait to give it to her."

"I'm impressed!" Rudi exclaimed. "Especially that Hätele would help."

"Well – you know, she sort of helped. She picked out the fabric." Maria smiled. "I must say though, our Hilde has a lineup of young men, but apparently choosing just one is much too restricting. She is very flirtatious" Maria stated, lifting her eyebrows. Rudi looked a little concerned.

"That's dangerous," he said, "she's a heart breaker. And Anneliese? And Dietmar?"

Maria updated him, "She's fine. Tired. But happy. And Dietmar? Well - I am starting to see a resemblance to Mama's face. He's got the blue eyes and light, wavy hair." She explained, thinking how best to sum it up. "He's perfect, what can I say?" Rudi pulled her in closely and they walked home, arm in arm, deliriously happy to be together again.

Chapter Nineteen

HILDEGARD STOOD SHYLY BEHIND MARIA AS she opened the door to welcome their Onkel Gottlieb and his son Walter in from the cold. It was Christmas Eve 1951 at the Riekert household. All the guests had now officially arrived and were seated in the living room enjoying the lively conversation. They were all so thankful to be at the home of this beautiful family, taking part in this Christmas celebration. Germany had been through a lot and although it had been over five years since the war ended, their country was still recovering. Life wasn't easy, but times like this were incredibly special. Gatherings with family, celebrating everything that was important to them and going to church together, made them each more thankful in their hearts than they had ever been.

Maria felt a tug on her dress as she leaned in to give her uncle Gottlieb a hug. If she didn't know better, she would think that Hildegard felt nervous. Hilde; the confident, happy-go-lucky, flirtatious teenager – nervous? It was a new experience for Maria to see her little sister this way, a little flustered. Maria also gave Walter a quick hug to welcome him and then stepped back to allow Hilde to do the same. Taking her turn, Hilde indeed followed suit and reached out to give her Onkel Gottlieb a hug, but when it came to Walter, she gave him more of an awkward handshake. 'What is going on here?' Maria wondered. Puzzled by this strange atmosphere between Walter and Hilde, she led them into the living room to join everyone else and felt that the awkwardness between the two of them would melt away as the evening progressed.

"Take a seat Gottlieb," Maria's mother said as she motioned towards a chair, next to his sister, Anna. "And Walter, you can sit in Hilde's seat." Walter's eyes grew big and so did Hilde's.

"We are about ready to put dinner on the table." Maria's mother informed her guests. "so, I'm going to need your help in the kitchen Hilde!" Just as she motioned for Hildegard to follow her, Walter deliberately walked past her to take her seat, giving her a friendly shove. She stumbled momentarily taking no time to retaliate the gesture. The onlookers laughed at the light-hearted fun the two cousins were having. Hilde giggled and looked back at Walter as she was headed towards the kitchen. Anna noticed their flirty banter but thought better of saying anything. She offered her help in the kitchen as well but was strictly told to let the younger generation do the serving this time.

Maria gently tugged on her mother's sleeve, whispering to her in the corner of the kitchen.

"I need you to come and see Hilde in your room for a moment. I think we have a problem." Maria's mother didn't hesitate to quickly slip away to her room, following Maria through the door. Maria quietly closed the door behind her mother as Hildegard stood before her holding up a beautiful, full-length dress that was light blue with tiny red cherries and dark green holly for her to wear to host her guests in style.

The tears welling up in her eyes were thank you enough. Hilde and Maria exchanged smiles and quickly helped their mother get into her new dress for the occasion.

"I never..." she started to say, unable to express her gratitude.

"You deserve it, Mama." Maria said, leaning in to hug her. Hildegard did the same.

"Do you like the fabric, Mama? I picked it out!"

"I love it!" she said, choking back her tears as she admired herself in the mirror. Maria and Hilde looked at each other with pride.

"Now, let's serve our guests!" their mother exclaimed. Stopping just short of leading her girls back to the kitchen, she turned around to hug them both again.

"Thank you, my darlings. You mean the world to me. I can't imagine how much this cost you – with hours to make and everything." Maria put her head down, well aware. Hilde just shrugged her shoulders, happy to be able to be a part of it. When they walked back to the dining room, Rudi was already doing the honors at dinner; cutting the chicken and the pork meat.

Twice a year, at Christmas and Easter, they had roasted swine, which they kept after it was slaughtered, several feet underground. The earth was cold enough to act as a natural freezer. This was one such occasion where it paid to have an entire pig on hand to feed all the guests. Maria's mother had boiled ten pounds of potatoes and Maria and Hilde, and sometimes Anneliese between taking care of Dietmar, had been busy in the kitchen preparing the pies and cookies for days. Now they just had to warm the vegetables, which they had cooked earlier in the day. Once all were called to the table, Maria's mother said grace, and everyone filled their bellies to their heart's content. The conversation was sparkling, as was the wine that was served on this special occasion. Anneliese sat to the side perfectly content to be present, but not directly involved with the festivities. She was very attentive to Dietmar, whom everyone adored. Afterwards, Albert and Ernst made themselves useful by clearing off the table and helping to clean the dishes away in the kitchen. Rudi had done so much in preparation for this night, so Maria instructed him to go and sit down and enjoy the company of her family, which left Rudi in his element – socializing.

"You've got your heart set on Rudi don't you, cousin?" Albert asked Maria.

"I do. I really do." She answered as she looked at Rudi enjoying himself in the living room.

"You're not worried that he's from Berlin?" Ernst implored. Maria shook her head.

"Why would I be?" Ernst looked at Albert.

"Well just because – they like to indulge in the party scene a little more than us country folk, that's all. I'm sure that Rudi would have already shown you that side of him by now if he were like most 'Berliners'.

"Actually," Maria said, "You are right. His family is like that. When we visited them a couple of months ago, I did feel completely out of place, for that reason exactly. But I told him, and he was very accommodating to me." The cousins just looked at each other.

"Well, he better stay that way," Albert said, "or he'll have your cousins to deal with!" They all laughed, but Maria was thankful for their watchful protection. She loved her family.

"Hey, are you people almost finished in there?" Maria's mother asked. "It's almost time to get our boots on and go to church." Maria was just drying the last couple of plates while Albert and Ernst were hanging up their dish towels.

"We're just about ready Mama. No worries!" Maria replied. Albert put his arm around Maria as they were emerging from the kitchen. It was a familial gesture as he enjoyed the company of his cousin, but his friendly show of affection was too much for Maria's rather sensitive fiancée. The sharp turn of Rudi's head and flash of jealousy in his eyes did not escape Albert's notice. He immediately took his hand away and laughed it off.

"I'm sure that if I gave you a big squeeze just because I haven't seen you for so long, Rudi would be bounding over heads and chairs to sock me in the mouth. I had better just tell you that I have missed you, and it is wonderful to be here, celebrating all together as a family. It feels just like it did when we were kids." Maria was caught up in reminiscing with Albert and of course, as predicted, in the very next second Rudi was standing right next to him and put his arm around her possessively.

"If there is one thing I do know, you will be safe wherever you go with Rudi. He does not miss a single beat where it concerns his Fräulein. But you need not be jealous here my friend. Maria is my sister-cousin and anything outside of pure familial love for her and all the family would be so wrong."

"I know, I know" Rudi said, "I just wanted to be in on the conversation."

"I understand your love for this family Rudi. It is incredibly special and so I am just saying – you better treat your Fräulein here right, or you'll have her cousins to deal with." At that, he put his arm around his brother, Ernst, who was not generally a man of many words. "Not that we're worried."

Rudi laughed but understood. "I hear you, Albert. It's good, it's good." Maria stood stunned and welcomed the interruption from her mother.

"Get your boots on everyone. Time to go to church!"

"That's my cue to leave." said Anna, standing up to dress herself for her own trip home. Gottlieb, making his way over to her at the front door, gave her a brotherly hug.

"Tell Papa I said Merry Christmas and I'll be around to see him soon." He promised.

"Will do Gottlieb! He would like that. Nice to see you again." She said, warmed by his company this night.

The snow was deftly falling as Rudi, wanting to lead the charge, was the first to venture out the front door. In his exuberance to be first, he failed to take the time to test the slipperiness of the pavement. It only took three steps before he started to lose his footing. He panicked, trying to overcompensate by bending his body in half. But now, there was too much force towards the front of his body, so just before he dove nose first, he threw his arms back to counter his weight, hitting a person walking past him right in the stomach, which caused the stranger to double over and stumble as well. Rudi's efforts to stay standing, while his feet seemed to spread apart from each other in opposite directions with his arms flailing about to somehow achieve some sort of balance, were quite humorous to his audience standing at the door. He did eventually fall, right on his behind, but stood right back up to make a quick recovery. As soon as he did, he looked back at the door, to check everyone's reactions.

The onlookers tried extremely hard to act concerned without making fun of him. All except for Maria's mother. She burst into a hilarious fit of laughter which broke the tension of the moment. Rudi began to laugh at himself, not so much because of what he had done, but because Maria's mother made it seem so funny. She laughed so hard her whole belly shook. She wasn't trying to embarrass him in any way at all. She just expressed the hilarity of the moment. Her laughter, which was contagious, gave license for everyone else to do the same. What seemed like a faux pas at the moment, served to draw everyone into an even closer-knit family circle. Everyone linked arms or held hands as they set down the street determined to make it to the church without breaking any bones on the treacherously slippery pavement.

"Merry Christmas!" Anna called to everyone, as she headed out very carefully in the opposite direction. She could hear the calls from behind her.

"Merry Christmas Anna!" as she walked down the street to the train station. She felt a thankfulness within, to be part of such a loving family. She would tell her father all about their wonderful Christmas when she got home, including Rudi's antics on the ice.

It was dark and they could see their breath in front of them, but the nip in the air did not stop the Dietrich clan from enjoying themselves. Their laughter couldn't be contained. It was heard all through the streets. Rudi supported his future mother-in-law's arm the whole way there, making sure she did not suffer the same fate he did.

When they arrived at church, the front house greeters at the Marienkirche told them to pipe it down a little, not wanting to disrupt the service. They didn't even realize how loud they were, having just come in from outside. Right away Maria's mother took authority and had everyone reign it in respectfully. Maria and her family were regular attenders and they felt extremely comfortable in this church. They all sat together in the front row. Maria's mother was closest to the isle, then Rudi, Maria, Albert, Ernst, Gottlieb, Walter and Hildegard. Occasionally, Hilde would let out a teenage giggle thanks to Walter's teasing pokes. Anneliese thankfully stayed behind with

Dietmar and Siegfried; it was too late of a night for them.

The church service was beautiful and appropriately festive for the Christmas celebration, and everyone was entertained by the children singing and the youth acting out the story of Jesus' birth. They even had a real baby in the play to make it as authentic as possible. Maria hoped with all her heart that Rudi would come to know and love the Lord like she knew Him and loved Him. But he didn't grow up understanding anything about the Bible because he had never been taught. Who Jesus is, or what that means for him, would take him some time to absorb. Maria knew that he listened, was respectful, and made every attempt to understand, but she needed to be patient with him. And she was willing to do that.

After communion when everyone was walking home, Rudi held Maria back a little and started gazing at the stars. "Rudi, we're losing the group." Maria chided. "I know it's slippery, but we're going to have to walk a little faster to keep up." Rudi laughed.

"No silly. I'm not slowing down because it's slippery." She stopped and looked at him.

"What are you up to?" she asked. He smiled as he reached into the pocket of his overcoat to pull out the box that he had so long been waiting to give her. "Rudi, what's this?" She questioned.

213

"Open it," he said softly. He watched her intently as she cracked open the lid to reveal the pure gold heart-shaped necklace. Her eyes grew wider and then sparkled as she looked up at him and then back at the necklace.

"It's so dainty. So elegant," she exclaimed, almost breathless.

"Just like you." He spoke. "Merry Christmas Maria. I wasn't sure what to get you as a gift but when I saw this I knew, because I just want to give you my heart." His words melted her heart even more than the gift. Tears were starting to well up in her eyes, so she quickly leaned in to give him a kiss.

Suddenly Albert realized that Maria and Rudi were not keeping up with the group. He looked back to call them, but then stopped himself as he caught a glimpse of their shadows. "They'll catch up with us soon enough. No worries. Those two lovebirds have no idea how cold it is out here. We'll see them back at the house." At that, he turned around and gave Maria's mother his arm to keep her from slipping as they walked the rest of the way home.

Chapter Twenty

THE LOVE AND JOY THAT THE FAMILY SHARED THAT Christmas was a memorable and magical time. Every once in a while, the family gatherings were such a wonderful break from the realities of daily life that no one wanted them to end. These special times reminded them what life was all about; relationships and loving one another. This newfound familial bond that Rudi was quickly becoming a part of was so special to him. The love they shared for each other was so genuine. And everyone was important. No one was overlooked. He couldn't wait to officially be a part of Maria and her family. 'It won't be long now.' he told himself.

* * *

THE NEW YEAR BROUGHT WITH it all the planning and preparation that goes into a big wedding. Maria was excited to attend to all the details of finding a dress and of making sure that the church and the pastor were available on their chosen day. She busied herself securing all the particulars; flowers, music and the food menu. And aside from all the wedding details, she was also preoccupied with plans for herself and Rudi after the wedding.

"I want us to live and work in Stuttgart." She confided to Anneliese when they were alone in Anneliese's apartment while putting Dietmar to sleep. "Rudi has such a good job there and I'm getting tired of only being able to see him on weekends. I'm sure that I can find a job in the city once we move." Suddenly, the thought of separating from her twin hit Anneliese hard.

"It's almost impossible for me to imagine life without you. Even now, despite the fact that I'm married and have a baby, we're still living in the same house. We've never been apart." Anneliese responded. Maria looked at her sincerely, not knowing how to respond without hurting her feelings. Finally, she comforted her with a warm hug.

"You know that no matter how far apart we are, we're always together in our hearts. It's never going to be any different. We're simply a part of one another." Maria said.

216

Anneliese nodded, tears falling from her eyes. "Two parts of a whole." she said, squeezing Maria's hands. Maria went to her room, closed the door behind her and sat on her bed. She dreamed of the day that she and Rudi could live together on their own, not having to work in the milk business and not having to say goodbye at the train station ever again. From the time that they knew they wanted to get married until the wedding day, they would have waited two years. And even though it wasn't easy, the years seem to have gone by so quickly.

Hildegard would turn fifteen in February and even though she still seemed like a child sometimes, she was old enough to take over Maria's position in the family milk business. Siegfried was still young, barely twelve years old, but he was eager to step up to help in different ways. He was good at keeping the chopped wood pile supplied and tending to odd jobs around the house. If Maria's mother was worried about getting along without Rudi and Maria, she was not letting anyone know. It was business as usual with just a little added pressure of training a reluctant teenager. Despite having to live without the daughter who had become her right hand, Maria's mother was genuinely happy for her because she adored Rudi and was confident that Maria would have a good life with him. She was so excited about their upcoming wedding that she thought about it and talked about it to everyone. Many of the townspeople, including their customers and friends from church, along with extended family were happy for them and fully supported Rudi and Maria's nuptials. Everyone except for one; the pastor of the church.

He had known Maria and her family since they moved to Reutlingen when Maria was just ten years old. He had come to know that not only was the Riekert family a steady part of the local community, but they were also regular attending, solid church members. Since Maria had started dating Rudi, the pastor noticed that she was not always along with the rest of her family and sometimes when Rudi came to church with her, it was obvious to him that their relationship was passed innocence. But it was more than that. He knew that Rudi was only there to please Maria, he wasn't serious about his own faith in God.

"I understand Pastor Schafer. But I have firsthand knowledge of what it is like to not be welcomed by everyone into a family that you want to call your own. No one else in the community has expressed opposition to their union." Maria's mother pointed out.

"That's because no one else is considering the lack of spirituality in Rudi. He is not a man that is equally yoked for Maria. I don't want to put a damper on things, but how can I support that? She grew up in church. This church. And now this man whom she chooses to spend the rest of her life with, what does he have to offer her? Is he going to be able to lead her in God's way?" the pastor asked seriously.

"Pastor Schafer, he loves her more than words can express. I'm telling you if he was called upon to choose his own life or Maria's, he wouldn't hesitate a second to lay down his life for hers." The pastor was silenced for a moment.

"Yes Maria, I hear you. But please understand; God's Word tells us not to be unequally yoked with unbelievers. I think God wants to spare His children who do believe in Him, the hardship of living with someone who doesn't." Maria's mother almost laughed out loud.

"You don't know Rudi like I do. He makes all our lives happier and easier."

"I'm not only talking about right now. I'm talking about ten, even twenty years from now, when the bloom is off the rose so to speak." The pastor tried to relate. "That's when it'll matter that he loves God first, and if he did, it would be because of that, that he would strive to be a good husband, when the warm, fuzzy feelings of young love give way."

Maria thought for a moment. "Doesn't His Word also tell us that 'Love covers over a multitude of sins. Say what you want Pastor, she has chosen Rudi and honestly, I think he's a good match for her. I trust him. I would trust him with her life."

"I hope you still feel that way in ten years." He sighed for a moment and did not try to conceal his reluctance, but he could see that Maria's mother was almost as intent on having Maria marry Rudi as Maria was herself. "Alright then," he conceded, "in that case, I would sure like to see him in church and get to know him better." Maria's mother nodded.

"I know they will make the effort Pastor Schafer. I wonder if you might have May twenty-fourth available for the wedding? That would give you plenty of time to get to know Rudi. They were hoping for a wedding in late Spring." The Pastor stood up and moved directly to his calendar on his desk.

"Yes, it looks like that day is available. I will pencil it in. Maria Riekert's wedding." He looked up at Maria's mother and came around to the side of his desk to offer her his handshake and goodwill. "Maria, this is a serious matter. Do not forget. I'd like to get to know Rudi before I officiate a church wedding."

"Yes. I understand Pastor. I will be sure to tell them to make a point of attending regularly. And I'm sure that he would welcome a chance to sit down and chat with you privately. Thank you for saving the date Pastor." He forced a smile as she left his office.

Chapter Twenty-One

WHAT EXACTLY DOES HE WANT TO KNOW?" Rudi inquired, a little unnerved, as he leaned back against the stove in the kitchen. Maria's mother sat at the table with her hand sewing as she tried to explain to her daughter and future son-in-law the importance of visiting with the Pastor.

"He wants to be able to marry Maria in good conscience and he can't do that if he doesn't know you. It would be best if you went to visit him on your own first, Rudi. That way he can ask all the questions he wants and since there is nothing to hide, it will be just like making a new friend. He is a genuinely nice man and has a lot to teach you. I'm sure he will like you just as much as we all do, even if you are a bit, you know, rough around the edges." She winked at Maria.

"What?" Rudi protested "What do you mean? Rough around the edges? What does that mean?"

"Oh, you know I'm just kidding you. We kind of like you. I think we'll keep you." She nodded and winked at Maria again who just smiled back at her mother. Rudi laughed it off as he walked towards Maria. "Okay then, I promise to go see Pastor Schafer this Sunday if he has time after church." He put his arm around Maria. "How about we go for a walk around the block?"

"Now? Tonight?" Maria asked, surprised.

"Yes now. I've only got the weekend and I want as much time with you as possible if we must fit Pastor Schafer in our schedule." He turned to appease his future mother-in-law, "which I'm sure will all be to my benefit in the long run." He looked back at Maria "But in any case, let's just put on our coats and go for a walk under the stars." Maria finally agreed. Her mother just sat at the table and busied herself with her sewing, smiling to herself. Anneliese and Helmut were upstairs with Dietmar. Hildegard and Siegfried were fast asleep and now Maria and Rudi were about to step out for an evening stroll. As soon as they left the house, she took a deep breath, put her sewing down, leaned back in her chair and reveled in the few precious moments that she had to be alone.

"I'm a little nervous about meeting with the Pastor." Rudi admitted once he and Maria were a little further down the street.

"Why on earth would you be nervous?" Maria asked.

"You are very familiar with going to church and learning Bible things," he explained, "but what do I know about that? Nothing. What if he decides that I'm not good enough to marry you?"

Maria stopped dead in her tracks. She looked at him sincerely. "Now hear me in this, my dearest Rudolf Heinrich. There is no one who can stop the two of us from getting married. We are adults and we choose to get married in the church. The Pastor has known me for most of my life and he is just looking out for my best interests. He probably does wish that you had a little more knowledge or had a little more of a relationship or connection with God. He probably will be able to teach you some things if you let him. Keep an open mind and an open heart. He will learn to love you too. I'm sure of it. And if not," she clearly stated, lifting her chin, "we'll just elope." She took his arm again and started down the street. "Anyways – no one is really good enough to marry me, but eh – you're the best candidate, so you'll do." She took off running and he chased after her. When he caught her, he swung her around and then set her down and kissed her.

"What makes me the best candidate?"

"Because" she teased, tipping his fedora backwards to get a better look into his eyes. This time it was her that held onto his coat lapels and pulled him in closer. "You are...silly, but smart, fun-loving, but hard-working, sincere, but funny, kind, but still honest, cheerful and generous and I Love You!" she answered.
He was so happy, he picked her up and twirled her around again. She laughed and enjoyed how happy she felt at that moment. When he finally set her down, they started walking home again.

"So, Mrs. Heinrich?"

"Yes, Mr. Heinrich?"

"We need to think about where we are going to live once we are married."

"Why don't we stay in the apartment you are living in right now, for the time being? I'll just bring some of my belongings and once I am able to find a job, we can think about getting a place of our very own." She simplified everything for Rudi in such a decisive way, which he appreciated because it alleviated a lot of stress from even taking root in his mind.

"Sounds like a good plan to me. Rudi said. He pulled her close and the two of them walked home together with their arms around each other.

Chapter Twenty-Two

"TURN AROUND A TINY BIT SO I CAN GET THE hem pinned evenly all the way around," the dressmaker instructed. Maria was trying to do exactly as she said. Her mother was always so busy with the business, she didn't have time to make clothes for her children anymore, so she often sent them to their local dressmaker. She was an acquaintance from their hometown who had several local families as clients. It was exciting for her to be making Maria's wedding dress because she had known her for so long and Maria was happy too because she trusted her work. She always made beautiful dresses and she was already used to fitting Maria's petite frame. She was very pleased that Maria's desire for her dress was a simple, long gown, all the way to the floor, which she was planning to have shortened after the ceremony to just below the knee so that she could wear it again. She chose a V-neck style with a tightly fitted bodice, which was perfect to display the gold heart necklace Rudi gave her for Christmas. She had a simple veil and kept everything very sleek and elegant. All four of Maria's bridesmaids, including Anneliese, her Matron of Honor, were fitted for light blue dresses. Hilde was another of her bridesmaids as well as two of her cousins, Hannelore and Erika.

Rudi's side of the wedding party consisted of his friend Kurt, along with his wife. Kurt, not shy in front of a crowd, was also the master of the ceremony. Maria had met him while she was in Stuttgart visiting Rudi and found him and his wife to be very friendly. Unfortunately, no one from Rudi's side of the family was able to attend the wedding. Communist rules for East Germans were very strict. Travel papers outside the wall were not easy to obtain.

"I'm sorry that Rudi's family won't be present for the wedding." Her seamstress said, making conversation.

"I'm sorry too." Maria acknowledged. The seamstress stopped what she was doing to look up at Maria, knowing that there was no love lost between her and her future mother-in-law. "For his sake." she finished with a half-smile.

The seamstress stood up from the floor where she was pinning Maria's dress, taking a step backwards. "Can you turn around very slowly for me please? I want to make sure it's even." Maria complied with her instructions and had an opportunity to behold how lovely the dress was in the mirror.

"I'm delighted!" The seamstress exclaimed.

"So am I." Remarked Maria enthusiastically. You've really done a beautiful job!"

"With a perfect, petite figure like yours Maria, it's easy. And beautiful doesn't even begin to describe how you will look on your wedding day." Maria blushed.

"Well, it's easy to keep your figure when you work as hard as I do. Never having an opportunity to sit."

The seamstress conceded. "I can't imagine how hard it is to work with all those heavy milk cans. I couldn't do it."

"It's amazing what you can do when you have to." Maria said simply. "How much do I owe you?"

"I've already worked that out with your mother. See, hard work pays off. You are free to go. I'll call you when it's ready. It should be about a week from now. Two tops." Maria clasped her hands together. "I can hardly wait!" she opened the door to leave and called back, "Thank You!"

"You're welcome Maria! Congratulations!"

"Thank you again!" Maria shouted back. At that she twirled around and started to walk home. It would soon be dinner time, so she decided to stop in their milk shop to see her mother in case she might need some help wrapping things up for the day. Her mother seemed to be dealing with one last customer.

"Like I said Maria, it would be my pleasure." The customer said, feigning a grand gesture.

"I very much appreciate it Herr Schmidt." Maria's mother answered.

"Ach nein. Was ist ein bissien Bier zwischen Freunde?" What is a little beer between friends? Maria's mother looked disappointed. "I'm looking for more than beer. I was hoping for wine for all the guests at the table and then an open bar to put everyone in a festive mood and give them some courage to use the dance floor."

"Well then," Mr. Schmidt continued, "Let me roll out the red carpet for you; wonderful restaurant food served at the table, wine at dinner and an open bar afterwards and of course yes, there is indeed a dance floor. We certainly need a first dance for the happy couple."

Just then Maria realized they were talking about her wedding.

"Right Maria?" Mr. Schmidt asked, waiting for her response.

"What?" Maria asked, curious and confused. Her mother turned around to see her daughter standing there.

"Maria! I was just discussing your wedding reception with Mr. Schmidt. What do you think?"

"Mama, I don't think we can afford ..."

Carl Schmidt was quick to interrupt their discussion, looking right at Maria's mother. "How about it Maria? We have a room for big events like this. You'll have everything included. The food, the drinks, the music. What do you say? Do we have a deal?"

Maria looked over at her mother, who seemed to hesitate slightly.

"Mr. Schmidt, it is truly kind of you to consider hosting this, but I don't think we can afford your restaurant for so many people." Maria answered for her mother, as she noticed her contemplating the transaction.

Carl Schmidt looked over at Maria's mother.

"Your mother and I have a deal. Business to business," said Mr. Schmidt.

Mr. Schmidt just stood there with a smile. After a minute, he said, "I think we can work something out, so everyone is happy." Maria looked at her mother who just had a grin on her face, but Maria couldn't quite tell if it was a happy grin.

"Alright Mr. Schmidt, once my daughter and I go over the details of how many guests are coming and what to serve, I will get back to you." she finally said.

"Sounds great!" He picked up his milk, turned around and opened the door to leave the shop. Then he turned around as though he had forgotten something. "Congratulations Maria!"

"Thank you!" she replied, with a wave of her hand. Then she turned to her mother. "Mama, I just came from the dressmaker, and you paid for my dress and all the bridesmaid dresses as well! And now we're thinking of getting a fancy wedding reception?"

"Well, I'm not putting up four different borders in my house for nothing. I do have some money saved Maria. If we put our money together, we can afford it. I know that you and Rudi said you'd like to help pay for the wedding, but I'd like to contribute as well. Just say thank you and be happy!" She gave her daughter the biggest, brightest smile. Maria could tell it pleased her mother to be generous to her, especially with this wedding. "Now as far as Mr. Schmidt goes, he actually threatened to take his business away from us as our milk customer if we don't use his hotel and restaurant as your wedding venue." Maria started to protest, but her mother continued before she had the chance to say much about it. "In all honesty, it is a wonderful place, and everything would be taken care of. I know it will cost us a little more than we had budgeted, but I don't think you'll find a better deal. So, we'll just go along with it if it's okay with you."

"I certainly don't like someone coming in here with threats and ultimatums. That, to me, is bad business. He's so lucky that you are so easy going." Maria remarked, somewhat frustrated on her mother's behalf.

"It would actually take a lot of the work right out of my hands." Her mother countered. "He would provide the food, the drinks and everything! I mean, how good can you have it?" she said, raising her eyebrows and smiling at her daughter. Maria stood flabbergasted. She reached out her arms to her mother.

"Well, when you put it that way, I suppose it's worth it. Thank you, Mama," Maria hugged her and said, "I am truly grateful. More than you know."

"Oh, I think I do know." Her mother said. "I was young too once. I know how it feels to have to wait to have a proper wedding. We have worked hard Maria. You deserve it and I am thankful that God has allowed me to help provide it for you." They both stood, happily nodding, reflecting on the goodness of God. Maria was speechless.

* * *

IT WAS LATE IN THE AFTERNOON EARLY IN THE week when Anna, Maria's Godmother, came knocking on their door. Maria immediately went to grab her jacket because she figured that something had happened to her grandfather. Instead, they were puzzled when Anna went straight to sit down at their kitchen table. Maria's mother and Anneliese stopped what they were doing to prepare supper and gave Anna their full attention.

"Anna, can I get you something to eat?" Maria's mother instinctively asked.

"No. no." Anna said solemnly. "I have something to tell you all." Her tone of voice and calm demeanor made them all take a seat around the table. She had an air of seriousness that made them all silent, waiting for her to speak. Laying her hand on Maria's mother's hand, she looked deep into her blue eyes.

"Now I know how much he loved you all, and how much you loved him." She began.

"Oh no, no, no, no, no." Maria's mother already knew what she was about to tell them. "Oh Ähne!"

"He's gone Maria." She informed them as simply as she could. Letting everyone take in the news, she waited, allowing them to absorb the shock and giving them time to let the tears flow. "You know he's in heaven. We don't have to despair." Maria's mother looked around the table at her twin girls who were hugging each other and crying. She took both of Anna's hands in her own, questions arising. Anna answered them, before they were even asked.

"He was in so much pain two nights ago, that I had Gottlieb come and take him to the hospital. He had a ruptured appendix by the time we got him there. It was too late. It was very fast, Maria. The good thing is that he didn't suffer long." Anna related sadly, but calmly. She had cried her tears in private and was now able to console others.

Tears streaming down their faces, Maria's mother and her two girls held each other's hands and consoled one another. Hildegard and Siegfried weren't as affected because they simply didn't have as close of a relationship with him. But Maria and Anneliese were devastated. It was particularly hurtful because he was their father's father, who they grew up with on the farm. They even had memories of sleeping in the same room, separated only by a curtain when they were little girls. His passing seemed to bring up the memory of their father's passing all over again because their memories of him were connected to the memories of their dad. He was their closest grandparent. He taught them to pray in that small farmhouse bedroom and when his own son died, he helped them deal with his death. He especially treasured their family, according to Anna.

"Oh Anna, I'm so sorry. I'm so very sorry." Maria's mother said, giving her sister-in-law a hug.

"What are we supposed to do now?" she asked her. "What I mean is, how can I help with the funeral?"

"Well, I've been to the church already. Pastor Shafer says we can have a service for him tomorrow." Maria's mother nodded her head.

"Gottlieb is looking after the coffin and his boys can carry it to the church for us. We can come to your house if that's okay, first, and then walk from here?" she asked tentatively. "Tradition is to walk in a funeral procession through the street to the church, just like for a wedding."

"Yes, of course Anna. Whatever I can do." She said.

"Who knew that our next gathering would be for a funeral?" Albert whispered to Maria the following day. She looked up at him and fresh tears started to fall. Maria and Anneliese weren't quite finished grieving yet. Albert put his arm around Maria to console her. Maria's mother and Anneliese held each other close as well. Hildegard and Siegfried seemed oblivious because their grieving was not as personal as that of their sisters. Maria thought about the times that she and Anneliese would peak between the curtains to get a glimpse of their grandfather's naked bum when he dressed for bed. They giggled until they fell asleep, and he just let them. Maria had to smile to herself. 'He must've known.' She thought, but he just didn't bother with us. 'He knew we would have been in so much trouble. What a good grandpa I had.' She thought.

234

With emotions all over the place, the family started the procession through the streets, Albert, Ernst and Walter carrying the coffin in front, family following close behind. When they reached the church, Pastor Shafer, said a few comforting words. The beautiful songs of hope that followed lifted their spirits and helped take away the pain of the moment. Afterwards, the procession continued to the gravesite, where he was laid to rest. The words that were spoken over their beloved grandfather helped console everyone. He raised five children on his own, having lost his wife to mastitis after a cow kicked her breast during the period that she was still breast feeding their youngest child. He was remembered for his strong work ethic, his love for farming and his steadfast faithfulness to the Lord.

The singing continued and his 'home-going' became more of a celebration of his life than a sad gathering of mourners.

"Where's Rudi?" Albert asked. "I thought he'd be here for this." Maria was very sorry for never having had the chance to introduce Rudi to the grandfather that meant so much to her. She tried to convince him time and again to visit him throughout their courtship, but to no avail. Rudi always had an excuse to elude the meeting. At this moment, she was angry at Rudi over it, but her sadness was deeper than her anger, besides which she didn't want Albert to know that Rudi had disappointed her in any way.

"We just found out yesterday. He couldn't be here in time. It all happened too fast." Maria said. She turned her attention back to the service.

"He was a beautiful person." she whispered to Albert. "I know I'll see him again."

Albert smiled. "Absolutely."

Chapter Twenty-Three

"A THANKFUL HEART CANNOT BE SAD." MARIA'S mother said, helping them all to deal with the loss of their grandfather. So, kneeling beside her bed, the following weekend, Maria was thanking God for everything that He provided for her; all the good things in her life that had come about because of absolutely nothing that she had done. Her family was a great blessing and even though her father and grandfather were now in heaven, they lacked absolutely nothing. She was thankful for her health and her family's health which afforded them the ability to work hard and have thankfulness and joy in their hearts. The kind of joy that wasn't dependent on circumstances. The joy that helps you carry on despite the realities and the chaos in the world around you. She was also thankful that their milk business was successful. It allowed them to develop friendships and build community.

In turn people were generous towards them and here she was, affording a wonderful wedding celebration with her and Rudi's money and through the generosity of her mother and the relationships that had been fostered with her clients throughout the years. All be it through an underhanded deal on the client's end, the blessing ultimately came to fall on her. And even more than that; her husband-to-be came from out of nowhere and chose her from among all women. He was a loving and kind man. She knew he would walk with her through all of life's hardships which would inevitably come. All these gifts she knew were from God, be it a result of her ancestor's prayers or just favor from God, but in this moment, she was beyond thankful. It was almost too much – her heart was full. She decided to ask God to always fill her heart with gratitude to Him no matter what would come. To help her remember His goodness, even if she became blind to it. And one other thing...

"...and please God I ask that Rudi would come to know and love your son Jesus, just as much as I do?" It was so important to her and just then she decided that she would never stop praying that prayer until it was answered.

Tired and full of the peace that God gives to those who love Him; the peace that passes all understanding and a love that anchors the soul, Maria climbed into bed, pulled up her covers, turned out her light and fell fast asleep.

A loud crash jolted her awake the next morning. There was the sound of shuffling feet nearby. She opened her eyes to find Hilde's face looking at her from across the room. She was trying on Maria's hair combs and even some of her jewelry.

"What are you looking for Hilde?" she asked. Hildegard picked up the comb that had fallen on the ground. She turned around, feeling a little guilty for trying to get something without asking.

"I was wondering if I could wear this comb with the white pearls. It would go so nicely with my dress."

"Where are you going?" Maria asked, sleepily.

"To church silly. We are leaving in half an hour. You better hurry. I thought Rudi was supposed to meet with the pastor." Maria bolted upright in her bed. She forgot.

"Yes, you can wear the comb, but Hilde, can you please run upstairs and make sure Rudi is awake?"

Hildegard smiled and put the comb perfectly centered above the crown of braids on her head. "Okay. I will. Thanks." She said as she skipped out of Maria's room and up the stairs. Maria listened and hoped that Rudi hadn't slept in like she did.

"Rudi!" Hildegard called through the door. "We're leaving for church in a half hour. Are you awake?" There was no answer for a minute and Maria, listening intently from her room, felt her heart sink. Then suddenly, Rudi opened his bedroom door and stepped out in the hall dressed and ready.

"Sure I am. Let's get some breakfast before we go."

Maria could hear them coming down the stairs. As they passed her room, she heard Hilde telling him that she 'woke Maria up a few minutes ago.' At that, Maria raced to her closet and chose a classy yellow dress with little white pumps, quickly got dressed, washed her face, brushed her teeth and fixed her hair and make-up. She was just in time to grab a quick muffin from her mother's breakfast basket before they hurried out the door. Rudi moved in beside her and put his arm around her shoulder.

"Are you alright today sweetheart? I really am very sorry that I kept putting off going to meet your grandfather. I know that he meant the world to you. "

"I'm fine. I just needed some extra sleep I suppose. I don't even know why. And yes, I really do wish that you had agreed to meet him when I asked you to, but it's too late now. I'm disappointed about that, I really am." She looked at Rudi and saw the guilty look on his face. "One thing I'm confident of, is that I will see him in heaven again, so I'm not altogether broken about his passing." She shared with him. They were silent for a moment. Maria was forgiving and didn't like to dwell on things, rather she just accepted it as a missed opportunity. She was regretful about it, but not resentful. Her thoughts were already on the day ahead. She admitted to herself that she was a little anxious about Rudi's meeting with Pastor Schafer. She had always looked up to the Pastor and his opinion was important to her.

"That was a very good sermon, Pastor Schafer. I liked it very much." Rudi commented as he stood awkwardly in front of the man of God, not knowing what to say. He directed Rudi to take a seat in his study. They sat side by side in big armchairs.
"I'm glad you liked it Rudi. Tell me, what was it that you enjoyed about it?"
Rudi sat forward in his seat, very eager to have this man's approval who, by position alone, Rudi felt was somewhat in authority over him. "Well to be honest Pastor Schafer, I have never known about church or religion. My family are businesspeople. I suppose that is no excuse. Maria's family has a business too. What I mean is that my dad died when I was three and since then, well my mother has been busy with her new husband and the family business. She never really had time to teach me about church and Jesus. My grandfather is the one I spent most of my time with, but he didn't take me to church." The pastor just listened.

"I know Maria and her family come every Sunday." He looked away. "Well mostly anyway." He said, knowing that he was the reason Maria didn't make it to church on many Sundays since they'd started dating. "I would like to learn. I would like to know more. I find it amazing about Jesus dying for our sins. It's beautiful."

The pastor listened to Rudi explain his lack of association with the church and faith in general. It was obvious to him that he was nervous. He understood how alone he must've been as a little boy and somehow instead of feeling upset that he may be trying to lure Maria away from her faith, he understood that was not the case. He felt compassion and was encouraged that Rudi was open to learning about the gospel. But he still wanted more experience with him before he agreed to marry him off to Maria Riekert.

He noticed Maria coming to church with a couple of different suitors in the past, each of whom had a lot more to offer her, and yet Maria's mother was all for this 'young Berliner.' Not only did he not grow up in the church, but he also did not have much in material possessions to offer her. The other young men were different in those respects. What made Rudi so special? Pastor Schafer valued Frau Riekert's opinion. She was a strong woman; mother of four children, businesswoman, and owned a house. She managed a lot. And that, much more successfully on her own, than most of the men he knew.

"Would it be alright with you, Rudi, if I pop in to visit with all of you sometime soon?"

"At Maria's? of course." Rudi answered. "I come every weekend on the Friday afternoon train from Stuttgart. I don't leave until Sunday evening."

"I see," the pastor said, "Well then, expect to see me sometime in the near future."

"Sounds good to me." Rudi said. The pastor stood to his feet and held out his hand to shake Rudi's.

"I'll see you soon Rudi!"
"What? That's it? I don't have to sign anything?" Rudi asked.

"No. Not unless you want to." The pastor chuckled. Rudi stood up and headed towards the door.
"Actually Rudi, do you understand the reason Jesus came to die for us? Do you know the truth about it all?" he inquired. Rudi had never been so earnestly confronted with the biblical question and now standing in this comfortable silence, he was unable to give any account of his own spirituality.

"I'm sorry. I'm right at ground zero Sir."

"That's not entirely a bad place to be." The pastor shared. Rudi was surprised that he would say so, but also relieved. The pastor went on to explain. "We all have a free will. Our creator, God, took a chance in giving us that, knowing that we may not choose Him. I'm glad you at least have an open heart and are curious. Would you like me to share a little bit about God with you?"

At this point in his life, Rudi was not sure that he wanted too much "religion". But here he was, in the pastor's office to win approval from him so that he was at least willing to officiate his wedding to Maria.

"Yes. Go ahead." Rudi answered. Pastor Schafer had seen it before. Somehow Rudi thought 'as long as I say the right things....' Pastor Schafer was well aware of Rudi's semi-interest, but he accepted this time as an opportunity to plant the seed of salvation in Rudi's heart and mind, hoping that at some future date, when Rudi was more spiritually mature, he would come to delight in hearing and understanding the things of God. So, he continued.

"Long ago," the Pastor started, "when God chose Israel to be His holy nation, His special people, He called them to be separate from the cultural idol worship of their time and gave them ten basic rules to follow to keep them from sinning against Him. But of course, as is, and has always been the case, no one was able to follow all the rules. Not one person. Not even Moses, whom God chose to give the rules to the people on His behalf."

Rudi listened. The pastor was a good teacher and he had Rudi's attention.

"It was Moses' job to lead them to the promised land – a place that God was giving them for an inheritance. But as people tend to do, they mistrusted and doubted God so many times when things got hard. They 'forgot' the miracles he did to lead them out of slavery in Egypt." Rudi leaned forward, keeping his attention on the story. The pastor became animated. "Imagine walking through the sea, on the actual seabed, with walls of water on either side, and then watching as the water came back to engulf the enemies wanting to kill you? Hard to forget, I would think." He looked at Rudi for a response. Rudi just raised his eyebrows and continued to listen politely.

He continued, "But every time a new hardship surfaced, they complained and lost faith. So, God was patient and had them wander a long time giving them opportunity after opportunity to trust His care for them. But they would not, trust I mean. So finally, God had enough and swore that they wouldn't be able to enter the promised land. He only wrestled with them for so long. You see, even Moses sinned against God by having a prideful attitude. He dishonored and disobeyed God by being angry with the people. God simply asked him to trust Him and obey His instructions. But honestly, which one of us is willing to do that? We think we can take matters into our own hands, don't we?" he asked Rudi. Rudi simply nodded. "Well Moses' punishment was that after leading all the people out of slavery in Egypt and through the wilderness for forty years, he was not allowed to enter the promised land with the new generation – the children of all the people who had originally come out of Egypt. Sin always has a consequence."

Rudi's eyes were starting to glaze over, and the Pastor saw that he was starting to fidget.

"Stay with me for just a minute longer Rudi. This next part is about you." Rudi just smiled but didn't say a word. He let the pastor finish.

"People, that's us, have always been and still are so bent on sinning against God and against ourselves really. Without God, we have no morality check, and we are self-absorbed, and bent on self-destruction. And for that, all our sin, God requires a sacrifice of blood. He cannot be in the presence of unholiness. So instead of having to follow the rules of sacrificing the blood of innocent animals, God had a plan. In His great wisdom and love, He sent Jesus, His own son, to be born on earth to a very poor couple, live a sinless life and then shed His own blood to be the sacrificial lamb to atone for all our sins. All the sins, for all the people, for all of time."

He searched Rudi's face for an enlightenment, an 'aha' moment. "The sins were indeed paid for" he explained "– on Jesus' back. For you. For me. For everyone." Rudi was speechless.

"And because once He died, and God raised Him to life three days later, we also, through our belief and acceptance of His sacrifice on our behalf, will be raised to eternal life when we die. It was God's beautiful plan since the beginning, that we who believe, would be able to live with Him forever.

"Thank you, pastor." He simply said. "It is a lot to take in. I'm thankful that you explained it more fully to me. I certainly would like to take some time to absorb it all if that's okay."

"Of course, Rudi. And once you believe it in your heart, you can just tell God. Thank Jesus for sacrificing His body on the cross to carry your sins, so you don't have to. Ask Him to forgive you and be your Savior. That is all God wants. Your heart, your thanks, your belief. He wants to be in a relationship with you; to be the father you never had. And of course, part of that is your acknowledgement of your sin and your need for a Savior, because we certainly cannot come clean from our sin by our own doing. Otherwise, His Son died for nothing. He wants you with Him in His heaven forever."

"That simple huh?"

"Yes, simple, for us. Not for Him."

Rudi stood up. "Well like I said, I have to absorb it all…"

"Yes, it is a process Rudi. The Bible puts it this way, "For God so loved the world that He gave His one and only begotten Son, that whosoever believes in Him will not perish, but have everlasting life." Rudi nodded. "And if you need a little help in understanding it" he threw up his arms in welcome, "Well that's why we are here as the church. But thank you for coming Rudi. I look forward to seeing you soon." He held the door as he bid him farewell. If first impressions proved correct, he understood that Rudi was a very genuine young man and sincere in his love for Maria. He just wished that he felt that way about Jesus. It wasn't something that he could push, but it was something that Rudi could learn and would hopefully come to accept in his own time.

Chapter Twenty-Four

"HOW DID IT GO?" MARIA ASKED AS HE CAME around the corner with somewhat of a puzzled look on his face letting out a big sigh.

"I can't believe it." He stared blankly ahead at nothing.

"What? What can't you believe?" He stood in silence for a moment trying to formulate his answer.

"I thought I was going to be grilled and chastised for my non-righteous self. Instead, he was interested in my life and full of grace when I told him that I don't know anything about Jesus." Maria smiled and nodded. That's the Pastor Schafer she knew and loved. He was a fair man.

"Well, I'm sure when he heard that you didn't grow up in a Christian family, he understood that you can't possibly know what you haven't been taught."

Rudi smiled at her. "Yeah. That's exactly how it was. Although he certainly did his best to explain it all." He said, his eyes widening as if to express his feeling of being overwhelmed with information. Maria put her arm around him and started walking him down the street.

"So, he's fine with marrying us in May? All is well?" Rudi was still somewhat in shock and deep in contemplation over what he had just learned.

"Well not exactly," he remembered, "he said he'd like to get to know me better. He's planning on visiting us at your mother's house soon." Maria's steps slowed down a little.

"So, he's not okay?" she said, disappointed.

"He is not sure, but I think he's trying to get a better picture of how our relationship works, who I am and how we fit together and can build a future. I told him I'm here on weekends and it would be fine if he popped by anytime."

Maria nodded. "Well then," she said, "we better let Mama know. Just to prepare her."

"Good idea." said Rudi, "but first, let's have a wonderful Sunday together. How about we go on a river cruise this afternoon on the Neckar?"

"Yes! Let's do it!" Weekends with Rudi were always so much fun, especially Sundays, when they could take time away for themselves.

The pastor, alone in his study sat down to contemplate how powerful love can be. Having known Maria as a child, he understood her to be sold out to the Lord in all her convictions and yet this young man in his charm and gregarious personality managed to sweep her off her feet. It was puzzling to him because she knew that he was not a Christian man. In fact, he questioned whether she was merely concerned with approval for Rudi because she was set on marrying him no matter what anyone else said? Was she that blinded by her attraction to him? He questioned whether she was even concerned with God's approval. He wondered these things a long time, ultimately concluding that God has indeed given us all a free will. Whatever Maria's choices and her motivations, he knew that God would be able to work it all out for His glory and her good. He felt uneasy and simply decided to give the matter much time and prayer.

* * *

THE NEXT TWO WEEKS WERE DIFFICULT for Maria and Hilde. It was time to hand over the reins and train her little sister to carry on her position in the family milk business. Hilde was doing everything correctly, even though it was a tough job. Her frame was even more petite than Maria's which meant it was a real strain on her to carry and lift the forty-liter cans of milk. On top of that, it was tedious work to clean everything at the end of the day. She was a typical teenager and had other interests which did not involve working all day, every day with nothing to show for it. Maria was alongside her for now, but Hilde dreaded the day that she would not be there to help. She was especially thankful on weekends when Rudi came to visit because he always wanted to be with Maria and she was more than willing to accommodate him by handing over her position, so he could do that. Rudi was also aware of how hard the milk business was on Hilde and if anyone understood what it meant to be young and looking for ways to have fun, it was Rudi. They were birds of a feather, Hilde, and Rudi, and they knew it.

Siegfried also waited for Rudi to come visit on weekends. He was the only male in the house, other than Helmut, but Helmut was always away at the Sports plex and when he did come home, he was usually drunk. Rudi was the one who always spent time with Siegfried and helped him with his chores around the house even though he was only able to be there on the weekends. They also had some important coming-of-age conversations that Siegfried needed a man for. Rudi was like a father to him. He was like medicine for the whole household since they lost their dad. When Rudi came, there was singing and dancing and everyone was included. He genuinely lifted their spirits.

After his private meeting with Pastor Schafer, a visit during the week was no longer a source of anxiety for Rudi. He welcomed it in fact because he wanted him to see how much they functioned like one big family, and he knew he had a big role to play in that. And he loved it. Because he loved Maria. But he loved them all. And he knew they loved him. He felt it and he wanted Pastor Schafer to feel it too.

He got his wish when at the start of the first weekend in April, the Pastor came walking down Gerber Straße. His visit was unannounced, so no one was expecting him on that specific day. It was Saturday morning and Hildegard was begging Rudi, once again, to take her place at work. Rudi always did it for her, but he wanted to tease her a little first.

"Hätele, I have to get all the arrangements done for the wedding this weekend. There isn't much time." He fakely protested.

"The wedding isn't until next month!" Hilde argued.

"Exactly!" he said.

"Rudi, I just need a rest. I'll do anything you ask me to. Whatever you like. Please! Please!" She was on her knees pulling on his shirt at this point, purposefully being overdramatic.

No one had seen him yet, so the pastor slipped into the overhang of a shop on the side of the road. He watched with great interest exactly what was transpiring before his eyes. Rudi bent over to take her hands off his shirt and go nose to nose with this poor pathetic young girl.

"What's in it for me?" he joked. The pastor gasped. He overheard every word. He was in shock. He thought he was listening to some kind of sinister entanglement.

Hildegard was silent for a moment, trying to think of something worth trading a day off for. "I will make you and Maria lunch tomorrow?"

"Nope! Not good enough!"

"What can I do then?" Hilde asked nervously in case it would be something she did not want to do, even worse than working all Saturday.

"I have just the thing!" Rudi laughed "Mwah ha-ha. You must dance with me in the street. Right now." He took her hand, lifted her up off the ground where she was kneeling and swung her around. Hilde threw her head back in laughter as this was what she loved to do. She didn't mind being the center of attention and she knew how pretty she was and that all the boys would be watching. Rudi pulled her in at the end of the dance, "Now Hätele,"

"Yes Möpsle?" she asked.

"If I do this for you, this one time, and don't expect it again, then you must promise me not to break any boy's heart today. No crazy flirting with five different boys at the same time. One is enough."

"I'll try." She fake-pouted and giggled.

Rudi laughed and let her go. The pastor didn't know what to make of it. He started down the street again towards their house, baffled about what he had just witnessed.

"Hilde and Rudi!" Maria called "Stop horsing around. We need to get to work!" She started walking across the street to get the three-wheeler. "Are you coming Rudi?" She kept walking straight ahead, knowing he would follow. Hilde and Rudi gave each other a curtsy and a bow respectively to finish their little dance. Hildegard ran into the house and Rudi followed Maria.

The pastor did not understand what he just witnessed, but he was about to find out. He purposefully knocked on the front door. Maria's mother came to the door wearing her apron. "Guten Morgen Pastor Schafer! Willkommen! Come on in! Rudi told us you would be stopping by one of these days. Unfortunately, you just missed him. He left for the day with Maria. They are on duty for the milk business today. Would you like a cup of coffee?"

"No thank you Frau Riekert. I am a little disturbed by what I just witnessed in the street." He quickly confessed, not wanting to lose his resolve to get an explanation.

"What happened?" she asked curiously. "Well, I just saw Rudi and Hildegard. I started to think they were arguing."

"Oh no." Maria's mother corrected him. "They do that every weekend. She waits for him to come and take over her job. He teases her, lets her beg a little and then they have a little dance. Am I right?"

He cleared his throat. "That about sums it up."

"You have to understand Pastor Schafer, Hildegard is fifteen." He stared at her blankly. She went on to explain. "Fifteen means she's starting to want her freedom. She's a teenager. As you know, they want to be independent, but they are not quite ready. In any case, she works harder than most girls her age. She has to because I need her. Rudi comes and relieves her of her duties, so she can be a normal fifteen-year-old for a few days."

"I see. When will they be back?" he asked.

"Oh, probably around two o'clock. You're welcome to stay." Maria's mother answered.

"I have a lot to do today. Thank you anyway. I will see you later." He said and rose from his chair to show himself out the door. Maria's mother stood in the kitchen wondering what on earth he must be thinking. But she had a lot to do today too. There was no time to daydream and no point in worrying.

Siegfried had been waiting since lunch for Rudi to get back. He cherished every moment with him. Growing up just after the war as the youngest child and the only boy meant that he was alone. A lot.

Rudi understood because he was alone a lot too when he was little because his parents were always busy working. He knew. And he took his role in Siegfried's life seriously.

Rudi and Maria could barely get in the door when Siegfried pounced on the opportunity to claim some of his time. "Rudi, I have to show you what I've been working on. After you finish lunch of course. Hi Maria!" He vanished out the back door again.

"What's he working on?" Rudi asked as Maria's mother set a lunch plate before them.

"I wish I could tell you." She mused. "I've been too busy to keep track of him. He's been up in the shed all morning." Rudi nodded, knowing how much she had to work and how tired she looked sometimes. "Interesting..." was all he said. Maria's mother reminded herself about their curious visitor that morning.

"The pastor came by earlier today." she said. "He was looking for you." Taking a bite of his sandwich, Rudi said, "I was wondering when I would see him."

"I told him you would be back by two o'clock, so he'll probably come by soon." Rudi looked at Maria. "I guess we timed that perfectly. It's almost two now." They quickly ate their lunch and waited a little while, but the pastor didn't come.

"When can I show you what I made?" Siegfried pleaded. "I'm still waiting. It's been at least half an hour." Rudi shook his head.

"More like ten minutes Siegfried." He laughed. "But don't worry, I'm coming." Rudi agreed as he rose from his chair and took one last sip of his drink and followed Siegfried out the door. "Call me when he gets here." He called back.

"Anneliese was looking for you." Maria's mother informed Maria. "She came downstairs just before you came home."

"Okay. Thank you, Mama." Maria said kissing her mother's cheek on her way up the stairs. When she got to Anneliese's door, she could hear baby Dietmar crying and she was just about to go in, when she heard Helmut's voice.

"I don't have time for this Anne. I'm going to the Sportsplex. I have a game today." She could hear her sister starting to protest and she didn't want them to fight so she knocked loudly on the door. Helmut came to open it thinking this was his excuse to leave.

"Maria! Good timing." He looked at Anneliese. "See you can visit with your sister. You won't be here alone with the baby."

"You don't have to leave Helmut. I came to get Dietmar. I'm taking him for a walk." She winked at Anneliese who quickly got his bag and a bottle and handed Dietmar to Maria.

"Thank you so much" she said as she passed Dietmar to her sister's waiting arms.

"No problem. You two need to spend some time together." and just as quickly as she arrived, Maria disappeared and called back over her shoulder, "I'll have him home for his supper. We'll be gone at least two hours!" She didn't hear any arguing as she carried Dietmar down the stairs, so she was hopeful that she read the situation correctly and did the right thing. She knew her twin better than anyone and she could tell she needed a break.

"Mama, I'm going to take Dietmar out in the stroller for a while, is that okay?" Maria asked.

"Fine with me," she answered.

"Alright." Maria said. "Where's Hilde?" she asked, thinking she might take her along for a stroll.

"I honestly do not know." Her mother answered. Just then Rudi and Siegfried came through the kitchen door, Rudi holding out a wooden toy wagon.

"Look what Siegfried made by himself!" Maria made sure to make a big deal of his first attempt at a skillful creation. She then looked at Rudi questioningly for approval of what she was about to offer.

"I'd like to reward you for all your hard work Siegfried. I think your toy is truly amazing! You know what would be even more amazing is if I could get this baby to stop crying! Would you two like to come for a stroll with Tante Maria?"

"Come on Siegfried," Rudi coaxed, catching on. "I'll buy you an ice cream."

"Yes!" Siegfried exclaimed. "I'm coming!"

258

"Mama," Maria said on their way out the door, "we'll be back at dinner time."

"Okay. Don't ruin your dinner by having too much dessert!" she called after them. Not long after they had left with Dietmar, Helmut came bounding down the stairs. He put his arm around his mother-in-law and gave her a wink. Before she could turn around to ask where he was going, Helmut was gone. She could hear his motorcycle as he pulled away. But she did not have to ask. She knew Helmut was going to play soccer with his buddies and would likely come home drunk much later.

Suddenly, it was strangely quiet in the house, but not for long. Within half an hour, there was a knock at the front door. At first Maria's mother assumed it was a milk customer, but then she saw Pastor Schafer through the window. "Good afternoon, Frau Riekert. I have been trying to get back here all day. I seem to be swamped with personal visits today." He said.

"Oh, that's okay. We are just having a typical Saturday. No different than most" she informed the pastor, but sadly, you have missed Rudi and Maria again. They were here at two o'clock and they waited to meet with you, but they had just now left. They took Siegfried and the baby out for ice cream. They'll be back in time for supper if you want to wait." The pastor looked disappointed, and he was full of questions.

"So, let me get this right. Rudi takes the train in from Stuttgart every Friday after work. Saturday morning, he gets up early to take Hildegard's place in the milk business, so he can be with Maria, which also helps you. He finishes that, then spends time with Maria's siblings?" he asked incredulously.

"Yes. You left out the fact that he works with Siegfried in the woodshed above the garage. They chop up enough wood to keep all my four tenants and ourselves stocked with firewood to stay warm. It's a little too much for Siegfried because he's so young. Would you like to see it?"

"No, that's not necessary."

"And today Siegfried was proud to show Rudi something that he had made by himself. It was a wooden toy that Rudi had taught him how to make. Siegfried has become very attached to him." The pastor was silent for a moment. He considered the blessing that had come upon this household in the form of a vagabond 'Berliner' looking for a girlfriend and ended up finding a family and a home. He thought of the bible verse in Deuteronomy, 'You shall do what is right and good in the sight of the Lord, that it may be well with you.' The pastor stood up and walked towards the door.

"I've seen and heard enough Maria. I believe that Rudi has a good, kind soul and I think he may eventually come to know the Lord through your daughter and whatever God has in store for them. I still say it would be easier for her to be married to a man who already knows Christ, but I can see that Rudi loves all of you and works with all his strength towards showing you. I respect that. God is fair and Rudi is just now coming to learn about Christ. If God brought them together and is patiently working in him, I will be too. You can tell them that I agree to perform the wedding. In any case, I hope to see you all in church before then. I've had a long day too, so please give everyone my regards."

"Certainly, Pastor. Thank you for coming." Maria's mother stated. "And thank you for seeing into Rudi's soul. You see what I see, and I've never seen a couple more in love."

"Good night Maria." Pastor Schafer said as he left the house. Once he was gone, she plopped down on the couch and breathed a sigh of relief. She let herself sit there for a few minutes 'savoring' the quietness; the blessed peace.

Chapter Twenty-Five

STREAMS OF SUNLIGHT DAPPLED THROUGH THE window in the early morning of May twenty-fourth, 1952. Maria opened her eyes, excited and filled with a godly peace that she was in the Lord's hands on this, her own wedding day. She said the words out loud to herself and to God, "It's my wedding day." She heard the words as she spoke them and let the reality sink in. "It's my wedding day" she repeated. Her smile spread across her face as she said it yet again. "It's my wedding day." She threw her covers aside and ran to open her bedroom door. "It's my wedding day!" she shouted to the whole house. She listened to hear if anyone would respond. Nothing. She walked over to her nightstand to look at a very old pocket watch from her grandfather. It was seven o'clock in the morning. She walked over to the window to let the light in. "Mine too!" Rudi exclaimed from behind. Maria turned and ran straight into his arms. "Congratulations Mrs. Heinrich!" he exclaimed just before he gave her a kiss.

"Thank you, Mr. Heinrich." She answered. "You have a busy day today!"

"Yes indeed" he agreed as he let Maria out of his embrace. He held out his hand to her and asked, "are you coming?"

She gave him a smile he would remember for a lifetime and answered "Of course. Let me just get my hair up and get dressed." She brushed through her shoulder length hair and put a hair comb in, to keep it in place and rushed to get changed into her work clothes. "There. I'm ready." The two of them tip-toed down the stairs quietly. Maria slowly opened the door to her mother's room. Happily, she found her awake. "Mama" Maria whispered, "it's my wedding day!"

Maria's mother chuckled. "Yes, so I hear darling." Maria blushed as her mother walked over to her at her bedroom door. She took both of her hands in her own. "I'm so happy for you. I know your father would be too." She smiled at her beautiful daughter, so full of anticipation and joy. "Don't worry Maria, when you get back, I'll have your bath ready. I want everything to go perfectly for you today." Maria gave her mother a big hug.

It was indeed her wedding day, but people in their district still needed their daily milk supplied. Most did not even have a refrigerator and getting their milk from the Riekert's store was a daily necessity. Maria and Rudi got their day started early enough so that they could make it to the Milk Centrale and back again with plenty of time to get ready for their own wedding. The guests would be arriving all day because some of them were travelling from villages that were an hour or two away. And of course, they had to travel on foot. Almost no one owned a car and most of the horses were taken for use in the war. Walking just became a way of life.

Rudi and Maria were happily looking forward to living together in Rudi's current small apartment in Stuttgart. Little did they know that Rudi's landlord, Albert, and his wife, Brunhilda had other plans. They were invited to the wedding because they had gotten to know Maria when she came to visit Rudi on occasion and even stayed in his room while she was in town.

"I don't want them staying in our house anymore." Brunhilda sharply told her husband on the morning of the wedding. "We don't rent to couples, and I don't even want to start that." Brunhilda said to her husband emphatically. She felt no remorse over her decision. It was simply business and she had it in mind for a while. Now that Rudi and Maria's wedding was about to become reality, she felt she had to speak her mind, after the festivities of course. Albert knew better than to argue with his wife once her mind was made up. He kept his opinion to himself although he did find it wrong to turn them out on their wedding day. Still, he held his tongue.

"Hustle it slowpoke! You're going to miss your own wedding!" Rudi joked. Maria smiled at him and started walking very slowly just to incite his sensibility. Rudi started laughing, realizing there was no use in trying to rush the work that still needed to be done today. Trying to do so would only frustrate his very own bride. "I deserve that. Ha-ha." He promptly picked Maria up and started running to the truck. "I don't know about you lady, but I have a wedding to get to." He opened the door to the truck and placed her in the passenger seat. Maria just gave him a look and kept her silence. She knew that he was getting anxious to move everything along, so they could get home and start to get ready for their big day.

"Are you sure you want to drive? I don't want you rushing now." Maria asked.

"I'm sure" Rudi replied. He reached over to hold her hand. She gently placed his hand back on the steering wheel. "I'm okay. I know you love me. Just get us there safely." she said calmly.

He leaned over to look her square in the face. "Do you trust me? I promise to take care of you."

"I know Rudi. Settle down. I'm quite sure they won't start the wedding without us." He took a deep breath, faced forwards, both hands on the steering wheel and started driving the truck from the Milk Centrale back home to the store. After they unloaded everything and had all the big milk cans washed and ready for the next day, Rudi and Maria walked calmly hand in hand into the house where all the family were gathered and seated in the living room. They were all chatting with one another and helping with the final details for the after-party.

"Come straight to the back!" Maria's mother called as she heard the bride and groom-to-be arriving.

Maria smiled at Rudi and gave him a last kiss before her mother led her away. Rudi's friend, Kurt along with his wife, had travelled from Stuttgart. Rudi was thankful to see his best man and master of the ceremony. He gave Kurt a warm pat on the back and held his hand out to his wife, Ingrid. "I'm very glad you could make it my friend. Do you have a little speech planned?'

"I got you covered Rudi. I think you will enjoy it. Just leave it to me." Rudi smiled, trusting his friend to keep things light and entertaining.

Maria tried not to feel rushed as she sank into the warm tub that stood on one side of the kitchen. It was a private and secluded corner, and she was so thankful to have the luxury of a bath on her

266

wedding day. Maria's mother had wonderfully prepared the water on the stove to be the perfect temperature. She wanted everything to be beautiful for her lovely daughter. All the details, which were many, were particularly attended to with loving, nurturing hands. When it was Rudi's turn to bathe, Maria was whisked upstairs to dress in her room where Anneliese was waiting to help.

"Are you nervous?" Anneliese asked.

"Not really, no. We have been waiting such a long time. The novelty is somehow – not the same." Anneliese looked down, understanding that it was because of her untimely pregnancy that Rudi and Maria had to postpone their wedding for a year. "It's not like it would be if we were young in our relationship. I'm extremely excited, but not nervous, no." she looked pensively into the mirror. "It's better. I am marrying the man who is my best friend and since we've already championed so many hardships – come what may – I know Rudi will stand by me."

Anneliese listened, but could only imagine such security in a marriage, such trust. She fell in love with Helmut because he was so good-looking. He still was and just thinking of him made her melt. But hearing Maria talk made a part of her long to know that kind of love. "Can you help me with my veil Anne?" Maria asked, startling Anneliese out of her own thoughts. She got up and stood behind her sister as she fixed her veil.

"You look perfect Maria. So serene. So, at peace." Maria just smiled. She walked towards the door.

Looking back at Anneliese, one last time, she set her gaze straight ahead. "I'm ready." She stated confidently.

Anneliese took Maria's hands and sincerely looked her twin in her eyes, "Maria, our lives will really be separate now. We won't be living under the same roof anymore. I will miss my other half so much." They both had to wipe a tear away. Then Maria gathered her courage.

"It's time." she stated and opened the door, ready for her future with Rudi.

Rudi had been upstairs getting himself ready as well. He wore a dark suit with a white shirt. His hair was slicked back, and he was clean shaven. His best man, Kurt, checked his tie and gave Rudi a confident smile and pat on the back. Making sure the ring was safely in his pocket, he followed Rudi down the stairs. Everyone was waiting for Maria to make an entrance into the living room. Her mother raced to the bottom of the stairs the moment she heard her footsteps coming. She was in awe of how beautiful Maria was in her precious wedding gown. She looked like she was in a dream, her face aglow with love. Rudi stood behind Maria's mother. When he caught sight of his bride, his body froze. He did not have the capacity to connect brain to motor skills – he was incapacitated, almost breathless the moment he laid eyes on her perfect figure and beautiful face. He could hardly believe this beautiful woman whom he met by chance, took a leap of faith in getting to know him, and here they were, ready to be married. Kurt gave Rudi a nudge. He came to his senses and realized it was his job to take her hand and lead her to the front of the wedding procession.

It was tradition in Germany, at that time, for the entire wedding party to walk from the bride's house to the church. The happy couple in front, wedding party next, parents and finally guests of the bride and groom which included friends and family.

Rudi stood at the doorway as though his life were about to change when he took his first step out of the house. He looked at Maria and gave her a wink. He reached back to get her hand and link it through his arm. Anneliese was right behind Maria (Helmut looked after Dietmar), Kurt and his wife were behind Rudi. Following them were Hildegard and two of Maria's cousins, Siegfried and Maria's mother and grandmother. Trailing behind the main bridal party were the rest of the cousins and their families and finally friends and acquaintances like Rudi's landlords from Stuttgart, Albert and Brunhilda. It was the proudest twenty-minute walk Rudi had ever taken or would take in his lifetime and he knew it. This was the best moment of his life and he felt happier than ever. The fact that his mother, stepfather and sister were not able to share this most important moment crossed his mind briefly, but he was too happy to let it put a damper on the day. He knew they wished him the best.

As the bridal party walked to the church, people on the side of the street stood and clapped and a lot of people came to their windows to cheer them on. It was becoming quite a regular wedding tradition in their city. Maria felt so happy she wanted to shout it from the rooftops. When they arrived at the church, the bride and groom went around the side to find the pastor who was waiting for them. Everyone else went into the church through the front door. The side door led straight to the altar of the church, where Rudi and Maria were seated, waiting for the guests to sit down behind them and then for the pastor to begin. When he called them up, Rudi could only maintain his wits by looking straight into Maria's eyes. He felt like he could hardly breathe. 'The most beautiful girl in all the world, standing before me, ready to be my bride' is all that ran through his mind. He barely listened to what the pastor was saying. All he wanted to know was when to say, "I do."

"Do you take Maria to be your lawfully wedded wife? To have and to hold? In sickness and in health? For richer, for poorer? Until death do you part?"

"I do." He spoke loudly.

The pastor turned to Maria.

"I do," was all Rudi heard. He leaned forward, put his hand on Maria's waist and pulled her close. He sealed their covenant with a kiss to remember. When they were done kissing, they gazed into each other's eyes and smiled. Rudi took Maria's hand and led her down the aisle to the front door. As they passed by Maria's mother and siblings, they saw their handkerchiefs wiping away tears of joy. Everyone was in awe of their love for each other. It was solid. It was sure and it encouraged others that a strong love, despite differences and hardship, could still exist, even thrive. Everyone looked forward to celebrating their marriage. When they stood at the entrance to the church, Maria and Rudi waited for the wedding party and the guests to stand and follow them to the reception. Once again, the wedding procession moved from the church to the hotel where two rooms were prepared with food and drinks for everyone. Maria would have preferred the reception in one big room, as opposed to two separate rooms. It made for a little chaos in trying to greet all their guests and to thank everyone for coming as was the custom for the bride and groom to do together. More than once they found each other in separate rooms, but since the arrangement was made as a business deal, Maria conceded, once again, to keep the peace and to please her mother.

She did realize, however, that it was indeed a beautiful hotel and would have been out of their price range, had it not been for the forced agreement. The food was amazing, there was a wonderful buffet, and the alcohol was plentiful. Thankfully, all their guests kept themselves from overindulging. This union was a long time in the works and people felt completely in agreement with Rudi and Maria becoming husband and wife.

When everyone sat down to eat, Kurt took center stage, starting to roast Rudi and his single lifestyle before meeting Maria, albeit in a charming and witty manner. He had everyone laughing as he imitated his best friend dancing around the room, grabbing a new partner from every table he passed.

"This was Rudi at every party we went to." He joked. "Matter of fact, we crashed a lot of parties because Rudi danced his way from one end of the room to the other and then by the time he was done swinging with the ladies, he told his jokes at the bar and started dancing on the tables. No one cared if they knew us when we came in because he was everyone's best friend when we left." Everyone was smiling and nodding as Kurt related his experiences with Rudi. "Anyone know the feeling?" he asked sincerely. "Tell me I'm wrong – anyone?" All the guests roared with laughter because Kurt described Rudi to a T. He nailed his personality.

"You know, this quality was particularly useful when Rudi was a POW in East Germany. The enemy soldiers loved him so much, they invited him to all their parties, and no one was the wiser when he escaped." People were still smiling, but the laughing suddenly stopped. "Which was a good thing," Kurt continued, "because how else would he have met our girl, Maria? And who else would be bold enough to whistle at a stranger from across the street, from their boss's company car, no less?" Once again, people laughed, and Kurt continued to set the mood for a cheerful celebration.

"But underneath that jovial, happy-go-lucky persona, was a deeper character in search of an honest, sincere woman that he could build a life with. And once again, God smiled on this wanderer and gave him Maria. Talk about winning the lottery! – Let's all raise a glass to the nicest couple we all know and the luckiest man alive! Cheers to you Rudi and Maria!"

Everyone toasted the happy couple and then watched as they took to the dance floor for the first dance. They were surrounded by their guests, all wanting to witness their amazing love story, but the two of them felt like they were alone in the room. Once again, as happened on their first date, when the music stopped, they kept dancing. At that, everyone applauded because they were so lost in each other's love. Rudi reluctantly let go of her and asked his mother-in-law for the next dance and Maria held out her hand to Siegfried. Everyone else joined in and danced the rest of the night away.

After the reception, most of the guests went home, but Maria's two bridesmaids (her cousins), and Kurt and his wife came to finish off the night at Maria's mother's house. Along with that select group, Rudi's landlords tagged along. They didn't say anything, until they were at the door, about to leave. It was then that Brunhilda turned to Maria's mother.

"Guess what – we cannot have your daughter rent with us. Rudi is always welcome to stay at our house, but we cannot have Maria stay as well."

"Well, that doesn't make any sense." Maria's mother exclaimed. "They are married now. What do you mean Maria's not welcome?"

"We don't want to board couples. We cannot even start that. They'll have to find somewhere else…"

"And you wait until their wedding day lady?" Maria's mother was livid. "How can you do this after sitting as a guest at their wedding?" she started, realizing that her emotions were getting the best of her. Everyone in the house stood silent.

"Never mind." Maria's mother cut ties immediately. "They'll stay here with me." She stated as she shut the door behind them. Brunhilda and her husband cowardly fled the scene after their announcement.

Maria and Rudi stood in shock and dismay for a moment. No one saw this coming.

"What just happened?" Maria asked Rudi in disbelief. Rudi had no words.

Maria's mother quickly surmised the situation and took control.

"Stay here for now you two. We will figure it out. Tomorrow is a new day."

Chapter Twenty-Six

IT WAS QUIET IN THE HOUSE WHEN MARIA AND Rudi woke up the next morning. Hildegard and Maria's mother had left early for the Milk Centrale and Siegfried had gone home with his grandmother. Their thoughtful service gave the newlyweds some private time together. Maria and Rudi were happy but also exhausted from all the wedding festivities the previous day. "I must be honest Maria. I might have suspected that Albert and Brunhilda were up to something. They started acting weird around me a couple of weeks ago. I'm so sorry that I haven't done anything about it yet."

"I think it's despicable what they did. I wish you would have said something if you noticed, but let's not worry about them anymore." Maria wanted the greedy couple erased from their life. She didn't want anything to do with them. "When you go back to Stuttgart, you can get all your belongings out of their place. Do you think Kurt and Ingrid will let you stay with them until you can find an apartment for us?"

"Oh, I absolutely do. I'll go see them after work." Maria lay with her head on Rudi's chest.

"I think it's a blessing in disguise. It forces us to find something for ourselves immediately. Then I can come and get a job to help with our expenses. We'll finally be on our own." She lifted her light, blue/green eyes to Rudi's soft brown eyes. The spark between them ever present.

"Imagine that." Rudi said. "On our own and saving for a house. But let's never mind about that. We should take advantage of our time alone right now." Maria giggled as they rolled around and got lost in the sheets.

* * *

RUDI WENT TO STUTTGART THE following day and within one week he had found a small apartment on the black market. It was already furnished, but it was very cramped with a make-shift kitchen that consisted of two burners, an oven and a sink. When Maria made the trip to her new home for the first time, Rudi had already warned her about the cramped space, not wanting her to expect luxury and then feel disappointed. He also told her about the long commute to the city. They would have to take two different streetcars and then walk up a very steep hill to finally reach home. Getting an apartment in Stuttgart was next to impossible so, even though it was exceedingly small and required a lot of commuting time, they gladly accepted it.

Upon surveying her new surroundings, Maria, turning to Rudi, gave him a hug of approval. "It's wonderful Rudi! I'm so happy! It needs a little work, but I can make it a cozy home for us. I'm going to go and look for a job right away this week."

"Actually, I just found out today," he muttered, "that Mutti, my stepfather, and Rosi are coming to visit." Maria was incredulous.

"Now? But we just got married... and we have no room. And there is so much I need to do to set us up - just for ourselves, let alone hosting company right away." She looked at him as though it couldn't be true. Rudi walked over to her and reached for both of her hands. He stood calmly before her and attempted to smooth her ruffled feathers.

"I know. The timing of their visit couldn't be worse for what we had planned for ourselves, but you know they were not permitted to come to our wedding by the occupying authority. Now that the wedding is over, of course they are free to come, the governing forces knowing full well that there is no longer a reason to make the trip. But they have decided they want to come anyway, so let's just make the best of it. We can pick up where we left off as soon as they go home again." Maria's resistance was down, and her heart was starting to soften towards the idea. But she still felt the need to express her feelings a little further.

"Okay well untimely is not all it is. It is downright inconsiderate. I don't understand how they don't feel like they are intruding on a newlywed couple." She let go of his hands and busily started putting some things away in the cupboards, realizing there was so much she needed to get done to get them settled. She turned back to Rudi, "How can they not consider us? I don't really get their mentality."

Rudi knew that she was working herself up again, defending her position, and hoping to deflect the inconvenience that was about to be thrust upon her. "I understand Maria. Since we've used almost all our wedding money to pay rent for this place, maybe their visit will be a help to us. Either way, she is my mother. And even though I have never had a close relationship with her, I would like to keep the tethers in place that do exist and maybe build a better relationship for the future."

Maria was silent for a couple of minutes that seemed like an eternity to Rudi. She had to collect her thoughts and calm her spirit before she spoke again out of anger. "Okay." She finally conceded "We'll just do the best we can. I don't suppose there is anything else we can do." Rudi hugged her quickly and rewarded her generous spirit with his love, making it all worth it to her.

Chapter Twenty-Seven

I T'S SO QUAINT." RUDI'S MOTHER COMMENTED as she looked around their new apartment. Rosi quickly made herself comfortable in a chair by the small window in their living room. Maria felt as though they were trying to be positive, not condescending, although she could still feel the hint of superiority in their tone and expression. "We could still have the two of you come to Berlin. I mean it's a very big city and with Rudi's experience in leather, he could easily find a job."

"Thank you for wanting our best, Mutti." Rudi jumped in, "I think Maria and I are going to stay right here and work towards building our future in Stuttgart." Maria kept her silence as she busied herself in the kitchen. "We'll be fine" Rudi reassured his mother, "Maria is planning on getting a job here too and then we will be able to save for a bigger place." Rudi's mother, trying to make her intentions clear, pushed the envelope once again.

"Well, if you change your mind, you can always come back home. You too of course Maria. The city is filled with opportunity."

"Well I haven't even had the opportunity to look for work here yet. That was my plan for this week." Maria stated. If it sounded like she was trying to express her impatience with the untimely visit, it was intentional. Rudi was very quick to diffuse any hint of repressed anger trying to surface from Maria's lips.

"Maybe we could all go to the ice cream store in town. It would be a nice outing to show you around this area. Maria needs a few things for the kitchen anyway, so maybe we can do it all in one trip." He said, trying to sound positive. It was just the diversion needed to keep the atmosphere friendly. Internal turmoil always seemed to brew when Rudi's mother and Maria were together. But Maria had a plan that she knew she could always count on.

After consideration of the impossible sleeping arrangements with Rudi's family in the small, one-bedroom apartment, Maria thanked her mother for helping to accommodate her in-laws once again. "I don't know what we would do Mama, if we couldn't always rely on you to help us out."

"Never mind Maria. You know I am always happy to have visitors. I'm just sorry you didn't get much of a honeymoon."

Seeing that her daughter was disappointed in her in-laws she encouraged her to keep the peace. Instead of being negative or judgmental, she just raised her eyebrows to let Maria know that she understood. She then proceeded to help her daughter plan to make the best of the situation.

"Well you can take your honeymoon another time. Don't worry, you have your whole life ahead of you. Rudi's parents need a little attention right now. They want to join him in celebrating his wedding to you. Let's make it nice for Rudi so that he feels your support. Like you said, it's one week. His mother, of course, needs reassurance that all is well with her son. You can do that." It was thanks to her mother that the visit went so well, but Maria's mind was so focused on getting her future going, she almost hurried along the time to get back to Stuttgart so she could look for a job. As their visit was ending, they went back to the city and Maria wasted no time.

"I'm not a child!" Rosi pronounced after Maria expressed concern about leaving her in the apartment alone while she went to look for a job. Her in-laws had ventured into town, and Rudi was at work. She didn't want Rosi to be alone for long.

"Are you sure?" Maria asked. "You're only nine."

282

"Yes. Nine, not three! I am fine. Good luck! I hope you find something." Maria smiled at her little sister-in-law who was far too mature for her age. She closed the door hesitatingly behind her, but convinced by Rosi's reassurance, she went ahead, her mind focused on finding a job. 'If I can get a job at the Bleyle Dress Factory' Maria thought' then I can use my dress cutting skills. She was so hopeful as she approached the front door of the famous textile factory in Stuttgart. "I have experience in cutting." Maria stated, confident and hopeful as she stood before the woman who was at the front desk.

"I'm sorry Ma'am, but we only have an opening for a hand sewer, which is very intrinsic. The buttons and the hems and such. It requires careful attention to detail, an acquired skill and a very small stitch."

"Well, it just so happens that I can do that too." Maria stated.

"Oh. Well in that case," the young lady brightened, as she handed Maria an application, "Please fill out this paper and have a seat."

She was tired by the time she reached her apartment later in the day. It was a long journey home, but her joy could not be dampened. She had a job, and everything seemed to be falling into place. Her in-laws were about to go back home, and Maria would finally be able to settle into her new life as Mrs. Heinrich.

"I start on Monday!" Maria announced proudly as she opened the door to the apartment.

"Maria, that's amazing. Congratulations!" Rudi's mother exclaimed. At least she's a hard worker, she thought. Maria was not raised to nurse a lazy disposition. Her step-father-in-law also offered his heartfelt congratulations.

"I knew it." Rosi blurted out. "I knew you would find a job. You were so determined. I knew you could do it!"

"Yes, you did. And thank you." Maria said. Then she turned to Rudi, who stood with a big smile on his face and welcomed her home with open arms, expressing how proud he was of her. He would've liked to provide for them both, but he knew how important it was to Maria that they worked together to be able to save money and, in a few years, buy a home of their own to start a family. He knew he had a gem when he married her. She just kept proving to him every day what a diamond she was, and he fell deeper and deeper in love with her for all that she was and continued to give to their relationship.

Chapter Twenty-Eight

THE NEXT SEVERAL WEEKS WERE A BLUR; THE days ran into the nights and time seemed to escape them. Both Rudi and Maria had precious few moments together in the morning and they didn't sit down for supper until eight o'clock at night, exhausted and hungry. Through it all they maintained a positive attitude and kept their love for one another strong.

One day, on a very much needed break in late fall they went to visit everyone in Reutlingen. Maria and Rudi went on a hike up the trail to the Achalm mountain with Anneliese, Helmut and little Dietmar. Maria was suddenly reminded why children were not something she wanted in her immediate future. Carrying Dietmar close to her chest, she trudged up the trail close behind Rudi. First, he became very heavy very quickly. Then, all a sudden she burst out squealing as she held Dietmar at arm's length.

"Ugh! Ugh! No! Dietmar! Anneliese - Take your son! Ugh! Everything is warm and wet on my new dress! Ugh!"

Helmut fell out laughing on the ground as Rudi spun around to grab the small boy out of Maria's arms. He too, held the boy at arm's length.

"Oh, for goodness sakes!" Anneliese chided as she took Dietmar from Rudi's hands. "How are you two ever going to manage with your own child, let alone two?" Helmut's laughter started to fade. He had a strange look on his face that gave away the subtle hint Anneliese could no longer keep to herself.

"Anne?"

"Yes?"

"Are you?"

"Maybe. Yes. Okay yes. We have another one in the oven." She said tapping gently on her own belly.

"Oh my Gosh!" Maria exclaimed. "Are you kidding me?"

"No kidding." Anneliese answered shyly, unsure if she was allowed to feel happy over this new development.

Rudi was quick to congratulate them both, noticing how smug his brother-in-law was, looking very pleased with himself over the situation.

"Have you told Mama?" Maria asked.

"No. Not yet. I mean, not that it has anything to do with her." Anneliese blurted, afraid of how her mother would react.

"But not that it doesn't." Maria said, in defense of her mother's generosity.

"Helmut and I are planning to move to our own apartment." Anneliese stated, trying to explain their plan. "Helmut was offered a job at his company. He'll be an English translator. They really like him. They are offering him an apartment that is close to the factory where he works. It's a very nice package, so we'll be moving out before the new baby is born. We'll need the space anyway."

"Okay. Wow. this is all very good news." Maria nodded positively. "Congratulations all the way around!" she said. The sisters walked down the mountain together arm in arm as Rudi and Helmut took turns carrying Dietmar behind their wives. The sisters had not been together for a while and had so much to talk about, not the least of which was how to break the news to their mother.

Chapter Twenty-Nine

TAKING THE NEWS IN STRIDE, MARIA'S MOTHER was hoping that Helmut's new position would cause him to mature. She was waiting for him to become more of a steady husband and father figure, willing to spend time with his wife and children. It was with that hope that she gave Anneliese her full blessing and congratulations as she helped to move them out of her house on Gerber Straße and into their new apartment. It also gave her a little more focused time with Hildegard and Siegfried now that the baby was not in the house.

Things also seemed to move quickly for Rudi and Maria. It was already late spring in 1953 and Rudi could hardly believe that a whole year had passed since he and Maria were married. It was a beautiful Sunday and although it was still Spring, the sun shone so brightly that there wasn't a cloud in the sky and the air was warm enough for people to wear shorts and short sleeves. Trying to be frugal, Maria was creative in planning their outings. Despite their money struggles, they always had fun and were very happy. Wanting to make their first anniversary a very special celebration, she packed a picnic, and they ventured out to a local park to enjoy the sunshine. It was lovely just to rest and be together. Rudi leaned back on their blanket under an oak tree and looked up into the leaves of an overhanging branch.

"This is a really beautiful spot" he remarked. "I feel like we were meant to be here, under this tree, on this day." Maria was quiet, enjoying the stillness. "Beautiful." Rudi remarked again, only this time he was looking at Maria. A smile brightened her face as she turned toward him. He stroked her cheek gently and then turned to look skyward into the sun-speckled leaves that made an umbrella over them. After thoughtful reflection Maria broke her silence.

"It's God's outdoor cathedral." She said, turning toward Rudi with a smile.

"It does seem like a cathedral, doesn't it?" Rudi agreed. He took Maria's hand in his and playfully intertwined their fingers. "I wish we could freeze time." He said.

"So we could be young forever?" Maria asked, trying to follow his train of thought.

"Yes! And this happy. This much in love. I wish it could last forever."

Maria put her hand up to his face to gently stroke his cheek. "That's why we got married, silly, so that it would last forever."

"Yes, but I want us to be this happy... forever." Maria thought about his wish.

"We're as happy as we can be right now. And we will be as happy as we can be a few years from now – when we have children. Then many years from now, when we have grandchildren, and then still more when we bounce our great grandchildren on our knees. We don't have to worry. I think it's a state of being that changes and grows as life changes and grows." Rudi nodded his head.

"Yes, but I wish we could always be happy, never sad." He simply stated.

"Hmm...then we'll have to skip straight passed living and go straight to heaven." She mused.

"No." he protested, "I mean, I wouldn't want to miss the living part."

"No. We wouldn't. It'll be a journey, but through happy times and sad, we'll be together and hopefully we will be growing and changing together." Rudi was satisfied with that conclusion. He just smiled and kissed her. Then he jumped up abruptly from their blanket.

"Okay. Let's go find an ice cream place. This is a day for ice cream!" Maria stretched and reached out for his hand to pull her to her feet. They shook out their blanket and Rudi tucked it under his arm as they lazily walked up the street arm in arm in search of an ice cream shop.

"One last thought to add to our conversation under the oak tree." Maria said.

"Okay..." Rudi answered, wondering what she could mean.

"If we were never poor, how could we appreciate wealth? If we were never sick, how could we appreciate being healthy? And if we were never sad, how would we even know when we are happy?"

"You have a point my dear. I understand. I would just like to skip the poor, sick, unhappy part, so that we could forever be prosperous, healthy and happy. I know it sounds a little shallow, because of course, where then would the achieving and the satisfaction of these things be? I don't want to miss anything I suppose, I just really enjoy the good parts. But you have encouraged me simply by reminding me that we will be going through all the good and not so good times together."

"Even right now" Maria continued, "we are in the poor stage. We are working hand to mouth and live in a meager apartment, but because we are together, we are still happy."

"Agreed." Rudi said. Taking the last lick of his delicious ice cream, he was dreamily planning their romantic evening. "Tonight, we will get dressed up and meet in the living room. There will be candles and music for dancing and a wonderful meal of course. How about it Mrs. Heinrich?" he said, lightening the mood.

"Sounds like you have it all planned." She laughed.

"I do. Yes. I'm rather good at planning last minute, impromptu romantic rendezvous!"

"Ha-ha. Yes, you are. I must admit." Maria laughed. "I like your plan." The two lovebirds walked arm in arm the rest of the way home and had a wonderful time just being together, not thinking about work, until the night was about to end, when they were forced to look to the day ahead.

"The best days are nothing days, aren't they?" Rudi said, twirling Maria around their living room. They were enjoying a waltz together as their first anniversary was coming to a close.

"Sometimes, yes." Maria agreed. "It's a little tiring to have to spend so much time getting to and from work. Don't you think so Rudi? It certainly makes for long days. By the time we sit down to eat, I almost feel ready for bed."

"It's a bit of a rat race, isn't it?" Rudi asked.

"Well, it wouldn't be so bad if we could see ourselves getting ahead — saving money and building our nest egg to buy a house for a family. Rudi, we have not managed to save anything this whole year. All our money has gone to rent or food or what we need to live. It's a bit discouraging if you want to know the truth." Her words somehow felt accusatory, and Rudi started to feel a little responsible.

"Well, I don't think we can find anything cheaper." He replied.

"Yes, I know. It's just our economy." Maria stated, releasing Rudi from feeling at fault. "Germany is struggling, still trying to come out of its depression after the war. I just hope it improves soon." She confided.

"Me too. Of course. I want us to get ahead too. For all of us. At least we just have the two of us to consider. Imagine Anne and Helmut, about to have another baby!" Rudi said.

"Yes, well, she wants it that way. She's happy. So she says." Maria replied.

"Yeah, but sometimes I wonder about Helmut." Rudi confessed. "He's always running off to the Sportsplex, leaving her to parent alone."

"He is. I don't know how she manages, but when it comes to him, she's very defensive." Maria said. "We can only be here if she needs us. One good thing is that he is quite smart, and he has a really good job."

"Well I'm glad I got the right sister." Rudi said.

"Ha! You wouldn't have had a chance with her! To begin with, you're not over six feet tall..." Maria said.
"Oh," Rudi smirked, "in that case, this is probably the first and only time that I have, or ever will admit this, but right now I'm glad I'm short." Maria threw her head back in laughter.

Chapter Thirty

THE NEXT TIME RUDI AND MARIA VENTURED A visit to Reutlingen, Anneliese was proud to present her new baby. Mesmerized by the sweet, angelic face staring up at her, Maria contemplated what life would be like for this beautiful child. Anneliese's new bundle of joy was a blonde haired, blue-eyed baby girl whom she named Brigitte. She seemed like a bright and feisty little one, eager to communicate with anyone taking the time to hold her.

"It was a lot easier this time Maria!" Anneliese was happy to report. "You wouldn't have been anywhere near as stressed. As a matter of fact, her birth might even have encouraged you to consider starting a family yourself."

"Well I don't know about that," their mother chimed in. "Maria is essentially still a newlywed, Anne. She and Rudi have only had one year as a married couple. They still have plenty of time." Their mother was not only thinking of Maria and Rudi, but she also had her hands full with her own two teenagers. Another baby to care for seemed like an overwhelming prospect to her already overloaded schedule.

"Don't worry Mama. Rudi and I are still working hard and trying to save for a house or at least a bigger apartment. We don't have any plans to start a family yet." She saw her mother's face relax as she breathed a sigh of relief. "But I am glad that the birth was easier for you this time Anne." She nodded and smiled as she reiterated the sentiment towards Anneliese. "So glad." Maria would never forget Dietmar's birth, and she was not willing to relive it, which is why she made sure that she and Rudi arrived to congratulate Anneliese after the birth this time.

Rudi was already celebrating with Helmut over a beer in the kitchen. Helmut seemed to be incredibly happy about his new position.

"Work is going very well," he shared with Rudi. "They've asked me to translate several key documents and attend important meetings where they needed to have someone present who was able to communicate on behalf of the company. It is a lucky thing that I was able to learn English while

296

I was in the army." He took a deep swig of his drink and then waved his arm in a sweeping motion, "among other things." It seemed to Rudi that Helmut wanted to divulge certain things to him, in his half-inebriated state, but Rudi felt like it was too much information that he was better off not knowing, so he didn't ask about it and proceeded to steer the conversation in a different direction.

"I'm glad you enjoy your job Helmut and that it provides so nicely for your family. Good for you. For all of you. It is amazing that your company has provided you with such a nice apartment right across the street from your work. Maria and I are both working long hours just to make ends meet and our commute time is ridiculous. Count yourself lucky."

Helmut put a hand on Rudi's shoulder. "Everyone seems to be having a hard time right now. Germany is not used to being in a depression. We're all working like dogs to dig ourselves out of a hole that we let our government lead us into. We were blind-sided, not willing to look beyond what the reporters were feeding us. Propaganda from our own government, for their own cause. Well now we're all paying a high price for being so dumb, so willing to believe that we were better than anyone else in the world. We didn't even question the government's actions. I mean we just got swept up, didn't we?" Maria listened with one ear, agreeing with what her brother-in-law was saying.

She kept her attention on Dietmar and Brigitte though, trying to let Anneliese have some rest.

Maria was also home to soak up her mother's wisdom. She respected her so much for being such a smart businesswoman who knew how to draw an income from more than just an hourly wage. Her business sense along with her work ethic provided her family with financial security which spilled over to a sense of stability. She instilled the value of hard work and the importance of taking time for family celebrations. She made sure they always knew they were welcome, and, in her home, there was always laughter. In her mother's presence, Maria found strength to renew and rejuvenate and draw courage that she later applied to her own life wherever she went.

Once back in the city, Maria and Rudi bustled off to work every day. Rudi was a steady worker and seemed to really enjoy his job. His hardship was simply in the amount of time it took to commute back and forth from their home. Maria also enjoyed her job, and she was becoming somewhat of a leader in her department, which gave her a boost in morale and purpose, at least for the time being.

Hand-sewing was very intricate and tedious work that required concentration and patience. Sometimes she would imagine stories in her mind to provide the mental distraction needed to attend to the precision of each stitch. Maria's department had a quota to meet every day so there was pressure on the women to stay focused in their painstaking work. One day Maria started relating to her colleagues about a book she had been reading. It was a mystery romance novel. As she was telling the story to one of the women, she noticed that a few others were paying attention to the narrative account she offered. The women started to become extremely interested and Maria noticed that their attention to her storytelling was distracting them from their work.

"Let's try and help our owners do well," she suggested. "If we work hard, we can get our quota up." The ladies looked at one another, puzzled. "I will continue to tell the story as long as you continue to stay focused on your work. If I notice anyone slacking off from their handiwork, I will stop telling the story." The women looked at each other and heartily agreed.

"Yes, yes. Keep telling the story." They agreed. Maria had all six women sit in a circle so they could all hear. "Remember", she began, "if I notice anyone listening instead of sewing, I will stop. Understood?" Maria was a strict person, but the women loved to hear the stories she told. They respected her and were thankful for the relief from boredom that her storytelling provided. She was thrilled that her love of reading was coming in handy. At night she would devour her novels, and then turn around and recite an embellished account of her book, the next day at work. It wasn't long before the owner became so pleased with the production from the hand-sewing department, that he inquired about the reason for it. When he learned Maria was largely responsible, he made her a supervisor over her division. This, of course, gave her an incentive to keep up with the grind of the commute day after day.

The days started turning colder and before they knew it, the holidays were upon them once again. It was a beautiful time of year and Maria made sure to decorate their little apartment very tastefully. They had a small Christmas tree and after dinner they liked to have a few dances to the radio in the living room. It was beautiful, but still Maria's ambition to move to a better apartment did not seem to have a chance to become a reality if they weren't able to save any money.

"We work so hard," she complained to her co-worker one day, "and yet we barely have enough to cover our own expenses. I thought we could have saved something by now, but it hasn't been possible. Our rent is so expensive even though we live so far out of the city. It literally takes us an hour and a half to get to work." Her co-worker was sympathetic, so she proceeded to tell Maria of an opportunity she had recently learned about.

"It might seem like a long shot, I know, but you may want to consider it. I've heard that in Australia and in Canada, they are welcoming German immigrants and apparently, it's easy to get an apartment in the city and it isn't that expensive. I heard they have lots of work and you don't need experience. You just need to be willing to work. I cannot go," she said, "because I have two children and I wouldn't want to put that burden on my husband. Both of our families are here and so we have no desire to go, but my friend, who lives there, writes to me all the time. That's how I know. You don't have any children yet. Maybe you and Rudi would want to consider it. I could give you her contact information and who knows, it might just be the breakthrough you're looking for." Maria listened and took it all in. She pondered it in her mind and decided to bring it up with Rudi.

Later that evening the opportunity for the discussion presented itself. After a while Rudi answered her thoughtfully. "I know you want a house. I know you have ambitions for our future." He said.

"You too, right? I mean, don't you want to have a house for our future children?" Maria asked.

"Maria, I'd be happy with you in a house or an apartment, but of course I want us to have something to show for all our hard work, yes. I think the lifestyle we are looking for might be easier to achieve somewhere else, maybe. Plus, we wouldn't have to double check our every move under the watchful eye of occupying soldiers." He conceded.

"Yes. Yes." She heartily agreed. "And apparently, it is quite easy to find jobs and even a nice apartment if we're willing to work, which we are. We always have."

"Of course." Rudi said. He thought to himself for a moment and said, "It doesn't really matter what I do. If I can provide for you and our family, I'm willing. And at least for the foreseeable future Germany seems to be somewhat under foreign control. We have such a hard time visiting my side of the family in Berlin. Our leaving wouldn't change that situation much, so I am sure they would support us. But it's your family we would really miss. Your Mom and your twin. It wouldn't be easy to leave them behind."

Maria agreed and yet she added, "but we haven't lived there since we got married, so we have kind of already taken ourselves out of their daily life."

Rudi, in an unexpected moment of decision, changed the course of their destiny. "Okay, I say we make a break and take a chance. We can always come home if we don't like it, but if we're ever going to try, we better do it now before we have any children to consider."

"Are you sure?" Maria hesitated. Then, following his lead, she worked up her courage as well. "Alright. I'll get more information then," she said. "We want to have all of our bases covered before we present the idea to Mama." Rudi nodded in agreement, half excited and half anxious about such a bold step into an unknown future. But as was his custom, worry didn't last long. He considered it a worthless waste of time, so he simply put it out of his mind and went to sleep.

Chapter Thirty-One

I T'S A GREAT IDEA!" MARIA'S MOTHER exclaimed, "AND if it goes well, let me know and maybe I'll follow."

"What? That is not what I expected you to say!" Maria almost protested.

"What about, 'don't leave me? What will we do without you?'" Rudi added, half joking.

"Well, I think the latter half of those questions has been answered ever since you moved to Stuttgart. Somehow, we've managed to survive." She joked. Then she took their hands and declared seriously "Maybe this is what you are supposed to do. You are right. Germany will be on a long road to recovery, and you are just freshly married, and you don't have children yet. Things change when that happens; look at Anneliese. No, I support you. If you want to go and try to make a life in Australia or Canada, I say go now, before you have a family to support. You know you're always welcome here if things don't work out." Rudi and Maria looked at each other and burst into big smiles.

"Yes!" Maria pronounced. "We will get the ball rolling then. We'll submit the application." She turned to her mother again. "I know that we've been in Stuttgart now for a while, but it's not across the ocean. I couldn't go if you didn't want me to or if you felt like you ultimately needed us here."

"Maria, I have watched you two working together and sticking together despite people who were against you. Don't think that won't come in your future. It will. There will be times when you must fight to stay together, but I trust you and I trust Rudi. He will look after you. With him, I know you'll be okay. But most importantly, remember that with God all things are possible. He will go before you. And who knows, like I said, if you really like it, I might join you!"

Her optimism gave Maria the courage to move forward with their plans. The very next week she inquired about obtaining tickets on a passenger boat to Australia. They both needed to get a physical done and then present their papers as well as a fee to the immigration officials.

As far as the money for the ticket was concerned, Maria was planning on using wedding money and money that they would've used for their following month's rent. Luckily it was enough to purchase two tickets. She was so excited that everything was falling into place. She felt as if it were God's hand helping them until she sat in the doctor's office.

"'Can it be?" the nurse asked. "No, I don't think so." Maria responded. "Well, I mean, of course it could be, I'm married, but I don't think I am. I'm just very stressed about going over the ocean. I've never been on a boat. I've heard the trip will take about two weeks. I think that's why I'm late. I feel a little anxious, that's all."

"We're going to make sure. We're going to do a blood test." The nurse stated as she left the room with a sample of blood from Maria's arm. When she came back, she looked at Maria matter-of-factly.

"You are indeed pregnant. That's why your period is late." Maria's face fell with the news. She knew that the timing of this was not what she hoped. She did want children, but she had all her future planned for at least the next few years, and it didn't involve a baby.

"Don't worry dear," the nurse said, "we can take care of it, so you don't have to be saddled with a baby. Especially with your big dreams to start a new life in Australia. We'll just 'put it away quickly' and you can keep all of your plans."

"What?" Maria was shocked in the most horrifying way. "I would never! What? Oh no - I'm keeping my baby!"

"But honey you don't want to start a new life in a different country with a baby. Think of your husband. Come now, let us just handle that for you. We've done it so many times. It's no big deal." The nurse did her best to convince her that having an abortion was a viable option.

"Yes, it is!" Maria shouted "I'm not getting rid of my baby. The timing is not great, but we'll figure it out. Thank you." She picked up her belongings and went to the front desk. Once she had the receipt in hand for her physical, she almost ran out of the doctor's office. She continued straight home at a hurried pace, talking to herself all the way. "How dare they suggest I kill my baby. We will be just fine." When she arrived home, Rudi was already waiting for her. She nearly fell into his arms. She was sobbing so hard. He had never seen her like this before.

"What happened?" he asked. "Tell me why you're crying."

"Oh Rudi, it's so terrible. I've ruined it – all our plans." She explained.

"What are you talking about?" he asked as he guided her to the sofa, so she could calm down.

"Our new life in Australia. Our trip – I've ruined it. I'm pregnant!" she sobbed.

"What? Oh my goodness!" Rudi was so happy. "How does that ruin it? We'll be fine." He brushed it off as if it would not be a problem and his joy over the prospect of them being a family, made her feel guilty about overreacting.

"Oh I'm so sorry for making such a big fuss about it," she said, teetering on the verge of crying again.

"Okay" Rudi said, "Those pregnancy hormones are kicking in big time!" He made a point of looking straight into her eyes. "Don't worry. Don't stress. We're fine. We're going to go ahead with our plans and see what happens. If it's not meant to be, it won't be. Simple as that. But apparently it is meant to be that we start a family right now! I'm so happy! Be happy Maria. Be happy with me!" She let him wipe away her tears and then she joined him in the moment. After she calmed down a little, she was able to relay the other stressful situation that she encountered.

"I told the nurse about our plans to go overseas, of course, because I was giving her the reason for the physical. I had no thought that I could be pregnant, other than being late for my period." Rudi looked at her puzzlingly, as though that should be the first clue, but he let her finish, "and she had the nerve to inform me that it was okay – they could take care of it so that I wouldn't have a baby. That way I could just go about my adventures mindless of having had a child in my womb!" Rudi stared at her in disbelief.

"Well of course you told her no!" he breathed.

"Yes of course! But my first instinct is to do what the doctor tells me to do. I was shocked that they would just go ahead and kill a baby as if it were just another routine medical procedure."

"Wow." Rudi said. "Well that's not happening!"

"No!" she said, her disposition threatening to become somber again.

"Well don't worry." Rudi said, "you still have our baby and we're going to be a happy family. And we're going on our first trip." Maria grew serious.

"Rudi" she said sincerely, "how can we honestly go now?"

"Same as before." He said. "We'll get an apartment. I will work hard. Maybe two jobs, we will see. But if things really are better there, we will make it. Together." He kissed her and erased any doubt or insecurity in her mind that this might not work out as they planned.

Chapter Thirty-Two

THE IMMIGRATION LINE WAS BACKED UP AS people crowded on the platform to have their papers verified for passage to Australia. Rudi and Maria inched their way along until they were finally next in line. They handed the officials all their paperwork. He looked up at Maria and asked in a serious tone, "Are you pregnant?" Maria felt nervous and the words almost caused her to panic in her already anxious state of mind. Her heart pounded as she answered honestly.

"Yes, I am. I just found out. Does that change anything?" she asked.

The official was very direct. "Australia is not accepting anyone that is pregnant. You will not be allowed to go Miss. Sorry. You are denied." The words wounded her as he handed back her papers. He wasn't entirely callous. He did notice that his proclamation crushed her hopes. "You might want to try Canada Miss. They may accept you." And with that tiny seed of hope, he motioned for the next person to come forward. As she moved down the line feeling completely dejected, Rudi was ironically the one reminding her that it was in God's hands and that she should not give up so easily.

"I don't like spiders or snakes anyway," he said. Apparently, Australia has a lot of big spiders. And a lot of snakes. Maybe we should consider ourselves lucky. Canada is too cold for that. Let's go back to the immigration office tomorrow and try our luck again."

"Oh Rudi. Spiders and snakes? Really? Are you just trying to make me feel less upset about this rejection?"

"No. I'm serious. I'm afraid of spiders and snakes. So, this is not that disappointing to me."
Maria had to smile, even though she was feeling disappointed.
With hope hanging on a thread in her delicate, hormonal condition, she relayed the whole experience to her colleague at work the following day.

"I'll give you the name of my friend in Canada." She simply answered, not even considerate that Maria was disappointed at having been turned down from emigrating to Australia. "Having the name of a sponsor is very helpful once you arrive. Otherwise, they can assign you to work wherever they need you. This way, you can look for what you want once you are settled. Here!" she said, handing Maria a paper with her friend's information. "Go ahead and try Canada. They're friendly. So I've been told."

The next day, Rudi and Maria went to the ticket counter at the train station to try to purchase tickets with their refunded money for their Australian trip, for an overseas voyage to Canada. "Papers please Ma'am." The woman said as she reached out her hand to receive them. Rudi handed all their papers to her, giving Maria a confident wink. The woman looked up at Maria once she had looked over her papers. "Any health issues Ma'am?"

"No." Maria answered.

"Are you pregnant?" the woman asked without looking at her.

"No." she answered with hesitation. The woman looked up at her as if she knew. "Well, I suppose I could be. Maybe – I don't know." She lied. I mean we are married." She fumbled as she looked at Rudi.

"Here you go" the woman answered, and she handed her a ticket. She cross examined Rudi in the same manner and handed him a ticket as well. "They will call you when they have room on a ship.

It could take up to six months," she warned, "but you never know. You just have to be ready."

"Thank you." Maria beamed. "Thank you so much." Rudi was right behind her, gently pushing her along so she would not say anything further to reveal her pregnancy. He was also hopeful that it wouldn't take six months otherwise there would be no hiding her baby bump. Once they were out of hearing distance of the ticket agent, he grabbed her and swung her around. She let out a shout of joy. They were both elated knowing that their plans were coming to fruition.

"Here we go Mrs. Heinrich!" Rudi exclaimed as he set her down.

"Here we go!" Maria echoed.

"Let's go to Reutlingen this weekend and tell your family." Rudi suggested. "They think we're trying to go to Australia. Now we are going to the other half of the world. Viva Canada!" He looked at Maria for a response.

"Yes!" she called out. "Here we come Canada!" She quickly realized that she had not given Canada much thought. "We should find out everything there is to know about Canada. Like, how cold it is, what kind of food there is, what most people do for fun. I want to know everything!" Rudi nodded in agreement.

"Yes. And do eskimos live there? Where are the polar bears?" Maria shot him a sidewards glance. "Just kidding" he said, "but I think you're right. We should be somewhat informed. It'll help us to be prepared."

"Exactly." Maria said. "And we should learn how to speak English."

"Absolutely!" he agreed." I'm already getting started. 'Hello. How are you?'" he said, as he lifted his hat in a pretend greeting to her.

"No fair. Who taught you that?" Maria inquired.

"Helmut of course. He could probably teach us quite a bit."

"You're right, but then again, since he's so far away and we never know that he'll be home when we visit, maybe we shouldn't rely on that." Maria said.

"Understood. And agreed." Rudi said plainly.

"Why did you lie?" he suddenly asked her.

"About the pregnancy?" Maria looked down, feeling shameful. "I know. It was wrong. I should have told the truth."

"Well, she knew anyway." Rudi explained. "We turned in the medical reports."

"I know. It was wrong of me." They were both silent for a moment. "I'm not perfect, okay. I just wanted to fake it." Rudi didn't say anything. "I didn't want to be the reason we couldn't go." she finally said.

Rudi was quiet. He just squeezed her hand.

Chapter Thirty-Three

SIEGFRIED RAN OUT THE BACK DOOR TOWARDS the woodshed. He was terribly upset that Rudi and Maria were planning on leaving. Just when he was feeling secure that he had a father figure in Rudi, they announced their plans for departure. He was fourteen. An awkward, insecure, impressionable boy trying to figure out how to become a man. Rudi understood. He went after him because once again, he could relate to this brother-in-law of his, as no one else could. He found him crying on a stack of wood they had chopped together. Siegfried usually jumped up and gave Rudi a hug or a friendly punch in the arm, but this time he just stayed sitting and let the tears flow. Rudi walked into the shed, and it was all he could do, seeing Siegfried uncontrollably crying to not cry with him. He knew whatever consolation he could speak to this boy; the outcome would still be the same. In all their plans to leave their country, in all their dreams of a better life abroad, the heart of this fourteen-year-old boy was never considered.

For the first time Rudi realized how vital a role he played in this young man's life. If not for the circumstances of his impending trip to Canada, Rudi would have vowed to give Siegfried more time. He realized that time is the greatest gift you can give someone you love. Standing before this heartbroken child, all he could do was say sorry. "Siegfried," he began, "you will always be my little brother, no matter where I go." When Siegfried finally got himself together, he told Rudi something he never forgot.

"You were more like a dad to me. I have always wanted a dad and for the last two years I felt like I almost had one. And now you're leaving." Siegfried started crying again, baring his deepest heart's cry, even though he knew that it was no use. This time Rudi cried too.

"Well guess what?" Rudi thought to say to help lighten the situation for both, "Maria's going to have a baby." Siegfried's eyes grew big.

"Really?"

"Yeah," he confirmed, "I was surprised too. So, I guess in a way you helped me to figure out how to be a dad. Now I need you to do something for me.

315

Your mother and your sisters – they need a man around the house. They need you. You need to watch over them and protect them, you understand?" Siegfried nodded in response. He couldn't speak. "And always be good to your Mama. She has a big heart. She has no one to help her and here, look how she has provided for all of you all this time."

Wiping his tears on his sleeve, Siegfried said, "I was mostly raised by my grandmother, but I know. She had no time. I understand Rudi. I just wish you wouldn't leave. I will miss you very much." he said faintly, trying desperately not to keep crying. He wanted to be brave for Rudi.

"I will miss you too Siegfried. Promise me when you meet someone you love, you will treat her right and protect her, ja?" Siegfried smiled looking up at Rudi.

"I will. I've watched how you treat my sister. Like you really love her. Helmut just goes away – looks after himself."

"Right. You see the difference. It's not what you get – it's what you give. That will make you happy." Rudi instructed.

Siegfried listened intently to all that Rudi had to say and wanted, even yet, so desperately to please him, to win his approval. "Okay." He answered, as he jumped down off the woodpile. "I will. I promise."

"We'll come visit. Or you will come to us for a visit." Rudi said to make him feel better, but they both knew it would be years before they would be together again. Everything would be different. They would both change, and Siegfried would grow up alone.

"Congratulations Maria!" Siegfried said as he came back into the house through the back door, Rudi trailing behind him. Everyone looked at him. Maria looked at Rudi, her eyes giving away the question 'Did you tell him?'. Rudi just looked back at her and shrugged. She could see that he had been crying too.

"Thank you, Siegfried. You are the first to know." Maria said. Siegfried stood amongst the family a little taller upon learning that. Every eye was on him. Know what? That was the question on everyone's mind. Siegfried looked around and back at Maria questioningly. She just nodded to give him permission.

"Maria is pregnant." Siegfried announced. "They are going to have a baby." he said proudly. She smiled at her brother and gave him a nod of approval. Maria's mother was the first one to break the silence.

"Congratulations you two! Well, it's not the best timing, but I know you will make good parents." Her mind taking in all their plans to go abroad which they had just shared. "This will definitely make things more difficult in Canada for you, but..." she sighed "God never makes mistakes, and we can always trust Him. Our timing is mostly never His timing. You shouldn't worry. If God is making a way, everything will work out." She assured them. Maria was thankful for her mother's heartfelt support. She didn't say it, but it meant all the world to her.

"You are full of news today!" Hilde said as she stepped forward to congratulate her sister. "Canada and a new baby!"

"Congratulations Maria. Congratulations Rudi." Anneliese said. "it's about time. I'm so happy for you two!"

"Thank you, Anne, We're happy too." She reached for Rudi, and he leaned in for a congratulatory hug.

"I know if Helmut were here, he would want to say the same. All our best to you both. All three, unless you have twins, like Mama." They all laughed and agreed that would probably not happen.

"Don't worry." Maria's mom said. "It usually skips a generation. All of you should be in the clear. Ha-ha. Not that it would be horrible, but I would not recommend it if you were going to another country, where you have no family to help." Once the obvious was stated, Maria looked a little sad for a moment.

Hildegard, with her contagious charm, lightened the mood instantly. "I'm going to be an auntie again! I am so happy! What a lucky child to have you two for parents!" she exclaimed. And she really meant it. Maria had always been like a second mother to her because she was seven years older and Rudi, being the only adult male in the family took the mantle of the father figure as well as brother-in-law without really purposing to. After everyone had time to digest the news, they just spent time talking and laughing together well after dinner. No one wanted to leave because they were all aware that their time together was short.

Chapter Thirty-Four

"THE ONLY CONSTANT IN LIFE IS CHANGE." Maria said as she pondered the events of their adventurous life and how much time they had left in Germany. "Whoever said that first was a very wise person." She said to herself. "I must have read it somewhere."

The nurse was signing Maria's discharge papers as she gathered her belongings from her hospital room. She was dressed and ready to go home with Rosie who had come to pick her up and drive her back to her house in Port Dover. Unfortunately, they would be leaving without Rudi. A decision had not been reached regarding his accommodation for long-term care. If Rosie stayed in Canada, he might be allowed to go home, but because of his immobility, nursing care would still be needed almost around the clock. The problem was that Rosie did not want to give up her ability to live and work in the United States because her three children and two grandchildren lived there. It was a huge dilemma and Rosie was searching for a solution through other family members living close by, or through the system of community care. She needed more time and now that her mother was coming home, she could focus her attention on her dad's situation. His vertebrae were not yet healed, and doctors were thinking that at ninety years of age coupled with his inability to walk, he would be better off in a nursing facility regardless of Rosie's decision whether to remain in Canada or just visit. Maria seemed to be okay with that, but Rosie, having once worked as an activities director in a nursing center, was not happy with the prospect. Either way, there was time to decide; today was Maria's discharge day.

Before leaving the hospital, they walked over to visit Rudi at the opposite end of the same floor. Once they reached his room, they noticed his bed had been made and there was no sign of Rudi. Rosie almost ran to the nurse's station in a panic.

"Where's my dad? Rudi Heinrich is not in his room."

"Oh, they put him on the fourth floor Ma'am. They just took him there this morning. He's in the long-term care unit on 4B."

"But no one asked us, or even told us." Rosie said.

"I'm sorry Ma'am. We needed the bed." The nurse said matter-of-factly.

"I thought there was a C-diff outbreak on the fourth floor." Rosie protested.

"That was lifted today Ma'am." The nurse informed her.

"Oh, so you take him up to the floor where a highly contagious virus is, on the very day that the restriction is lifted? This is outrageous!" Rosie fumed. The nurse said nothing. Rosie stood and stared into her mother's eyes in disbelief.

"Can we go see him?" Rosie asked.

"Yes, but you'll have to wear protective gear. They have all that up there on the unit." The nurse answered.

"How about my mother? Can I take her up there to see her husband?" she asked.

"I wouldn't advise it Ma'am. I am sure he is fine. He's not up there because he's sick. We are just moving him up there to make room for more people in this unit. Considering the lifting of the restriction, she might be fine, but because she's just being discharged today, I would wait a little so her immune system can get stronger."

Rosie was taken off guard and faced her mother to apologize, even though the situation was taken out of her hands.

"Well there doesn't seem to be much we can do accept be thankful that he is still being taken care of and that they have a bed for him upstairs. We can come back. Come on, I'm ready to go home." Maria said. Rosie understood. She hesitated a moment, not wanting to leave her dad. She was also disappointed. The staff had consulted her and her sister about their plans concerning Rudi, but Rosie thought there was still time to decide. The hospital took it upon themselves to move him to the fourth floor. She did not want that. She didn't like it and yet, he was still being cared for, which she was thankful for. Rosie thought of possibly making Canada her home again, but the prospect of losing the right to live in the States where her children and grandchildren lived, held her back, at least while they were still young. Her youngest child was, after all, still in high school. It looked as if her path was decided for her, as was her dad's.

"Okay, let me just run up and see Dad for a minute Mom. Can you wait here?"

"Sure." Maria agreed. "Don't take too long." She sat down in a lounge chair opposite the elevators while Rosie quickly took the next ride up to the fourth floor.

The elevator door opened, and Rosie stepped off, not sure where to go. She looked to the right and quickly spotted her dad sitting in a therapy chair in the hallway. The nursing staff had placed him there to allow for a change of scenery and for the cleaning crew to freshen up his room. It was disheartening for Rosie to see him like this. Memories of her time spent working in a Nursing Home in North Carolina came to mind. She remembered the staff would get the residents up and do the same, but they would leave them sitting in the hall for extended periods of time. They didn't pay much attention to them because as was the norm, these long-term care facilities were usually understaffed, and the nurses had to focus on getting everything done that was required in their shift.

'My dad shouldn't be here.' She thought to herself. 'He's not even sick. I don't like this solution one bit.' As she came closer to him, she smiled to hide her worry and anger over the situation.

"Hi Dad! I'm so happy to see you!"

"Röschen. I'm up here. They changed my room." She immediately noticed a change in his cognition.

"Yes. I know. But I found you. Don't worry I will come and see you up here now, okay?" she assured him. He just nodded positively. Rosie noticed he had some spilled yogurt on the tray in front of him, which she cleaned up with a wipe from the sanitation stations set up in the hallway.

"Which one is your room?" she questioned him. He pointed to the direction behind him and said, "417." It encouraged her that he knew his room number and where it was. "They have an activities room up here with a big television." He began.

Noticing the look of pity on her face, Rudi reassured his youngest daughter. "It's okay Rosie. Don't worry. I'm fine." Even now she could see that he was trying to soothe her anxious heart, so she put on her best brave face.

"Okay. I know. You just have to stay up here until we can arrange something different."

"Okay" he said, sleepily.

Rosie wanted some answers from the first nurse she saw behind the desk, not even knowing if she was assigned to her dad,

"I'm Rudi Heinrich's daughter." She started. "Why is he so groggy? He was not like this the last time I saw him, which was yesterday."

"Oh, I'm sorry Miss. He has just come on this floor today and the move has caused him quite a bit of discomfort. We're giving him some pain meds for his back to help him cope, but they can cause drowsiness." Rosie understood, but she was still frustrated.

"Shouldn't he be in bed then?" she asked.

"Not always." The nurse answered. "He needs to get up too, so that he doesn't develop bed sores."

"Okay. I'm sorry," Rosie said, "I just don't like to see him in a mental fog like this. That's not my dad."

"Yes Ma'am. I'll ask the doctor if there's something else he can give him." she offered.

"Thank you." Rosie said. "I appreciate that." Realizing that her dad could hear every word, she turned back to him and said, "I'll come visit later when Mom is sleeping. She is waiting for me downstairs. They wouldn't let her come up here yet because she's still too weak, but she gets to go home today." Upon hearing that news, Rudi got a big smile on his face. "Wunderbar!" he said. "Give her my love."

Rosie kissed him on the cheek and said "Okay. I will be back Dad. I'll see you later."

"Okay" he said, smiling. "And thank you."

"Of course, Dad. I will see you later." Rosie promised.

As the elevator door opened to the waiting room on the third floor, Maria jumped to her feet. Rosie stepped out and offered her mother her arm. "Okay young lady" she joked, "are you ready to go home?"

"Yes!" Maria answered. "I'm ready. How's Rudi?"

"Oh, he's a little bit foggy because of the medicine, so I asked them if they could change it for him. Other than that, he seemed to be okay." Maria nodded, satisfied with that answer. She turned her attention to her own situation. When she stepped out of the hospital doors, she took a deep breath of fresh air.

"You sit here Mom. I'm going to bring the car around." Rosie said as she guided her mother to the bench. On the ride home, Maria noticed how green everything was. She commented on the flowers in full bloom and all the flowers in people's yards and even the wildflowers along the roadside. She took

326

in all the natural beauty she could, cracking her window open slightly to feel the air on her face. Looking at her mother enjoying the outside world again gave Rosie a sense of normalcy. Her mother was alive and well and all seemed right with the world.

"You need to remember to take it easy" Rosie reminded her. "The doctor said you wouldn't have much energy for five or six weeks. Your lungs are still recovering. Plus, your body is dealing with new medication, the blood thinners, that you haven't had before and the pill to keep that stomach ulcer from coming back. Even so Mom, you only have to take two pills. Most people who are getting close to ninety have to take a lot more than that."

"Yup." Maria agreed. "And Dad didn't take any medicine either. Well now he has to because he is in pain, but not because he's sick."

"You're right. That is pretty good for ninety years old. Well you know what he likes to say – you can't kill a weed." They both laughed and enjoyed remembering his carefree personality.

"I'll be right here with you" Rosie assured her mother, seeing how she was starting to worry about her husband. "I'll just go see Dad when it's time for you to have a sleep in the afternoon, and then I'll be back in time to make us supper okay?"

Maria was thankful. "I'm glad you're here Roschen."

"Me too." Rosie said. "Do you want to drive down to the beach for a bit to see the water?"

"Oh yes!" Maria exclaimed, "I love the water." As Rosie was driving, Maria glanced at her from the corner of her eye. She was happy to see her youngest daughter again. She had been away from home for so many years. It was a pleasure that kept her heart from breaking because she was going home from the hospital without Rudi. She instinctively decided to focus on the good things and to trust God with the rest. Stepping out of the car, Rosie motioned to a bench on the pier. Mother and daughter sat side by side taking in the lake air as they listened to the surf lapping on the shore. It felt as though Rudi were with them. He loved the water. The pier was his favorite fishing spot; enjoying himself for hours with a fishing rod in hand. It was also one of his favorite things to do with his grandkids.

"Dad would love it here today." Maria said.

"How about I take a picture of us Mom, so I can show him when I visit him later?" Rosie stretched out her arm, phone in hand, and snapped a photo of their first day out of the hospital. They sat a while longer, taking in the scenery. The sun glistened on the water so brightly, they had to squint to look at it. In the distance they could see families playing on the shore right in front of the deck of the Beach House Restaurant, a scene they would've been a part of in years gone by. The seagulls were flying above calling out in search of food. It was a typical day at the beach. The wind gently lifted the hair off Maria's forehead as she breathed in the lake air.

"I almost died you know." Maria stated.

"Yes. You certainly did, and yet here we are, and you are fine again." Rosie said, squeezing her mother's hand, reassuring herself, as well as Maria, that all was well.

"God gave me a miracle." Maria said. "You know I was so ready to go home and see Jesus. I felt so warm and comfortable. I was happy as could be. Either way would have been fine with me." She spoke. "I saw all of you standing around me and I thought I must be pretty sick, and I was ready to go. Now all of a sudden, the doctor came in and said, 'we're taking you to surgery' and I just seemed to get better from then on." Maria recounted to the best of what she could recollect.

"Yes Mom. You gave us all a scare. I'm glad you're still here though." Rosie said, squeezing her hand again. Maria winced. "Be careful with that. They poked me quite a bit."

"Oh sorry." Rosie said. "I remember. You were so brave. I know I couldn't have been as brave as you. You're pretty amazing Mom." Maria smiled.

"Well, you just have to let them do their job, so I tried not to complain. But right now, I think I need to go home and rest." she admitted. Rosie recognized that her mother was very frail having just been released from the hospital, but she wanted to show her a glimpse of the beautiful sun sparkling on the aqua colored waves of the Erie shore. These are images, temporal gifts from God that can only be enjoyed to the fullest while you are experiencing it. No second-hand description of this scene could do it justice. Especially to share the experience between mother and daughter. Even the little moments meant so much to Rosie. She savored every memory-making opportunity.

Once Maria was settled in her own room, in her own house, she knew she would probably fall asleep quickly.

"I won't be long, Mom. I will be home soon. I told Dad I'd come see him again so I'm just going to go back to the hospital to make sure he's doing okay for the night and before you know it, I'll be back to make supper okay?"

"That's fine Rosie. Don't rush. I'm okay. It's nice to be in my own home again." Rosie turned around and looked at her sweet mother from her bedroom door. The love swelled in her heart, and she wished once again that she would have come home sooner.

"I know," she said, "you have a wonderful home. Just rest. I'll see you later." At that, Rosie drove off to the hospital once again and this time when she arrived on the fourth floor, Rudi was in his bed receiving his lunch tray. Rosie put on the full hospital gown and mask and gloves they had outside her dad's room. Someone in his very room had the C-diff virus and the hospital staff made the protective gear a requirement for visitors.

"Now you look more comfortable" Rosie said. Rudi looked up and saw his youngest daughter, bright and cheery as he always remembered her. Her disposition caused his own to brighten, even though he was in a lot of pain.

"I have a picture to show you Dad." Rosie said as she drew near his bed and pulled out her phone.
He looked closely squinting his eyes to see it clearly. Ninety years old and still only sometimes needing reading glasses. "Nice day on the Pier huh?" he remarked.

"Yup." said Rosie. "We took a picture just for you. Mom said you would have loved to be there with us today. It was sunny and warm." He smiled. He loved seeing Maria.

"How is she?" he asked.

"Mom? She is okay. Tired. The doctor said she needs to take it easy for the next five to six weeks until her strength comes back. She had blood clots in both lungs. Apparently, it's very normal to be tired after that." Rosie said sarcastically. Her dad was quick witted, and he understood that she was saying she needed serious rest. "But she's fine now. She is glad to be home. She misses you of course." He nodded satisfactorily.

"How are you?" he asked.

"Me?" Rosie asked puzzled.

"Yes you. Taking care of your old parents like this. Back and forth all the time."

"I'm doing fine. I wish I could do more. I want to do more..." she sat shaking her head looking down. Her Dad understood.

"I was in pain earlier" Rudi finally volunteered. Rosie had forgotten to ask him how he was doing today.

"Oh. Did they do anything about your medicine?" Rosie asked.

"Not yet." He said. "Maybe I will ask again. I don't like how it makes me feel." He complained.

"What do you mean?"

"It makes me sleep all the time. And I dream of funny stuff. Not funny, but strange. Almost like weird nightmares. I don't like it."

"Okay. I'll go ask your nurse. Or your doctor if he's there." Rosie went out to the nurse's station, and it didn't happen often, but thankfully Rudi's doctor was indeed there, and Rosie explained the situation. The doctor stood up and personally went to talk to Rudi in his room so they could get the medication agreed upon.

"Okay," the doctor explained to Rosie, "I can change his medicine and hopefully this new one will still take the edge off his pain. It's not as heavy of a dose, but at least he shouldn't experience the dreams that he's been having."

"Thank you so much doctor. I appreciate you taking the time to do that." Rosie said.

"Well luckily, I'm here today. I only come twice a week. Otherwise, the nurses run the show up here." He informed her.

"What if he does need more for the pain?" Rosie asked. "What do we do?"

"You can ask a nurse and I will write down how much I am willing to allow him to have. We do not want to start at that level though. He has broken vertebrae. He is ninety. It's likely not going to heal. I'm sorry." Rosie stood in her tracks. She had assumed that maybe he might yet pull out of this. In her mind, he still could, because she knew her Dad and she also had a great deal of faith. She heard his words, but she wasn't ready to give in.

"Thank you so much doctor." She simply said and went back to sit with her dad. After he had his lunch, she spent some time with him chatting the afternoon away. By three o'clock, he was ready to lie down and sleep again.

"This is going to work out with our timing pretty well Dad." Rosie calculated. "When Mom sleeps in the afternoon, I will come see you and when you need to nap just before dinner, I'll go back to her." Rudi smiled.

"Okay. Good plan." He said. "And when she starts to feel better, then she can come along with you."

"Of course." Rosie said. She stayed a while next to his bed and then left as he started dozing off. Rosie gathered her belongings and quickly headed back to her mother in Port Dover. As she left his room, she wondered about his roommates. One of his fellow patients, in particular, who was at the far end of the room, was in and out of the bathroom, leaving the door wide open. There was only a curtain between the beds, which the staff kept drawn, but Rosie was not impressed. One consolation was that her dad's bed was at the other end of the room, next to the window and there was a bed in between the man in question and her dad's bed. Nevertheless, it was concerning to her, and she decided she would say something about it next time. In any case, the nurses were nice and seemed very attuned to their patients as did his doctor. This would be life for the foreseeable future. Back and forth to the hospital until Maria was well enough to join her. It would be a long road, but she knew with the Lord at the helm she could trust the journey.

Chapter Thirty-Five

WHEN SHE ARRIVED BACK IN PORT DOVER, Rosie brought dinner to Maria in her bed. She was too tired to come to the table. Rosie knew that she had had a long day and that it was likely normal. She didn't worry. She simply gave her mother dinner on a tray and sat in bed next to her.

"Can you tell me more about your journey coming to Canada, Mom?" Rosie asked. Maria laughed.

"Well first we needed to learn how to speak the language..."

* * *

"MY NAME IS MARIA." SHE REPEATED after her English teacher, who moved to her next student.

"My name is Rudi." He said. Maria giggled, hearing his pronunciation and the teacher peered at her over her shoulder. That was enough to silence Maria who had always been a profoundly serious student. The classes seemed a little boring to Rudi, but Maria reminded him that they were not just doing this for fun. Even so, Rudi managed to spice things up a little.

"What would you like to eat?" and "what would you like to drink?" in English turned into "Why don't we all go out for a drink after class?" Rudi suggested that they could continue speaking English all evening and learn the language in terms of ordering food and drinks in a real setting of course. He liked to celebrate with lots of people. The more the merrier was his mantra. One day, after they had both come home from their evening English classes, their neighbor, who had a telephone, came knocking on their door.

"They called!" Maria and Rudi looked at one another and then back at their neighbor, puzzled. "You said you gave my phone number to the office of immigration because you don't have a phone. They just called!"

"What?" Maria gasped. "What did they say?"

"A ship is leaving the Hamburg harbor on May fifteenth at ten o'clock in the morning. They said to be there on time with your tickets ready." Maria was in shock. She had waited for this moment, but suddenly, she didn't know what to say.

"Two weeks." She whispered.

"Thank you." Rudi said, "Thank you for letting us know."

"Good luck!" the neighbor said to Rudi as he closed the apartment door behind her. He turned to his wife.

"We haven't finished our English classes yet." Maria said.

"Well then we better stay." Rudi joked. Her eyes grew big, and he lifted her and swirled her around in their living room. They were both excited and a little scared.

They lay in bed that night staring up at the ceiling. "We're so crazy!" Maria said. "I'm pregnant, we can't speak English..."

"Yet," Rudi quickly countered, "we're so fortunate." He was confident and ready for adventure. "Don't you want to see?" he asked her.

"See?" she repeated questioningly.

"Don't you want to see if we can do it?" Germany is not a good place to build up a life right now. A lot of the younger generation are going to places of opportunity. Like us. We're healthy. Hard working. Willing. We will be fine. We have each other."

"Yes." Maria calmed herself as she lay in her husband's safe embrace. "We'll always be fine together." The very next day, they both handed in their notice to their employers, they notified their landlord, and it was time much sooner than expected. Rudi's parents were supportive when they told them what they were about to do. His mother was a little worried, but she understood their reasons for leaving the country and gave her blessing which was important to Rudi. The older German population witnessed such a mass exodus of young adults without children in that time. It was mostly the people who were looking for work and charting a new course to build up families elsewhere because they hadn't yet started to do that. Once Maria wrote the news to her mother, they spent the next couple of weeks with the family having shut down their jobs and the apartment they occupied in Stuttgart.

The morning of their departure, they were saying their farewells in the kitchen. Maria's mother and Hildegard were awake anyway to work the business. Anneliese and Helmut and the kids even came to see them off. Siegfried wanted to walk them to the train station where they would be on their first leg of the journey, a train ride to Hamburg. Hilde was the first to say goodbye.

"I love you. I wish I could go with you!" she said and really meant it. Maria and Rudi gave her a tight hug goodbye. Even though she was very free-spirited, Maria thought she was a delightful teenager. She was forced to work hard in a situation she didn't choose for herself. Maria respected the fact that she stepped up to take her place helping her mother in the work she had to do to sustain their home. And she knew firsthand how hard it was.

"Goodbye Hildegard. Maybe you'll be the first to come visit." Maria said.

Anneliese stepped forward, hardly able to speak because she had a lump in her throat.

"My schwesterhertz" she said. It was a term of endearment they both used for one another because they were closer than sisters - sisters with one heart. When she said it to Maria as they embraced, it released a flood of tears. "We will always be one in spirit." Anneliese said. Maria held on to her sister very tightly and whispered in her ear, "I will miss you most." The twin sisters finally let go of one another and stepped back to let Helmut say his goodbyes. Rudi and Maria each gave the children last hugs for years to come, and then it was Maria's mother's turn.
She hugged Rudi first. "Take good care of my new son." she said to Maria seriously.

"I will Mama." Maria answered obediently. Then she gave her dearest Maria a very long goodbye hug. When she let her go, she looked at Rudi sincerely.

"You are getting gold here you know. You take good care of her, you hear?"

"Yes Mama. I will with all my heart. I promise." She hugged them both again and then pulled back from her embrace and looked Rudi square in the eyes.

"I know Rudi. I trust you. You have brought us so much joy. And you were such a big help to all of us. I don't know what we would've done without you." She spoke. Then she turned to Maria. Remarkably she remained composed, while Maria was in tears. Her mother had suffered great loss in her life and knew how to handle it. She took Maria squarely by her shoulders and looked in her eyes. "You will be strong." She instructed, "because you have to be. And God will help you." Those words of advice stuck with Maria forever. She would recall them every time she would face adversity. Her mother was an amazing woman. Strong, yet loving. Kind and gentle and incredibly wise.

"Thank you, Mama. I will write to you often."

"Thank you, Maria. I know you will. God be with you."

Rudi picked up their bags and not another word was said. Siegfried went down the street with them as the others stayed in the house and watched. At the train station Siegfried stayed glued to Rudi's side. He took the liberty of carrying his bags, while Rudi carried Maria's bags. Rudi bought the train tickets and then all three of them waited on the platform. The moment of dread arrived for Siegfried. First, he hugged his sister. "I love you Siegfried." Maria said. "Take good care of all your girls at home." He smiled and hugged her back.

"I love you too Maria. I'm a little mad at you for leaving, but I suppose I'll get over it." he said, as he fought back the tears that were threatening to break through his eyes.

"You will Siegfried. You will." Maria said. Then Siegfried turned to Rudi and gave him a tight hug. Rudi had to fight a little himself to maintain his composure.

When Siegfried stepped back, Rudi said "Remember our talk. You are the man of the house. Be good now. I love you."

"I love you." Siegfried said, "Very much." The doors of the train opened. Maria helped Rudi with the bags and then they stepped on the train. Siegfried pressed his young face to the window of the train, trying to hang on to Rudi as long as he could. When the train was out of sight, he turned around and took the long way home.

On the train, Rudi and Maria sat in silence for the first few minutes. Finally, Rudi said, "That was hard."

"Mama helped me." Maria said. "She helped me again." She looked at Rudi. "Don't worry," she soothed, "Siegfried will be eighteen before you know it. Time goes fast, and then he'll only be thinking about girls." Rudi squinted his eyes and looked out the train window. "He will understand when he gets older." Maria said. Rudi knew that was true, but it did take him a little while to stomach his emotions from saying goodbye to everyone who he considered his true family.

When the train pulled into Hamburg, Rudi's demeanor had improved, and he was optimistic once again for the path he and Maria had chosen to take. They made their way to the boating docks and followed the crowd. Everyone was laden with luggage and a line was starting to form. Their ship, the Arosa Kulm, was a passenger ship bringing German immigrants and students to Canada post World War two to start a new life. A lot of passengers seemed to have family members along that they were saying goodbye to, but having already done that earlier in Reutlingen, Rudi and Maria were able to sail right through the line-up and make their way directly to the stewards who were waiting to help passengers board. One such young man took the time to help them with their luggage to their assigned cabin and then was kind enough to show them the dining rooms and the deck area. Maria and Rudi then decided to join the other passengers on deck even though they didn't have family members present. The excitement of the crowd elevated their own spirits.

When the ship was finally leaving the harbor and the horn officially blew, Rudi waved and said "Have a good trip! God Bless You!" just to join in with the others. They didn't have anyone to shout it to them personally, so they said it to one another. Maria stood waving a handkerchief on the deck as the ship pulled out to sea. She felt sad, forsaking her country and all her family, but she also felt elated.

All the pain from her past, especially of her dad dying in the war and so many of her uncles, was something she wanted to leave behind. They were both eager to escape the trauma of the war itself and the fallout that it cost them.

They needed to start a new chapter in life. They knew it wouldn't be easy. Rudi especially, but he was willing to shoulder the responsibility of being the provider for his little family. Focusing on their future, they were young and invincible. They felt ready to forge a new path, so they set their faces like flint and looked forward to their new beginning across the ocean.

END OF PART ONE.

PART TWO – ACROSS THE OCEAN

PART THREE – GENERATION GAP

PART FOUR – SEE YOU TOMORROW

Anneliese, Hildegard, Maria and Siegfried.

Rudi waiting to board the Ocean Liner to Canada.

Maria and Rudi's wedding day — May 24, 1952.

Acknowledgements

Maria Heinrich

For your daily wisdom and your memories...Every time we talked about your younger days, I was amazed at how much you remembered. Now that you are 93 and the memories are starting to fade, I am thankful that I had the opportunity to reminisce with you while they were still clear in your mind. I love you Mama with all my heart.

Craig Heinrich

Thank you for sharing all your memories of your time with your Oma and Opa. You were more like a son than a grandson to them. Thank you for your generous heart.

Ray Heinrich

Thank you for your honesty. Even though some memories were difficult, I appreciate your willingness to share them and your faithfulness in service of helping Mama to age beautifully and with dignity.

Christine Heinrich

Thank you for sharing all the memories that filled in the gaps of when I had moved away. And of course for your faithful service and love which you've always given to both your parents but especially to Mama in her old age.

John Voss

Thank you for making me a better writer. It was painful to be edited honestly, which is why I only asked twice. Your advice was hugely appreciated.

And to my 3 children, Melissa Angell, Matthew Angell and Brittany Angell

Thank you for making sure that I didn't write a boring book and for helping me with the cover and design. And of course for your patience with my preoccupation of getting this work done. I love you all with my whole heart. It is my desire that you will be enriched with a history of your grandparents in their younger days. I hope the pages of this book will make their life come alive to you.

Stay tuned for Book Two: The continuing story of Rudi and Maria's journey.

Across

The

Ocean

About The Author

Rosemarie Heinrich, born in Hamilton, Ontario Canada is the youngest daughter of Rudi and Maria Heinrich.. She fondly remembers her growing-up years steeped in rich cultural heritage of German traditions and deeply rooted in faith. She has always had a keen interest in her family heritage which inspired her to begin writing a book about it.. What started as one book, quickly developed into a four-part series.

She worked as a Canadian journalist with Global News and for WPTF News Radio in Raleigh, North Carolina. She has also written several screenplays, one of which was produced by her church and won several awards at a film festival including Best Film Overall.

Rosemarie lives in Wake Forest, North Carolina and enjoys spending time with her three children and two grandkids, Noah and Nathan and her Rough Collie, Jake.

Made in the USA
Columbia, SC
18 May 2024

20ad79ea-0a2a-4519-9007-032adc986894R01